BREWSTER FLATS

Tony DeSabato

This book is dedicated to my son, Patrick, who inspired me
to begin writing when he was two and who continues
to inspire me in whatever I do that has value.

THE DRIVE UP

The memorial service will take place at dusk.

With the sun hovering above the Atlantic Ocean, Nicholas Amadeo DiDominico, Nad to his friends, parks his car as instructed on the grass lot a few miles from the ocean, across from the sprawling Cape Cod home that looks like a mansion to him.

The drive from suburban Philadelphia has been a typical August trek—convertible top down, music blasting, heat waves from the sun refracting off an asphalt surface threatening to bubble. He can't remember when he took his first ride up to the Cape or many of the trips preceding this one, but on this trip, as on all the rest, his decision points are few: the George Washington Bridge, if relatively clear, is faster than the Tappan Zee, but the Tappan Zee always has a lower risk for delays. Same thing with I-95 and the Merritt Parkway. He factors in that the more scenic routes on the Tappan Zee and Merritt provide an expansive view over the Hudson and a canopy of trees over the parkway until he exits near New Haven. Each time, he tries to process whatever information is out there, but in the final analysis, he relies on an intuition honed by experience. Today he feels a time pressure but one more fluid than if he were on a deadline to catch a ferry from Woods Hole to Martha's Vineyard, his usual destination. He picks the George Washington Bridge and I-95 and gets lucky— the trip takes just slightly more than six hours. He's accompanied only by Tom Rush, the Stones, Dylan, Cream, Joni, the Who, Bob Marley, the Doors, Shawn Colvin, Dire Straits, Bruce, and on for 360-plus miles. This is music he knows she liked, music they had listened to together.

The tunes and the turbulent air mix, and he rummages through thoughts and feelings accessible only in solitude. He feels the sadness of losing her and can't help but wonder about what might have been. Their relationship, if that's the right thing to call it, started off with such promise. The week on Martha's Vineyard was too storybook even for a storybook. But the substance below the fun had permeated everything. They shared their most important values. They both believed in community, integrity, loyalty, a pursuit of excellence. Their aesthetics aligned: They shared a passion for many types of music, for various forms of art, and for literature from the Greeks through Chaucer and Chretien de Troyes to Hawthorne and Hemingway. Even Seamus Heaney and Patti Smith. They always had something to talk about, and the discussions—sometimes arguments—were always challenging and thought provoking. Too bad they hadn't had more debates.

He does his best to prepare himself for feeling somewhat out of place. The only thing he knows about Brewster Flats is that she said they were beautiful and that he and she would go there together. He probably won't know anyone at the gathering, although during her illness, he had spoken to one of her friends, Doreen Lyle, a few times. Oh yeah, when she was in hospice, he'd met her friend Karen Langley. Actually, whether or not he knows anyone doesn't really matter. This is not about his comfort zone, is it? It's about Dr. Elaine

Olivia Neal—Eon, as he called her. They are supposed to scatter her ashes into the ocean at twilight.

Although the day is beginning to run out of steam, a solar blaze still overheats the Cape, and no clouds offer relief. The thermometer tops ninety at six thirty, and a heavy dose of humidity prevents him from cooling off. A musky, swampy salt air percolates from the grass lot. He has made the trip nonstop—no refueling and he didn't even pull over to pee. He noses the car into what he thinks is a parking space. Jane Siberry's "Calling All Angels" crops up on the playlist, and he waits for it to finish. They'd discussed that song in one of their many animated conversations.

> Oh, but if you could, do you think you would
> Trade it all, all the pain and suffering?
> Oh, but then you would've missed the beauty of
> The light upon this earth and the sweetness of the leaving
> Walk me through this one, don't leave me alone...
> We're trying, we're hoping, but we're not sure why...
> Calling all angels, calling all angels
> Walk me through this one, walk me through this one
> Don't leave me alone

She thought she might be willing to trade it all. He wouldn't.

He unsticks himself from the driver's seat. His legs are stiff from the ride, but they rally to prevent him from going down into the thick brown puddle he's parked in.

He walks slowly. The normal jump in his step is gone today. He catches himself looking down as he steps toward the house, then remembers that he's looking for someone. He wonders whether he belongs at such an intimate farewell. His only extended time with Elaine was more than ten years ago—and even that was for less than a week—a great week, but still only a week. When it ended, they talked by phone frequently and spewed e-mails at one another. She often told him about friends she saw all the time, friends she had history with, friends Nick considered her real friends, especially Tim Cavendish.

TIM AND ELAINE

Tim pedaled his new cherry-red tricycle, a birthday gift from his parents, as hard as he could. His blond hair blew in the wind, but the old deep-green three-wheeler inched ahead. Elaine's shrieks filled the air as she powered past the old Estes' walkway. They were now halfway between the starting line at Tim's front door and the finish at her house. She held on to the slim lead for the next few seconds and threw her hands up in victory, blasting over the checkered flag they had drawn with chalk on her front sidewalk. It was her third win out of six races that bright spring morning—with one more race to go.

"This is it!" Tim screamed. "Next one's for all the marbles. I'm gonna smoke you."

"Let's go for it!" Elaine screamed back. "You're gonna eat my dust!"

These races happened almost daily, and they were still happening when their tricycles became bicycles with training wheels and then ten-gear road bikes—even when they became two-door four-wheelers with power steering. Sometime around then Tim and Elaine stopped racing against one another but continued to run around together.

Did the tricycles come first, or was it the sandbox? Tim's father had someone build an enormous sandbox in his backyard where Tim and Elaine often teamed up to make castles with lots of rooms and turrets and tunnels. Sometimes they would build a moat and use a few Popsicle sticks as a drawbridge. Years later whenever he would hear Don McLean sing "Castles in the Air," Tim would think of them in that backyard, sand in their hair, in their ears, and in their mouths. Or maybe her birthday party came first—even before her sister and brother were born. They were the only little kids there, but that didn't matter. They played well together. It didn't matter what came first; they were friends.

Tim Cavendish and Elaine Neal. Their families were neighbors close in age and in the same social circle: Mr. Cavendish was Lincoln's preeminent attorney; Dr. Neal was the town's most respected doctor. The ladies, like most Nebraska wives then, worked in the home and wore sundresses with floral patterns in the summer and beige cardigan sweaters in the fall. The families often spent time together: dinners, swimming in the man-made lake at Holmes Park on Normal Boulevard, trips to amusement parks in the summer and to county fairs as the season wore on.

Tim and Elaine played together, went to movies together, listened to music together, walked to and from school together, ate lunch together, and studied together. They were more like twins than neighbors. Together they stormed into high school. At Pius X High School, Elaine bridled at the uniform requirement. She irritated her homeroom teacher by not standing still when Sister tried to measure the distance between the uniform hemline and Elaine's knee. And as soon as she left homeroom, Elaine would fold the waistband of her skirt in violation of the rules. Boys were required to wear a collared shirt and a tie. Tim usually knotted his tie around the collar of a knit golf shirt to comply with the letter of the dress code without ever conforming to its spirit. Elaine soon discovered she didn't like talking about nail polish, eyeliner, or movie stars. Although she liked running and bicycling, she wasn't really into sports. Tim didn't like discussing box scores, motorcycles, and hunting or fishing. They both liked acting and singing. They joined the debate team, the chess team, the science club, the drama club, the glee club, the newspaper, and the yearbook. Together, they smoked their first cigarettes, drank their first beers, and toked their first joints.

The rigidity of a Catholic education didn't sit well with Tim and Elaine. They were tough to handle in any discussion class, especially in religion, where they questioned everything. Tim would start the ball rolling with a couple of innocent-sounding questions. Then Elaine would jump in. Her questions were different—insightful, penetrating—and she showed no mercy. After three or four questions, Father Brennan would throw up his hands as if reaching for the sky to surrender and shout, "Neal, you just have to have faith!" That was the cue for Tim and Elaine to exchange congratulatory smiles and allow the class to proceed.

The crowd they spent time with was small: Tim and a few boys from the chess team and science club—guys who could keep the conversation going on any academic subject—and Elaine and Chloe Lang and Mary Sumner, girls from the debate team and drama club who never wore makeup and who could talk about political events and Edward Albee plays. But, basically, it was Tim and Elaine. They hung out together all through high school except for the last part of junior year.

They were walking home from the bus stop when she started the conversation.

"Richard Adams asked me to the prom." She spit it out from above a black turtleneck, her red ringlets swirling toward an already womanly body.

"Richard Adams? The basketball player? I didn't know you knew him."

Tim's big Irish face foreshadowed the adult version and was topped off by permanently unruly chestnut-brown hair. He had been telling her she should be branching out beyond their small group. Richard Adams was well outside their circle. The cliques overlapped cliques: athletes, popular kids, artsy kids, smart kids, dumb kids, bad kids, working kids, goody-two-shoes kids. Elaine and Tim were in the smart and artsy groups. Richard was an athlete in the popular crowd. Those worlds seldom crossed over. Although Tim made occasional voyages outside his groups, Elaine never did and in fact even know that certain groups existed. She didn't care about such things. Tim cared only enough to break through the boundaries.

"Well, I don't know him," she answered. "Not really. I can't even guess why he asked me."

"Don't you ever look in a mirror?"

"He's not my type."

It always irritated him that she habitually brushed compliments aside, almost as if she didn't hear them.

"Oh really? And why's that?" Tim said with a laugh in his voice.

"Jock. Superficial. Pretty boy. He looks like the kind of guy who's always checking himself out in a mirror, and I'll bet you he copies somebody else's homework."

Tim laughed out loud. He recognized the look she flashed. Her eyes shifted left to right, then down to up. It was her tell that she was about to launch into something witty or biting.

"He probably thinks that an isotope is a cold tope, and I guarantee you he's never read *Catcher in the Rye* or *To Kill a Mockingbird*. Not that he would understand them anyway."

"So, what's your type?" Tim asked.

This was an unusual conversation for them. Ordinarily, they talked philosophy or music or religion or history. Each of them had done some dating, but neither had ever caught the fever.

"I'm not sure I know what it is," she said, "but I'm pretty sure I know he's not it."

"You just talking or asking for advice?"

Tim knew from experience that if he offered advice when she was just venting, the conversation would carom into a sideways skid.

"Just talking, but advice would be okay, too."

Although she wouldn't actually admit it back then, she admired Tim's sense of balance. In reflective moments, she wondered whether she was too serious.

"I think you should go with him. I'm asking Holly."

"Holly who?"

"Holly Crews."

"Who's she?"

Elaine stopped walking. She turned to face him and put her hands on her hips like a Hollywood actress, glaring at him.

He stared back. "You should get to know the 'popular' crowd a little bit. Holly's a cheerleader. Captain of the cheerleaders."

She started walking again, but now it was a slow, pensive walk.

"Why?"

"Why what? Why should you go with Richard? Why am I asking Holly? Or why is she captain of the cheerleaders?"

"Sometimes you can be such an ass. I don't care why she's captain of the cheerleaders. The other two."

"You should go with him because he's somebody different and you need to meet some different guys."

She didn't acknowledge his reply.

"Why Holly?" she asked instead.

"Because she has big…"

Elaine shouldered him hard into the street.

"Bad idea, Don Juan. Chloe or Mary would be better choices."

"Not for me."

Tim turned, laughing, and opened his front door. Elaine slammed her front door even though Tim was already inside.

That night she went to the library rather than to his house to study. Tim didn't think anything of it. She didn't talk to him on the way to or from school the next day or the next. She invited him over to her house for dinner and to study, and she still went over to his place every other night, but they didn't talk about their homework. She gave one-word answers to anything he asked. It was as if they were taking a test and weren't allowed to confer. They went days without debating hot issues in the news. After a few weeks, Tim suggested that they double-date to the prom. Elaine told him to go to hell.

Prom night was clear with a slight chill. Tim gingerly guided his father's Lincoln into the Crews family driveway. A moment after a tense-looking Mrs. Crews ushered Tim into the foyer, Holly appeared at the top of the red-carpeted stairway. He immediately thought of *Gone With the Wind*. Dressed in his standard tuxedo, Tim waited for her descent, and she glided down the stairway without touching the walnut bannister. She greeted him with a two-handed, palms-up hand grasp and a light cheek brush, almost a kiss, that would not disturb her makeup. Her pale yellow gown contrasted with her deep-brown shoulder-length hair, exposing silky shoulders and the cleavage Tim had anticipated. He tried to keep his vision up to her eyes but inwardly chuckled remembering how his reference to Holly's endowment had gotten him pushed into the street a few weeks ago. He gently placed the orchid corsage on her wrist and wrapped her mother's chenille stole carefully around those shoulders. Smiling and eager, they eased into the Continental and headed toward school.

A few blocks away, Elaine was continuing her reading about the search for Amelia Earhart while waiting for Richard. When a white stretch limo pulled up seven minutes late outside the front window and Richard bounded out, Elaine rose slowly from the sofa, opened the door, and looked down at her watch with an exasperated frown. Richard stood angled sideways to the doorway looking out at the limo. He wore tails and a ruffled blue shirt adorned with a mahogany-colored bow tie and cummerbund.

"Is your watch okay?" She said it softly with a light smile in her voice and a totally neutral expression on her face.

"Yeah. Sure." He looked down at the oversized Tag Heuer. "Why?"

"Oh, I just thought we said seven o'clock, that's all."

"Sorry. I left without your corsage, and we had to go back to get it."

It dawned on Richard that Elaine now looked nothing like the everyday version. He didn't know that it was her mother who had to convince her to dress up. She even went to a hairdresser, who swept her long deep-auburn hair into a swirl off her neck to the top of her head. This effect highlighted her blue eyes, tonight with the hue of sapphire. Tim would have seen the reluctance in them, and he also would have seen how the radiance of her hair and the shimmer from her blue satin gown contrasted with her fair skin. Her eyes needed no makeup. An aura of elegance surrounded her—a luminescence that Richard didn't notice.

With the corsage in his right hand, Richard wrapped his left hand around her waist and leaned in slightly to kiss her. Elaine turned her head toward the corsage, and he awkwardly missed her entirely.

"Flowers? Nice," she said. "Thank you. These are my parents, Dr. and Mrs. Neal."

"Nice to meet you, Richard." Richard and the doctor shook hands.

"Thank you, Doc. Same here. And you too, Mrs. Neal."

Her mother smiled but didn't speak.

"And this is my sister, Ashley."

"Nice to meet you, Ashley."

"Hello." Ashley smiled and took a half a step back.

"And who's this little guy?" Richard asked.

"That's my brother..." Elaine answered as Stephan pushed his way to the front and grabbed Richard's right hand with both of his and gave it four enthusiastic pumps.

"Hey, Richard Adams. I'm Stephan Neal. Man, I saw your game against Central. You know, the one where you dropped in thirty-five with seven assists and nine rebounds. Great game, man."

"Yeah. I had a few of them like that last season. Say, I'll give your sister an autograph for you on something from the prom."

"Awesome. Thanks."

Elaine's eyes fluttered up to the ceiling over Richard's left shoulder.

"So, I think we should get going. Here, give me the corsage. I'll have my sister put it on."

"No, I got it, E."

He fumbled to take the flower out of the box and awkwardly began to pin the lily corsage just above her left breast, brushing her shoulder and breast with the back of his hand. He didn't say "excuse me." She recoiled, and he stabbed her with the pin. She grabbed the lily from him and handed it Ashley, who finished the job.

"Richard and Elaine, please get together there so I can get a picture." Mrs. Neal had the camera all ready to go.

"Thank you, Mother," Elaine interrupted. "You have enough pictures already, and we have to go. We're already getting a late start."

"I'll take a picture with you." Stephan moved next to Richard and smiled.

"Some other time, Stephan. We have to go."

Elaine shooed her brother away. She didn't care how good Richard was at sports. She asked herself why she had allowed Cavendish to influence her.

During the short ride to the high school gym, they didn't speak. Richard fiddled with his gold cuff links and kept smoothing his thin eyebrows and the sides of his hair. Elaine studied the back of the chauffeur's head. His hair was neatly trimmed and didn't touch the top of his white starched collar. It pleased her that he wasn't wearing one of those silly driver's caps, but that was the only pleasure she was feeling. She looked at her watch and tried to figure out how long she'd be able to last at this thing and what excuse she'd be able to come up with to get Richard to take her back home. She didn't go against her better judgment often. Damn it, she thought, and on and off clenched her teeth, wishing she had brought the Earhart book with her so she'd have something to do.

When they arrived at school, Richard bolted from the limo and got seven or eight steps away before the chauffer called out to him.

"Sir, your date!"

Richard turned back to see the chauffer opening the back door and extending his hand to help her out.

"Oh yeah. Right."

He backpedaled to the limo, grabbed Elaine's hand, and firmly positioned it on his arm. They took but three steps before she dislodged it. They did not walk in arm in arm.

Once inside, Richard took the most direct path to his teammates, gapping her en route. The guys immediately began running through a play-by-play of the basketball season, throwing out examples of Richard's clutch shooting, smothering defense, and deft passing. Their dates chitchatted off on the side, giggling and admiring one another's jewelry. For a moment Elaine closed her eyes tightly, fighting through the ascending nausea, trying, and succeeding, not to scream and run out of the building.

When Richard wasn't talking about himself or the team, he tried to parade her around like a display doll. He held her too close when they danced, and he groped shamelessly. She fought him off through the night and then insisted that he take her home right after the prom: no after-prom party for her. When the limo arrived back at the Neal home, she ripped the lily off her dress and tossed it on the seat as she slid to the door.

"Good night, Richard," she said. "I'm sure you'll be able to catch up with your friends at the after prom."

"Yeah. I'll find them."

Back in her room, Elaine stared into the mirror. As soon as she let her hair down, she shook her head violently first from side to side and then up and down. Slow brushstrokes helped restore the normal chaos. She felt that she looked better with her hair down. She admitted to herself that the gown was beautiful and that she was glad she had gotten dressed up. But she knew she should have gone with someone else or even with a whole crew who decided to go without dates. She would have danced more and had more fun.

Tim's night went much better. Holly amused him with her primping and preening. They talked about music and movie stars and laughed at one another's stupid jokes. They danced all night and left smiling, breathing heavily.

The next Monday, Elaine wasn't on the bus to school. She ducked away from Tim between classes and afterward that day and the next and the next. She didn't take their regular bus home, either.

On Thursday he set out to find her, starting with the school cafeteria after class. When empty, the cafeteria emitted a chemical smell—disinfectant, Tim once remarked—that didn't penetrate through the hustle and bustle of the lunch periods. (Over the next twenty or thirty years, every time he'd go into a high school cafeteria and get smacked by that same smell, it would take him back to his high school days.) He finally found Elaine on the far side of the cafeteria that day, head buried in Shakespeare's *The Tempest*.

"So, where have you been?" He spoke softly trying to put a smile into his tone. "I know you've been ducking me."

"Go talk to Holly. Jerk." Her voice was a whisper. She didn't look up.

The ninety seconds he stood there felt like ninety minutes to Tim. Then, suddenly, she slammed her book, stood up, and walked away.

"See you later," he called out to her. She didn't turn around and didn't reply.

It didn't blow over. She avoided him for several more weeks. But then, one day, out of the blue, she cornered him in an empty hallway at school after hours.

"Are you still seeing Holly?" It was more of an accusation than a question.

"I was never seeing Holly." His tone was cheery. "I just went to the prom with her."

"Well, you should've taken Mary, a girl with some substance, or Chloe."

"It wasn't a big deal to me. I just wanted to go with somebody different and have a good time."

"That was an awful choice. You don't have a clue, and I'll never take your advice."

They both knew she didn't mean what she said.

"It didn't work out with Richard?"

"You're a fool. I was a lunatic to listen to you."

In their senior year, the crew of six went to the prom together without pairing off as couples. Richard Adams and Holly Crews went together and were prom king and queen.

From that point on, Elaine and Tim did everything together, except date. During the summer before senior year, they began talking about colleges. They had the grades and test scores to go pretty much anywhere they wanted. They looked at the Ivies, Georgetown, Duke, Stanford, Berkeley, and upper-echelon small schools like Wesleyan, Williams, Middlebury, Swarthmore, and Haverford. When it came time to decide, they both chose to stay close and enrolled in Creighton University, where they'd heard the Jesuits were known for their intellects and inspiring teaching.

In the fall they both packed up and trekked the fifty miles up to Omaha, and after that, neither of them returned home often. They lived in separate dorms but spent almost as much time together as they'd done in high school. They took classes together, studied together, and joined the debate team together. Their circles expanded.

Eventually, Tim met Joy, who would later become his wife. Elaine's relationships, meanwhile, seemed to last about the length of a semester: after the initial physical attractions wore off, either she or the young man would realize they were on different intellectual levels, and one or the other or both would allow the relationship to fizzle.

One night after dinner midway through their junior year, Tim and Elaine decided to go to a coffee shop to do some reading. Despite their one falling-out, he had total trust in Elaine. In an isolated corner, Tim spoke to her in something just above a whisper.

"I'm not so sure about law school," Tim said.

For years, he'd made it clear that he'd be following in his father's footsteps. Everyone expected it. He expected it.

"Why's that?" She was surprised. "You've always been so clear about that. I respected that, especially since I don't have a clue on what I'm going to do. I envied you for figuring it out. I've wanted to be as clear and sure of things as you are."

"Well, being Jim Cavendish's son in Lincoln has had some advantages, hasn't it? But, you know, if I go into law back there, there's going to be some expectations, too."

"Like what?"

Elaine always knew that Tim had a sensitive, introspective side to him, but he always seemed so confident, so self-assured. She thought it odd that he had never shared these concerns with her before.

"You know, comparisons. I'd always be Jim's son. Not sure I want that."

He lapsed into silence, toying with his coffee mug. The Cavendish name was precious to him and his family. Tim had a strong relationship with his dad. He admired and respected him, but the famous Jim Cavendish cast a big shadow—former chancellor of the bar, icon of the Lincoln legal community, often mentioned as an eventual state Supreme Court justice nominee. The man's reputation was a bit intimidating, even for someone as self-assured as Tim. All through his days in Lincoln, Tim had made sure that he never did anything to blemish the Cavendish name. Over the years, the self-imposed pressure had accumulated. It followed him to Omaha.

"Don't go back to Lincoln, or don't go into law."

Her comment didn't come off as cavalier.

"I've never seen myself anywhere else doing anything else. I'll figure it out. Plus, Joy likes Lincoln. She likes it better than Omaha. She wants to live there. Thinks there'll be better opportunities there. She likes the school systems in the area and thinks she'd enjoy teaching there. Plus, she feels close to my parents. I have more concerns about myself."

Tim felt better by just talking to her. She had always been someone who could reassure him even with silence. He was always able to draw from her strength, her penetrating insights, and her ability to say the right thing at the right time. Later on, he would think of her as his own singular version of Gordon Lightfoot's "Rainy Day People." One year, for her birthday, he wrote out some of the lyrics in longhand as her birthday card, omitting only some of the "rainy day lover" parts:

Rainy day people always seem to know when it's time to call
Rainy day people don't talk, just listen till they've heard it all
Rainy day people don't mind if you're cryin' a tear or two
Rainy day people all know there's no sorrow they can't rise above
Rainy day people all know how it hangs on a piece of mind
Rainy day people always seem to know when you're feelin' blue
High-steppin' strutters, who land in the gutters, sometimes need one too
Take it or leave it or try to believe, if you've been down too long
Rainy day lovers don't hide love inside, they just pass it on

He finished it off with, "You truly are a rainy day friend."

"We've known one another our whole lives," Elaine responded. "I think I know you better than anybody else. You've never had a problem being your own person."

"I guess, but sometimes I wonder."

"Come on, you were definitely your own person in high school—the same high school where your dad was valedictorian. You're that way now here at Creighton, even though your father went here, too."

"But he was long gone by the time I got there. His presence in Lincoln is huge," he countered.

"He's physically gone, but you know he's still involved. On the board of trustees and all."

She didn't have to remind him that he was smart as hell. She knew he was confident in his intellectual ability, but she did point out that he had the benefit of great parenting.

"You'll carve out your own identity and build on what your dad started," she continued. "Here's what they'll say about you: 'That Cavendish boy—what a man! What a lawyer!' You are no smudged-up carbon copy. You're the new, improved model."

She kissed him lightly on the cheek.

"Thanks."

Once again, she had the right words. He relaxed.

"What about you? Back home, too?"

As much as they talked, she never spoke much about life after college.

"Doubt it."

She had known for years that Creighton would be the beginning of her escape, but she never let on to Tim or anyone because she wasn't ready to go into any explanations.

"Why's that?"

Tim had no idea of the gravity of the conversation that was about to begin.

"You know, there's one thing I've never talked to you about. Not sure I should even now."

She staged a quick debate with herself on whether she should tell him and decided the time was right.

"You can talk to me about anything."

He knew she knew this already but said it anyway.

"My family's not normal." Her tone was on the light side.

"No family's normal," Tim answered.

"You're probably right, but I think mine's a little less normal."

Her tone of voice became slightly more serious like she was beginning the opening statement of a debate. The normal rhythm in her speech flattened.

"So, did the great Dr. Neal scream at you once for not eating your lima beans?"

Tim was used to them bantering back and forth, and although he noticed the change in her tone, he didn't completely pick up that this conversation might be different.

"I'm being serious now. I need you to just listen to me on this. Please?"

With these words, her affect changed completely. A slight quiver crept into her voice. Her cobalt eyes became laser focused, and the normal brightness in her face shadowed over.

"Sorry, go ahead."

He now understood that this would be a different kind of talk. Elaine blanched and shuddered as her childhood story leaked out. She wasn't clear on when or how it started, but she knew it predated her teen years.

"It seemed that the great Dr. Neal had a thing for little girls, even if the little girls were his daughters." Her outward smirk concealed her clenched teeth.

"His daughters? No!"

"Afraid so."

"I'm so sorry."

Tim stopped talking and just looked at her. After a short recovery, she continued.

"At night, he would come to my room with a book to read to me. Then, he…"

She couldn't go on for a moment.

"It was almost every night until my sister got a little older. Then it was still a couple of nights a week. I thought he was stopping, but I figured it out. I tried to make it impossible for him."

"How'd you do that?" He forced the words out.

"Remember all those nights I had dinner at your house?" Her eyes filled, but she managed to hold back the tears.

"Yes." He reached to touch her hand.

"How about the nights I had you come over to do homework and listen to music until my parents went to sleep?" She allowed him to hold both of her hands in his.

"I remember them, too." He squeezed lightly.

"I tried not to be home without you there." She squeezed back.

"Why didn't you tell me?" Tim removed one of his hands and placed it on her shoulder.

"I was ashamed and afraid. It eventually ended in the second half of high school, but it had lasted a few years by then." A single tear traced crooked paths from each of her resolute eyes.

"*Years!* Where was your mother with all this?" He drew her to him in a brotherly hug.

"Drunk most of the time, but I'm pretty sure she knew."

Her labored, staccato breathing started to settle into a normal rhythm. His supportiveness comforted her and helped her relax.

"How?"

Tim was beginning to feel angry with the Neals. He knew that there would be a better time to show it. For now, he just wanted to take care of his friend.

"I have a feeling that she walked in once, early on, saw what was going on, turned around, and walked away. I think she just pretended not to see. There was no way she was going to take on the great Dr. Neal."

As a young girl, Elaine had taken her mother's reaction to mean that her father's behavior was okay.

"What about your sister?"

"I tried to warn her, but she was always 'Daddy's little girl.' She told me I was imagining things—that I was a drama queen. I have no idea how any of this affected my brother. He was still little when I left. So, anyway, I'm not going back to Lincoln. I'll go anywhere but Lincoln. I'll tell you what—if you go to law school, I'll go with you."

"Why would you do that?"

"Everybody has to do something, sometime."

She began to emerge from her dark mood. She pulled her hands from his so they could shake on it.

Tim wanted to apply only to Creighton Law School, but Elaine insisted that they look at five schools in total; he could pick the other four.

"Fate will decide where we go," she said.

Elaine was happy to start an adventure. Tim picked Stanford, University of Chicago, Georgetown, and Columbia. They changed the number to six schools because Tim wanted to add the University of Pennsylvania. He liked the phrase "Philadelphia Lawyer." Elaine researched all six, and they applied to all of them. After a few months, the responses came in; they had been accepted everywhere they applied. They were both A students with high LSATs. They put off the final decision until just before the deadline.

Although initially he was thinking only of Creighton, Tim soon gravitated toward Stanford. As Elaine delved into the background of the schools, she read about how Creighton Law School began and was impressed. In 1903, Rev. Michael Dowling, SJ, then president of Creighton, wanted to start a law department, and he went to Count John Creighton, the school's benefactor, for support. Creighton didn't like the idea because it was "common knowledge that all lawyers are scoundrels." Dowling replied, "that is one of the best reasons why Creighton University should [do it]." The patriarch found that argument persuasive. That vignette resonated with Elaine. Plus, she was well aware of the Jesuit adherence to the tradition of *cura personalis*—care of the whole person. When she found out that Creighton was among the first schools to provide women and minorities access to high-quality legal education, that ended the discussion. They entered Creighton University Law School the next fall.

Law school went as expected. They were both summa cum laude, coeditors in chief of the law review. Tim wrote articles on various kinds of business issues, while Elaine wrote on professional responsibility and legal ethics. By the time they earned their Juris Doctor degrees, counting kindergarten, Tim and Elaine had spent twenty years in school together. He returned to Lincoln, where he and his new wife, Joy, began their lives together hoping to start a family. Elaine fled to Boston and a law practice that lasted only a few years before she got bored and decided to get a PhD in philosophy.

Distance intervened, but the bond between them never weakened.

INTRODUCTIONS: TIM AND NICK AND DOREEN

Tim Cavendish sips on his Samuel Adams Summer Ale and scans the area—under the tent and out on the lawn. He figures that almost all of the guests have arrived. He finishes the introductions in a group of three husband-and-wife couples—Carl and Doreen, Padraig and Sonia, and Karen and Justin—and two women, Lena and Evangeline, who each arrived solo. Tim's wife, Joy, stands off on the other side of the yard, playing hostess with another small group of folks that Tim met today for the first time. In fact, other than Tim's own family members, Doreen and Carl were the only ones he'd actually known before today.

Everyone tries to keep cool on this typically humid New England August day—almost tropical. At this stage of the late afternoon, most of the conversations center on how each person fits in, how they knew Elaine, and why they were invited to be part of this select group. The conversation is light and friendly, cordial, not sullen or morose. Between pulls on his beer, Tim continues his lookout for another unfamiliar guest, the final invitee to arrive, he hopes. The group starts to disperse into the tent just as he hears the throaty growl of a sports car approaching. He suspects and hopes it is Nick, who said he would be driving up from the Philadelphia area, rather than Wayne, who likely would not be driving a sports car. When he sees a man about his age hesitate up the driveway, Tim rushes to greet him.

"You must be Nick." A bellowing sound belts out from Tim's ruddy face.

Nick notices just a trace of Nebraska in the accent—not southern, not cowboy, but not northeastern, distinctive and strong but warm and welcoming. His brain registers the flashing thought that this voice could easily belong to a radio announcer or a TV talk show host, baritone and clear.

"I saw the picture you sent Doreen and a couple more that Doreen found in the house."

Tim's big presence, with that dominant voice, bushy graying beard, and stevedore arms extending into bear-claw hands, would fill even a carnival tent. Nick matches his height—a tick or two above six feet—but Tim looks like the linebacker he never was, while Nick is more marathoner, which he continues to be. The brightness of Tim's tie-dyed Grateful Dead tee shirt and madras shorts looks dim beneath his smile. From what Nick knew, Tim had been Elaine's best friend. They had grown up together, did much of their schooling together, and remained close regardless of how much geographical distance might separate them at any given time. Nick intuits that Tim is the patriarch of this group and perceives that his own place is more that of a peripheral cousin.

On the other hand, Tim knows Nick's unique position here: the man Elaine loved beyond friendship. Although he's fairly certain Nick doesn't know this, doesn't know that he, Nick, was at the very center of Elaine's adult life and that this memorial service is as much to bring Nick into other facets of Elaine's life as it is to give her a proper send-off. Maybe by the end of the night, Nick will have a deeper appreciation of his role. Probably so, Tim surmises. Regardless, Tim's mission is to bring Nick to that point. He has as a secondary objective to keep Nick and Wayne Marlow isolated from each other if Wayne actually makes an appearance.

When Doreen told him that she had invited Wayne, Tim immediately realized it as a mistake on her part, but he didn't tell her. They were all emotionally thin, and he didn't want to hurt Doreen's feelings. In any event, Tim hoped that Wayne wouldn't show up, especially with the girls present. Elaine had told Tim how angry Wayne was when she broke up with him many years ago while she was on Martha's Vineyard. When Wayne found out she had something going with Nick, he threatened both Elaine and Nick. Doreen either didn't know about this or had forgotten.

"I am." Nick smiles back. "And you must be Tim."

Nick extends his hand. He hopes he'll fit in here for Eon's sake. Nick knows nothing about Wayne.

"I go by Cav or Cavendish. Everybody calls me that."

Nick knew that Elaine always called him Cav, but he wasn't sure whether that was reserved for her or if it was his regular handle. Cav grabs Nick's hand and, to Nick's surprise, engulfs him in a man hug.

Cav had vowed to make Nick feel comfortable, a pledge to Elaine. He would stand next to him the entire night if he had to. She thought that Nick might feel a little bit out of place. She told Cav that when she and Nick were together, Nick asked to meet some of her other friends and that it never happened. Elaine shared with Cav more information about Nick than she normally did on people she was seeing. That was one of the first clues to Cav that Nick was so special to her. She let Cav know that from Nick's upbringing in an Italian family in the inner city, he was used to having close contact with a wide circle of family, friends, and acquaintances. Elaine's culture was different. Tim was keenly aware that, for some reason she couldn't explain even to herself, she had all these segregated enclaves of friends. Friends from one silo never crossed over to another; she felt more comfortable keeping them apart. She was aware of her idiosyncrasy, but she didn't fully understand it. All of her friends seemed to know this about her, but Cav was the only one she ever discussed it with. It started many years ago. She once told him once it might have something to do with her family life in Lincoln. She went on and on to Cav in that last week that it would be his responsibility to make Nick feel comfortable at the memorial service. Cav promised he would.

"Great, Cav. I go by my initials—Nad—something I picked up from my dad. Quite a place you have here."

Nad swivels his head to get a panoramic view of the setting. The massive front lawn, now under a gigantic protective tent, preambles a stately Cape estate house. Classic white columns support a peaked slate roof over the third floor, unusual for the Cape. Black shutters flank the white windows on the first and second floors. On the top level, three dormer windows jut out, and two red brick chimneys add symmetry to the green shingled roof. The front entrance boasts a covered porch large enough for three oversized white wicker chairs and an old-fashioned slider. The deck, hidden out back next to a dug-out fire pit surrounded by stones like the kind Nad was accustomed to seeing on the Aquinnah Beach on Martha's Vineyard, overlooks the kind of woods normally found on the Cape—trees with long, spindly trunks topped off with green, bushy wigs. The type of trees that would supplely bend with the ocean winds but wouldn't offer enough resistance to be in danger of snapping midstorm. Not-yet-waning sunlight beams through lush foliage. Cicadas chirp, and soaring gulls choir a background serenade. Fairway grass carpets sandy turf. Everything feels right...except...Eon isn't here in the flesh.

"Our guest of honor found it for us. We started renting here about ten years ago, after the girls were born. Before then, we'd come out every year to visit her and stay at her place. She still had the horses back then. It was great to go riding on the trails through the forest, but after that, we were getting to be too many to stay with her, under the circumstances."

"Circumstances?"

Cav catches himself before he says too much too soon.

"Just a lot of people. Five of us in that house would have put us all on top of one another. We're all glad you could make it. I know how special you were to her. I have something to give you when you leave tonight."

In her last few days, she had gone on and on about Nad and what he meant to her, reinforcing what Cav already knew. Under heavy medication, she kept repeating herself. Cav wondered how he would react to him. Eon had always been reticent about the men in her life over the past fifteen years. She never described anyone in much detail, saying that there was no one special. She even described Wayne that way, although he seemed to have been her guy for a few years. She labeled that relationship as casual. She talked differently about Nad. He was special to her. She thought that he might have been the one, but she blinked early on, and they parted. Her descriptions of him were all positive—personable, engaging, intelligent, sensitive—but, as she would have expected, Cav had to judge for himself. She could influence his thoughts and feelings but not control them. His initial impression of Nad is that Elaine was right on target. He expects to learn more as the evening wears on.

"Okay. What something?"

Maybe this will be okay, Nad thinks. Maybe he won't be an outsider. Cav is very reassuring. Nad wonders again why Eon never introduced him to any of her friends.

"Just something she wanted you to have. Remind me."

He's interested to see how Nad will react to this parting gift, knowing its significance. Regardless, he'll be there to support Nad; he had given Elaine his word.

"Will do," Nad replies. "I'm glad I could make it. I've wanted to meet you for quite a while. I know you were her special friend. I wanted to become a bigger part of her life, so I really wanted to get to know all her close friends, but it never seemed to happen."

"I know," Cav responds. "She always kept everybody separate. She was funny that way. But tonight you'll get the chance. It's important that you meet everyone—Doreen and Carl, Karen and Justin, Lena, Padraig and Sonia, and Evangeline. Our girl made a special request that they get to know you and vice versa. I'll be sure to make it happen. Who'd you like to meet first?"

"Which one is Doreen?"

"Here, I'll introduce you around. Like I said, almost nobody knew anybody else here before tonight."

Nad begins to understand that Doreen and Cavendish orchestrated this gathering not only to celebrate Elaine's life but also to pull together the diverse friends she assiduously quarantined from one another. The realization filters in that there is no inside group to be outside of. That understanding brings him some comfort about how the evening will go.

They work their way through the tent over the manicured grass dotted with tables and easels adorned with photo collages punctuating the scene—a scant outline of Eon's life. Nad glances at them as they ease their way to the other side of the yard. He sees no baby pictures of her and no pictures of her family. He didn't expect to. Her only mentions of them teemed with anger or sadness or both. Her father's abusiveness resulted in her vow never to marry and never to have children. Her adamancy about kids might have been a stumbling block had she and Nad tried to make a go of it. She described her mother as a passive, overly tolerant woman who abdicated her own life and happiness in deference to her husband's demands. It wasn't until after her father passed that Eon could begin to work on any kind of positive relationship with her mother. There just wasn't enough time for that, as her mother passed only a couple of years after her father's death. He first met Eon only a few months after her mother's death. Eon mourned her mother's passing and regretted that the healing process between them had only just begun. He also knows she didn't get along with either her sister or her brother; she said both of them were in total denial about the way both parents treated all three of them. And, her siblings had conspired to deny her her share of the family inheritance. They succeeded when she decided that she'd rather disengage than fight. The greater her distance from her family, the better she felt. She thought of herself as an orphaned only child.

The visual story of her life begins with her high school days. The first four photographs are clearly her official school pictures. He can see how she matured from a young teenager to almost a woman. She went from pixie to petulant to pretty. By senior year, she was beyond pretty. It seems odd for him to see her in a school uniform, knowing as he does how much she detested that kind of imposed conformity, really conformity of almost any kind. She was as unique, original, and genuine a person as he had ever met. The next pictures seem to be from high school, too, but are outside the school context—lots of denim, long hair, and skinny bodies with smiling faces. Cavendish appears in almost all of them. In one, Elaine is playing the bongos and apparently singing with Cav dancing off to the side. In another, she sits majestically on a regal chestnut horse. She's decked out in full riding regalia. Cav stands next to the horse, petting its neck. Another picture, probably from the yearbook, shows her dressed in a contoured suit, standing at a podium, her left arm extended in midgesture. Cav, also in a suit, is sitting at a table off to her right. Probably from a debate tournament, Nad concludes.

The college pictures glow with Elaine's halcyon smile, red hair, and a few with a cigarette dangling from her lips. Her hair cascades in long ringlets in these shots, well below her shoulders. She wears no jewelry and no makeup. Again, Cav appears in several of these. The final picture in this grouping features them embracing in their caps and gowns, diplomas in their hands.

The next arrangement shows her standing between two beautiful, elegant sculptures. He's pretty sure he knows how these fit in—Karen Langley. He hopes to get to talk to Karen tonight.

Elaine's professional career is captured in the next set of photos. Only one shows her in a law office. Many were taken in classrooms and lecture halls. In those, she looks comfortable and relaxed. There is nothing stiff or officious about her appearance. She seems happy and at ease.

The final grouping of pictures confuses him. It's the largest collage of all. One eleven-by-fourteen photo captures her awkwardly holding an infant in each arm, standing in front of this very same Cape home. The children look to be three or four months old, dressed identically in white frilly dresses. The one on the right has dark curly hair, dark eyes, and a darker complexion than Eon; the one on the left has fair skin and strawberry-blond hair. They both display happy smiles, hugging Eon around the neck from either side. Probably Cavendish's kids, Nad guesses. Eon is smiling in the picture, but it seems to Nad that it's more posed and awkward than her natural, relaxed smile, almost quivering. The next photos are normal four-by-sixes of her—in front of her Brewster home with her small black cat named Hypa, standing outside of the Brewster Library, in front of the Cape Cod Museum of Natural History, and on the Cape Cod Rail Trail in Nickerson State Park. It surprises Nad that he's on that easel and that there are two pictures of him without her. She had taken the first with him posing like an ectomorph lifeguard on the Menemsha beach with the about to plummet into the ocean behind him. In the second he's standing in a bookstore, A Bunch of Grapes, in Vineyard Haven, paging through one of Peter Simon's annual Vineyard photo calendars.

The final picture in this display is an eight-by-ten in landscape orientation. It's the only picture he has of her, a group shot taken of the Martha's Vineyard writers' workshop class where they met almost eleven years earlier. He had sent this picture to Doreen just last week. All of the writers plus the head of the workshop are in this photo. Everyone looks happy in colorful summer garb, but the focal point is clearly the front left-hand side, where he and she kneel side by side next to three others. The rest of the group stands behind. The two of them jump right out of the picture. Above her barely visible mid-calf chino pants, she wears a dark-blue wrinkled linen blouse with a scalloped collar. The top two buttons are open. She left them that way intentionally, revealing a white gold starfish pendant he recognized. She had rolled the short sleeves halfway up her forearms so that the simple, ropelike titanium Guy Beard bracelet is obvious on her left wrist. The watch on her right arm is a classic Bulova with a plain black leather band. Eon's hair—he would have to ask if anyone else called her that—is pulled into a ponytail, so her subdued smile, aimed slightly away from the camera, projects out unblocked. With her hair pulled back, the white gold starfish earrings that match the pendant are visible. He had bought them for her at CB Stark when she wasn't watching early on that week on the Vineyard. When they arrived in town, they had grabbed muffins and coffee at Mrs. Miller's Muffins in Edgartown. They sat on a wooden bench by the dock next to the Edgartown Yacht Club feeding crumbs to the ducks, peering over Edgartown Harbor to Chappaquiddick through the masts of sailboats of various sizes, shapes, and colors. They meandered through town, stopping in several of the stores—Island Pursuit, Chappy, Sun Dog, Dream Weaver. In CB Stark she admired these elegant starfish earrings and necklace, so, later on when they continued their walk, he stole off to the restroom, hustled back to CB Stark, and picked them up for her. He surprised her with them that night before they went to sleep. She had that same jewelry on when he visited her in hospice. In the picture, he's on her right, looking more toward her than straight ahead but trying not to be too obvious about it. They are touching in a way the photo doesn't capture.

Memories of that week start to collide for him: a beach picnic dinner by the setting sun at Menemsha; walks on the stone-littered sand under the cliffs on the nude beach at Gay Head, mounds of chocolate ice cream cascading over sugar cones from Mad Martha's in Vineyard Haven or Ben and Bill's in Oak Bluffs; listening to the

Vineyard Sound belting out tunes a cappella on South Water Street in Edgartown.

His gaze slips back over all the pictures in this collage, eventually coming to a stop on the first one, where she's trying not to drop the two small children.

I wonder who the babies are, Nad thinks, not realizing he had actually spoken the question until Cavendish replies.

"I'll introduce you later. Good pictures, aren't they? Doreen put everything together, but I made sure your pictures got put into that one."

"Uh-huh," Nad acknowledges but refrains from asking why.

They make their way to the back of the tent. Cav turns him toward the food and gestures toward a buffet layout.

"We have plenty of food for you."

Over by the far end of the tent, a food table set with cheeses and crackers, fresh blueberries and strawberries, jumbo shrimp, and sliced carrots and red peppers abuts the beverage table displaying red and white wine, a couple of different kinds of beer, and a large bottle of Jameson's. White cotton table covers embroidered with various lighthouses found on the Cape and Islands hide the bare wood of each table. Over by that end of the tent stands a tall, blondish, graceful woman, made more real by her khaki shorts and orange tee shirt, matching toenails poking through flimsy sandals. She and a smiling man sip wine in married conversation.

"Doreen and Carl, this is Nick—Nad. Nad—Doreen and Carl."

Carl vigorously shakes Nad's hand. Doreen hugs him warmly.

DOREEN AND ELAINE

Doreen Lyle was excited about beginning her private-sector career in health-care administration as the new assistant administrator of a long-term care community in Boston. She had been on the job for only two months when her boss suggested that she attend a symposium at Massachusetts General Hospital because there were several breakout sessions on issues involving health and geriatric care. Doreen quickly agreed. The agenda included several topics that would be very helpful to her and the facility. They covered various state regulations, federal reimbursement issues, staff training, patient privacy, technological systems, and so on. The symposium was to conclude with a presentation on Ethical Principles and Problems in Health Care. These were all things she needed to know more about to be successful. She was pleased that her boss thought enough of her to send her there.

She arrived early armed with an eager mind and an opening latte to help her through each of the relevant units. At lunch she had the chance to meet other administrators in her field, more experienced professionals who were very open to share thoughts and experiences with her. They told her that the featured speaker was renowned and an insightful and creative thinker. Doreen could expect a dynamic final presentation. After the last breakout session, she made her way to the large lecture hall, which was already filled almost to capacity. She was interested in medical ethics but felt she had a big gap in her familiarity with issues in this area. She listened attentively as the program coordinator completed the introduction of the featured speaker. He recited many of the presenter's credentials—publications and awards like her highly regarded textbook on medical ethics, part of the curriculum in many medical schools across the country. He spoke about her six consecutive distinguished professor selections. He mentioned several of the scholarly articles she had authored. Doreen reviewed the speaker's education in the program—JD, magna cum laude; PhD philosophy, summa cum laude—and her position, professor of public health, family medicine, and medical ethics, Tufts University School of Medicine. The program coordinator came to the actual introduction: "Dr. Elaine Olivia Neal."

The next hour seemed to vanish as Dr. Neal cogently linked public health and philosophy. To her own insights, she mixed in some classical philosophical principles. Early on, Doreen decided not to take notes, allowing her to focus all of her attention on listening as hard as she could. At one point Dr. Neal referenced Aristotle.

"If we believe men have any personal rights at all as human beings, they have an absolute right to such a measure of good health as society, and society alone, is able to give them."

She recited Aristotle's virtue theory set out in *Nicomachean Ethics*, that man is virtuous when he "experiences pleasure and pain at the right time, toward the right objects, toward the right people, for the right reasons, and in the right manner." She related that to the five rights of medication administration: (1) to administer the right medication, (2) to the right person, (3) at the right time, (4) in the right amount, and (5) in the right way. She deduced from these principles that health-care providers have the ethical obligation to know what they are doing, to choose to act for the benefit of the patients or families to move them toward health or, in some cases, to ease their pain pending death, and to act consistently for the benefit of the patients or their families. She affirmed the efficacy of these principles and lamented that the American system of health care undermined them by often allowing, if not encouraging, decisions to be unduly influenced by financial considerations. She talked about the way she thought it should be, weaving Plato into the discussion:

> The free practitioner, who, for the most part, attends free men, treats their diseases by going into things thoroughly from the beginning in a scientific way, and takes the patient and his family into his confidence. Thus, he learns something from the sufferers and at the same time instructs the invalid to the best of his powers. He does not give his prescriptions until he has won the patient's support, and when he has done so, he steadily aims at producing complete restoration to health by persuading the sufferer into compliance.

But her best-received quotes came at the very end.

"I've already talked a bit about what Aristotle and Plato had to say on our subject today, but I'd like to conclude with the words of a more acclaimed scholar, that time-tested philosopher Groucho Marx. Two of his statements are appropriate for this moment."

She reached to the shelf of her lectern and whipped out Groucho glasses with bushy eyebrows and a thick mustache. As she grabbed the unlit cigar, she raised her eyebrows and brushed away imaginary ashes.

"'The secret of life is honesty and fair dealing. If you can fake that, you've got it made.'" She paused for silence. "'These are my principles; if you don't like them, I have others.'"

A robust and genuine applause gushed up from the audience. When it subsided, the question-and-answer session began. After an hour and three quarters, the program coordinator cut off the questioning and brought the session to an end.

Doreen scans the faces of her audience. Cav and Nad are paying close attention. She is clearly enjoying retelling the story of how she met her friend. The words keep tumbling out.

"I learned so much from this talk," Doreen tells Nad. "I'd never studied much about the classical philosophers, and I had no idea they could be relevant to modern health care. It was revealing. I was really impressed. And, she made it fun, understandable. And, of course, I do like Groucho Marx."

Doreen stops for a minute, not quite sure whether she should go on. Cav urges her forward.

"Tell Nad about how it went from there."

She explains that after the presentation, many of the participants approached the dais to try to get in more questions or to have mini discussions with the doctor. Doreen bided her time, waiting patiently off on the side of the lectern until the crowd began to thin out. When she saw signs that Dr. Neal was about to leave, she swooped in for an introduction. She wanted to meet this woman; she felt a connection.

"Hello, Dr. Neal, my name is Doreen Lyle. I very much enjoyed your presentation. I was wondering whether I could contact you so that we could have coffee to talk about some of the issues you touched on in your speech."

Doreen told Nad that she had felt very stiff and self-conscious when she approached Dr. Neal but that the good doctor immediately put her at ease.

"Pleased to meet you. I prefer Elaine—'Doctor' is for introductions and publications. Actually, you can call me Eon."

Doreen would later learn that when Dr. Neal introduced herself as "Eon," she felt a connection with the person she was meeting. Doreen was forever flattered that Eon's first impression of her was so positive.

"I'd love to chat," Eon told her. "I need to unwind. That q and a was fast and furious. It kept me nimble. I have some time now. I need some coffee and something to eat. Does that work for you?"

"Absolutely."

Doreen was surprised and thrilled. She didn't expect to be able to have this conversation so quickly. She was a little concerned that she didn't have time to refine her thinking so that her questions could be more focused. She knew she would have to improvise.

On the way to the coffee shop, Eon directed the conversation.

"You heard me speak, so you know something of the way I think. You read about me in the handout and the introduction, so you have me at a disadvantage. You know about me, but I don't know a thing about you. Tell me your story."

"Not much to tell, I guess. I grew up in Weston, went to Weston High School. I did pretty well there, but nothing spectacular. My grades were solid, and I was in a few extracurriculars—the newspaper and glee club. After Weston I took a few years off. I wasn't sure what I wanted to do, plus there was no money for college, so I decided to take some time to 'find myself.'"

Eon smiled. "How'd that go for you?"

"Pretty well. Still working on it, though."

"Aren't we all?"

That comment impressed Doreen, especially coming as it did from such an accomplished professional.

"Where'd you go to look for yourself?" Eon asked.

"I went waitressing at first. You learn quite a bit serving other people. You see all kinds when you waitress. Plus, I worked part-time in a shoe-repair shop, learning a craft, and at an art-supply store. I paint some. I was having a hard time sorting out what I wanted to do. I thought that maybe starting college would help me figure things out, so I enrolled in BU. I wasn't sure what I wanted to do there either, other than to listen to some music, drink some beer, go to some parties, and dabble in writing and drawing and painting."

Doreen was worried that she was being too detailed, but Eon encouraged her to keep talking.

"That sounds about right. Let's circle back to that after you get me caught up to how you got to where you are now."

"Toward the end of school, my grandmother's age started to catch up to her, and so she went into an assisted-living community and then a nursing home. Going to visit her got me interested in health care. I saw some great things and some not-so-great things going on, and I decided that I wanted to get involved to help the elderly spend their final years with respect, dignity, and proper care."

Doreen was feeling less and less intimated and continued to hope that she wasn't boring the doctor. She hesitated for a sip of coffee and for a status check.

"Interesting. It sounds like a path opened up and you started down it. What next?" Dr. Neal asked. She liked this woman, liked something about her from the very beginning. There was a freshness about her, a sparkle, an innocence, and a depth. The doctor liked to forge friendships.

"I entered the master's of public health program at Boston University. I graduated a couple of years ago and worked for the state, thinking that might help make a difference. I was wrong. It was frustrating and bureaucratic. It seemed to be more about administrative ease and convenience, and more about money, than care and respect. Some of the things you talked about today. I figured out that it wasn't the place for me. I decided to go into the nonprofit world, so I'm at the Watercrest Residential Community, an assisted-living facility, as the assistant administrator. I started a few months ago. Living in town now." Doreen stopped there.

"I know of Watercrest. It has a strong reputation. I hope it's working out for you there, but, you know, I'd really rather hear about the music, the beer, the writing, the drawing, and the painting. After, of course, we can talk about what's on your mind."

During this two-hour conversation, they failed to run out of mutual interests. They soon discovered they looked at life the same way.

"We started meeting for coffee at least once a week whenever we could. I don't think I would've had a career if it hadn't been for her. She kept me focused on the things we talked about that first day—made it really simple for me. Think about the welfare of each individual patient. Put patients first. They're the ones that matter. Not my boss. Not the docs. The patients were what it was about for her, always."

Nad observes a glow in Doreen's eyes. She immediately had become more animated when she started to tell the story. He can almost feel Doreen's love, admiration, and respect for their friend.

"When was all of this?" Nad asks.

He has the sense that Eon and Doreen went way back and that he was a relatively new friend. Eon talked to him about Doreen often and in detail. Hearing the timeline is helping him understand where he fits in.

"It was about fifteen years ago," Doreen confirms.

"That was a few years before I met her," Nad tosses in. "She told me about you. She really loved you. You and Cav were her closest friends."

From what he had picked up over the years, Nad knew that Eon's friendships with Cav and Doreen were very special. He's surprised that Doreen and Eon met only four or five years before the writers' workshop.

"I would put you in that category, too, Nad," Doreen says. "We got together to talk pretty much every week. There were only two significant breaks—one when we had a bit of a disagreement and one when she went away for an extended sabbatical. But other than those two times, it was pretty consistent. And, our friendship had a strong nonintellectual side. We became going-out buddies—to the beach, to bars, concerts, plays, and movies. We both loved to dance. If either of us found a place where dancing was going on, we were always eager to check it out. It was at one of those places where the only rift in our friendship began. This is the disagreement I mentioned."

"I'd like to hear about that," Nad responds, "if you're willing."

"Of course. No problem. We were always looking for new places to dance. Neither of us had men in our lives at that time. There was this new club that opened on Newbury. One night we decided to check it out. We went in, and it was pretty retro. They were having a history-of-rock-and-roll night. The DJ spun old-time and classic rock and roll—Bill Haley, Elvis, Chuck Berry, Jerry Lee Lewis, Fats Domino. He kept working his way through time. He played the Doors and the Who. We danced up a storm, especially with the early jitterbug songs. At one point we needed a break, so we went to the bar to recover between songs. In midbeer, this really handsome guy comes over in a maroon cashmere sweater and a light-blue oxford shirt."

She nudges Carl.

"He asked me to dance. Eon waved me off with a smiling 'Enjoy.' After the first dance, he asked me again. She went out on the dance floor, too, but then I lost track of her. Later on, when Carl and I got back to the bar, she was gone. She didn't say good-bye, didn't leave a note. I was pretty surprised. We'd never left one another without making contact. I called her the next day, but she didn't answer. I left her messages, sent letters and postcards. She didn't return any of them. I tried for weeks, months even. She just erased herself from my life."

"Sounds familiar, right?" Cav adds.

"About a year later, she called to yell at me about that night. She thought I was being too girly, too needy. She thought I was throwing myself at Carl and making a fool of myself. She was afraid I would be taken advantage of. When she finished, I asked if she would be willing to hear how things developed after that night. She listened. Carl and I got very serious about one another during that year. That night was the beginning of our great relationship. I told her all about it and how much Carl meant to me and about how wonderful he is. At the end of my explanation, she shouted, 'Congratulations.' After that, everything went back to normal. We were friends again. We would hang out sometimes just the two of us, sometimes with Carl. She and Carl became good friends, too. When Carl and I got married, she was my maid of honor. I still remember the toast she made."

"Really? I'd love to hear it," Nad says.

"The best man made the first toast, and then he handed her the mic.

To my sister and brother, Carl and Doreen,
Who met in a bar, where things usually go only so far,
Who first danced to 'Twist and Shout,' then found out what
life's really about.
I've watched your love grow and grow.
You know how it should flow.
May you continue to talk openly every day,
To share what you think and feel in every way,
To eat together, walk together, sleep together,
Dance together, laugh and cry together, and love together in
all kinds of weather,
Now and tomorrow and next year and forever.

I'll never forget that toast." Doreen is smiling.

"I can understand why," Nad says.

"Yeah, she knew about love, and she believed in it. Probably for everybody except maybe herself," Doreen adds.

Cav nods in agreement.

"I think I know what you mean," Nad says.

"Even after we got married, she remained close with us," Doreen pulls Carl in closer. "Through both of my pregnancies, she was like the sister I always wanted. Always there to help but never in the way."

"When it was time to name the girls," Carl adds, "Dor and I decided to name them after her, so we have an 'Elaine' and we have an 'Olivia.' She really cared for our girls. She was more than an aunt. She had an instinct about children, well, with our girls anyway. She always seemed to know what to do with them and what to say. They loved spending time with her. She took them to all kinds of places—carnivals and fairs, concerts, hayrides, haunted houses, and Easter egg hunts. She was constantly looking for the chance to give us some time to be alone as a couple. We all miss her."

"I would love to meet your children," Nad adds.

"We'll make sure that happens," Doreen says.

Doreen focuses her attention on Nad. She had heard so much about him over the years from Eon. She had hoped early on that he would be a strong presence in Eon's life, but it seemed that Eon, as with all of her other relationships, would go only so far and then stop, push the other person away, build a wall around herself. Doreen thought that this guy from Pennsylvania would be the one to break through that wall. She shared that thought directly and clearly with Eon, who said that maybe she was right, that this would be the one, but then, as always, the relationship collapsed. Doreen had a strong positive feeling about him and regretted that it never worked out. She is eager to get to know him better face-to-face. She hopes she and Cav can keep him talking about himself so that they can get a real insight into this man who got further along with forging a true relationship with their friend than any other man had.

"I'm so glad you're here. You might be able to fill in some missing pieces of her life. She spoke about you cryptically."

"Cryptically?" Nad asks. "Well, that's cryptic. What do you mean?"

His emotions swirl. He's beginning to feel too much the center of their attention. He thinks of himself as a peripheral person in her life.

"Well, years ago she came back from a trip in Martha's Vineyard and was all excited, like she just woke up from a glorious dream. She was eager about everything. She told me she broke up with the guy she had been going out with for three years. I had met him only briefly. She tried to keep the various parts of her life separate. And oh, by the way, I invited that other guy, too. His name is Wayne, but like I said, I don't really know him. She said it wasn't really working out with Wayne and hadn't for the past year. I think for her it was just a casual thing—somebody to go to the movies with or out to dinner. I got the feeling that for him it was more serious. She didn't want to go there—at least, not with him. She said she met some guy from Pennsylvania, you, on Martha's Vineyard. She talked about you non-stop after the Vineyard trip—your writing, your running, your music, your law practice—on and on. I pressed her about meeting you, but, like always, she made excuses. You lived so far away. When you came up for the weekend, the visit was so short, and you were pressed for time. It was about a month or so that you were the primary topic of conversation. But then after a few months—poof—you seemed to vanish."

Doreen gestures like a magician making something disappear.

"I thought this was just her typical way of retreating from what could have been something great for her, a real, durable relationship, something that could bring her the happiness and fulfillment that I knew had eluded her. And then after a few more months, *she* disappeared. She took a one-year sabbatical. Went out west. I never even heard from her that year."

Doreen's really wound up. Cav gives her a break to catch her breath.

"It was a similar thing with me, Nad. Eon and I always spoke at least once a week, and we e-mailed pretty much every day. She e-mailed me when she met you, and Doreen is right, it was nonstop Nick this, Nick that. She called you Nick to me. Then, boom—you were gone. The only difference with me was that she stopped in Lincoln on her way out west for her sabbatical, and she stayed with us again on her way back to Brewster when it was over."

"By the time she got back from California," Doreen continues, "it seemed like you were totally gone from her life. I asked her about you, but she just said your paths had diverged. She seemed melancholy about it. I was very disappointed. I had hoped she had finally found the partner I wanted for her. Things went on that way for a couple of years, and then you materialized again. She would talk about you from time to time but not like at the beginning. That's how she was." Doreen pauses.

"That really fits in with how I remember things. I wonder why she never told me about the sabbatical."

Nad remembers the feeling of shock and abandonment when he first lost contact with her. He had never experienced anything like it. Someone who was so present and intertwined with his life and then suddenly gone. He questioned his own judgment and perception of what he really had with her in that short time. Was he mistaken about this person? Did he misunderstand what had gone on between them? The connection, the chemistry, the fit, the shared life vision and values, the aesthetic they both seemed to embrace seemed so real, so right, so tangible. He wondered whether he was seeing a mirage in the desert, an illusion like the heat waves on a highway. Now he's glad to have some of the missing pieces come into place—particularly the sabbatical and Doreen's experience with Eon's flight.

"I need to backtrack for a minute so that you can understand something. When she first came back from the Vineyard, everything seemed to be different this time. She told me you were one of the most important people in her life," Doreen replies.

"She told me that about you, too," Cav confirms. "And she continued to say that to me during her sabbatical and even after she came back and mainstreamed back into her life in Brewster."

"Really!" Nad feels the temperature in his face rise. "I can't imagine why she would say that. We were close, but we didn't see one another very much."

"That's just what she said—often," Doreen insists. "She even called you the most important man in her life."

Cav again nods in agreement. Somewhat flustered, Nad senses the inflow of thoughts and feelings. He responds without filtering them.

"I know about what kind of man her father was and how he treated her. I know that she detested him for what she called his duplicity and depravity. And, I know she wasn't close to her brother. She rarely talked about him, and when she did, she talked mostly about his intellect. She said a few times that he was exceptionally intelligent. For someone of her intellectual status to call someone else exceptionally smart carries quite a bit of weight. But, she said he was very flawed, weak in character and resolve. I know that he wasn't that prominent a male figure in her life. I didn't know about that Wayne guy, but if they were together for a few years, maybe he could have been it. Tim—Cav, you more than anybody, as her best friend, her lifelong friend, you had to be more that guy than me."

"I was never that guy to her. We didn't see one another as male and female. We were friends. We grew up together—just two Lincoln kids who shared large chunks of time together when we were meandering through childhood, adolescence, and even adulthood. We stayed in touch consistently, and we trusted one another. I know I was special to her as a friend or maybe even as a brother. But, I wasn't that guy; you were. I agree with Doreen. Eon told me that meeting you, knowing you, having a relationship with you changed her life, made it better, gave her focus and direction, broadened her perspective. Doreen is correct—you were that guy. But I'm not sure we really know that much about you. Could you fill in a few blanks about yourself?"

NICHOLAS AMADEO
DIDOMINICO

Nad isn't prepared to take center stage. He'd had an inkling that Cav and Doreen would be directing the activities, but he thought the interaction would be more like at a cookout or a dinner party with the focus on Elaine. He didn't expect that he'd be asked to talk much about himself. But, he wants to be polite to his new friends.

"Absolutely, but I'd like to go pretty quickly so I can meet more of the people here, okay?"

He scans the area and realizes there are many more people he wants to meet. He already feels a real connection with Cav, Doreen, and Carl, a very strong positive reaction, so he's willing to share his story with them.

"No problem," Cav replies. "Our girl insisted that I make sure you get to know everyone, but she was even more adamant that we get to know you. She said for her life to be complete, all the important people in her life had to come together. And we know she treated her relationships more like a jigsaw puzzle than a fishing net. She even admitted to me that she had done that. She said it was time for all those pieces to be put together so the picture of her life would become clear. I have to let you know up front that she tipped me off that you might try to gloss over a lot of things about your background. Even in her weakened state, she told me she would find a way to come back and haunt me if I let you. So, you're up—hope you can put a lot of the pieces in place."

Cav's manner is warm and welcoming. His strong, clear statements aren't alienating or offensive. Nad wants to put the pieces together, too, and he wants to strengthen the bond with these folks, not only for Eon's sake but also for his own. He figures he'll be able to read cues from their reactions to things to let him know if he's going on for too long. With this encouragement, he lets more details of his life tumble out.

"Okay, then. Here goes. All four of my grandparents were born in Italy. They both had relatives in America, in the Italian section of Philadelphia. Everybody in my parents' generation was born in South Philly. I grew up in the inner city. Went to a Catholic high school like you and Eon did, Cav. Oh, by the way, I always called her 'Eon.' Is that okay? It seems like you always call her that. Is that what she usually went by?" Nad wants to be appropriate.

"She was 'Eon' to those she was closest to," Cav responds. "I gave her that name. I started to call her that when we were just kids, you know, because of her initials. But then it took on a greater meaning. Her knowledge and her wisdom spanned a period of time way beyond her years. She was one for the eons. She acted like she thought the nickname was stupid, but I knew she liked it. If she wanted you to call her Eon, that meant she felt a connection with you. You were in her inner circle. Most of the time she could tell right away how you would fit into her life. Like with Doreen. To most, she was Elaine. Only rarely was she Dr. Neal. With people who know her, I call her Elaine until I find out what they call her."

"Got it. At the writers' workshop, she introduced herself to the group as Elaine. It never came out in public that she had a JD and a

PhD. On our first walk, she told me I could call her Eon if I wanted to."

With Cav's explanation fresh in his mind, Nad is flattered to learn that she brought him close into her world so quickly.

"That's just like her," Cav explains. "She would never bring up her credentials. She was totally unassuming in that way—very understated. She was a giant in her field, but the way she interacted with everyone she came in contact with was so warm and informal, you'd never know that she was this renowned scholar and sought-after expert. You'd never learn that directly from her."

Cav knew her better than anyone else.

"So, Nad, born in Philly of Italian descent. Eon said you had a proud Italian identity. She admired that about you. So what were those early years like?"

"Like I said, second generation, living in an Italian section of Philly. My parents insisted that we learn English, but during the early years, we had to adapt to English outside the house because most of the time, Italian was spoken inside. All of my aunts and uncles spoke Italian, and that was how they communicated with my grandparents. Italian was the first language in the house except with us kids. From what Eon told me about how you two grew up, Cav, I would guess that my early years were pretty different from what you experienced in Lincoln."

"We didn't come across too many Italian-speaking kids in Lincoln. Of course, many of the kids we grew up with didn't speak English very well either."

They all laugh.

"In our neighborhood it was mostly just Eon and me. There weren't many others to play with. Even in high school, our network was small."

Cav stops to allow Nad to continue.

"That's different from my world. Back in South Philly, your block was your neighborhood, and there were hundreds of blocks in South Philly packed with kids of all ages. No matter what age you were, you had a whole troop of kids to play with. We played street games every day. Some of the games were pretty rough, and we got into fistfights all the time. Some of the older kids made up some dangerous street games. I even wrote a short story about one of those games in that writers' workshop Eon and I were in."

Nad can tell by the way they're locked in that they are enjoying this little journey through his past.

"Interesting. Is it published somewhere?" Cav asks.

"No, I mostly write for my own pleasure. I haven't tried to publish anything. That feels too much like work. I'm pretty sure Eon asked me for a copy of it, so it might be with her things."

Nad remembers that after the workshop, he typed the story up for his files, and Eon asked for a copy.

"Great. I'll check. If not, could you send it to me?" Cav asks.

"Me, too?" Doreen requests.

"Will do, but remember I'm a lawyer who writes on the side, not an author."

Nad continues to feel a bit self-conscious about his writing even though Eon had repeatedly encouraged him to publish his works or at least circulate them around to a wider audience than a few family members and friends.

"Could you give us a little tease about it?" Cav asks.

"Sure. It was for an assignment in the workshop on things we could take back if we could. I put together a story based on one of the street games that became lore on my corner, a game where kids dare one another to do some stupid, sometimes illegal, things. I gave the characters crazy names. The story is wound around that game."

Nad pauses to take a sip of water. He doesn't want to be talking too much and wonders whether he should stop right here. Cav gives him a cue.

"Great. Were there gangs in Philly back then?"

Cav recalls from his many conversations with Eon that Nad's environment was shockingly different from theirs, even though they grew up at the same time and their educational situations were similar. For all Cav knew, Lincoln, Nebraska, and Philadelphia, Pennsylvania, were as different from one another as Saturn and Pluto. He'd been amazed that their lives had converged given the differences in the paths they took. Because of Eon's comments, Cav wants to find out as much about Nad's background as he's willing to share. He's pleased Nad is being so open.

"Lots of them. Virtually each corner, each block, each neighborhood had a gang. Turf fights all the time. As we started to get a little older, it became obvious that the choices were clearly divergent, and you had to make a choice. You could pick the gang route or something else, but you didn't straddle both worlds. If you tried, you became a gang member by default. Some of the kids in my neighborhood went that way—hanging on the corner, getting into fights, stealing radios from cars, the whole street bit. In about sixth grade, I became friends with a bunch of guys from school who lived on the other side of the parish. That was another thing—your specific identity came from your block or your corner. The next level up was your parish. Even after all these years, if I meet somebody from South Philly, the first thing I find out is what street they grew up on. If it was Eleventh and Christian, I immediately say, 'Oh, Saint Paul's,' and we go on from there. Does that ring a bell for you?" Nad asks.

"It wasn't that way for us in Lincoln," Cav explains.

"Not in Weston, either," Doreen adds.

"So, what happened when you crossed over to the other side of the parish?" Cav asks.

"Well, it got me out of the immediate neighborhood and into sports. We played ball together all year long—football, basketball, baseball—and we studied together. So, I sidestepped the gang scene."

"I'm fascinated by that street gang thing," Cav explains. "We didn't have anything like that in Lincoln, at least not that I was aware of. I would love to hear more about it. We have time, and I'll make sure you meet everyone before the night is over. Deal?"

"Deal."

Cav's probing brings back strong memories.

"There were so many kids around the same age in the neighborhoods in South Philly back then that you could find twenty or thirty guys hanging on a corner, and four blocks away, which was like crossing the English Channel for the few of us who knew what the English Channel was, you could have another twenty or thirty guys. Times were different in the city then. A few but not many street guns. Knife fights here and there. Sometimes chains and bats, but mostly it was just fists. It didn't take much to start one. Somebody from one corner walks by another corner at the wrong time. He gets jumped and pummeled. He goes back to his corner, gets his crew. They jump a couple of guys from the other corner. It would escalate from there. Before you know it, you have a full-fledged gang fight. The cops get involved. Some guys are locked up overnight. Things simmer down until the next something or other triggers the next thing."

"Wow! Were you ever a part of that?" Doreen pulls her head back and her chin in. She tilts her head to the left, and her eyes seem to grow bigger.

"No, I was on the outside. It usually started in high school, and I was in with the other crowd by then," Nad replies.

"How did you avoid it?" Carl asks.

"Well, each neighborhood had at least a couple of guys who didn't hang out on a corner. Once it got figured out that you weren't from Tenth and Carpenter or Ninth and Wharton or wherever, that you weren't a corner guy, you sort of got a pass. But, you had to make sure there wasn't any connection between you and any corner. Sometimes, you had to fight your way through a jam before they figured out you weren't a corner guy. I plowed through a couple of gauntlets but nothing serious. You had to show courage without inciting anything. And, you could usually talk your way through a neighborhood, but, again, you had to be careful. A wrong phrase or a wrong tone of voice or even a wrong facial expression or gesture could get you in a lot of trouble pretty quickly. It was a lesson in street diplomacy."

Nad lets out a little laugh. He's remembering the first couple of days when he ventured out of the neighborhood to play ball on the other side of the parish at Pizzi Square. He had to pass the corner at Twelfth and State. He didn't know too much about the gang that hung there, just a few stories he'd heard from some of the guys in his neighborhood. Most of the guys in the Twelve-S gang were three or four years older than he and were led by a couple of kids with colorful nicknames—Butchie Pur, short for Purlini, and Plucker, named for what he supposedly did to a live chicken one day at the Italian Market on Ninth Street. On that first day on his way to play ball, Nad got ambushed by the gang and tried to talk his way out of it. When he couldn't slide by, he tried to maneuver his way into a one-on-one fight, a "fair one" in street lingo. It worked for a few minutes, but as soon has he started to get the better of the kid, a couple of other guys jumped in, and he got sucker punched. He escaped that day with a black eye and a bloody nose but without any permanent damage. On the second day, he got jumped again. Once again he stood up for himself. It helped that two guys who would have been in the Twelve-S gang if they weren't ballplayers vouched for him. They explained to Butchie Pur and Plucker that Nad wasn't disrespecting the corner— just going to the playground at their invitation. He earned his rite of passage those two days.

"I eventually earned a pass because I was crossing turfs to play ball. They made fun of ballplayers, but, by and large, they left us alone. I learned it was important to carry some sort of sign or symbol to make clear what was going on. You know, like dribbling a basketball while walking, or tossing a football up in the air, or carrying a baseball glove."

Nad could talk about this all day.

"Life in the inner city, right?" Cav asks.

"That was about it. I wouldn't have traded it for anything. I got to see a couple of different worlds, worlds that many people never see. I picked up some skills along the way that have helped me through the years. It gave me the opportunity to acquire some guile that I might not have gotten in a different setting. There was a certain toughness you could pick up. And, you learned when to engage and when it would be better to walk away—carefully, but walk away."

Nad looks over at his new friends. Doreen still looks like she's watching a collision. Carl is standing with his right hand holding his chin. Cav is slowly shaking his head left to right.

"It sounds like you put together some street shrewdness with some good old-fashioned luck to survive there," Cav says. "Eon told me you had a lot in the way of street smarts to go with your other smarts."

Cav is getting a stronger understanding about why Eon was so taken with Nad. He senses that the he and Eon could have had quite a life together with a couple of tweaks in circumstances. Over the years, Cav tried time and again to help Eon break through her reluctance to go all-in with relationships, to stop throwing up insurmountable barriers. He's sorry he failed.

"Thanks. I felt all along that I'd picked up some street savvy, but it's really great to hear that Eon portrayed me as smart in other ways as well. That's quite a compliment coming from her. As far as pure intellectual horsepower goes, she was an Indy car tooling through city streets and blasting over open roads—the smartest person I know."

"Amen to that," Doreen confirms.

Doreen's as interested in Nad's story as Cav is, especially knowing how Eon felt about him, how he was the undeclared love of her life.

"It sounds like more skill than luck," she adds.

"Well, maybe, but I definitely got lucky. I fell in with a good crowd. We played sports and had parents that really elevated the importance of education. We did well in school and managed to stay out of trouble. Some of the guys got more seriously involved with crime and violence and drugs. Some of my friends never made it out of their teens. Some of them spent some time in jail. Some of them wound up getting entangled with the mob. One guy I grew up with was found stuffed in a trash bag in the trunk of a car when he was in his twenties. It could be rough, but you could always make another choice."

Nad decides that this is enough about this part of his life. He's ready to move on to begin to meet some other folks, when Carl jumps in.

"This is really interesting to me. What was actual high school like? Can you give us some more detail?" Carl asks.

"I went to a Catholic high school like Cav and Eon did, but my school was all boys. The Philly Archdiocese believed that mixing the sexes in one school would lead to an increase in sin and teenage pregnancies," he jokes.

"Well, who would have believed that Lincoln, Nebraska, could have been more progressive than Philadelphia?" Cav interjects. "We had a mix of priests and nuns at our school. How about yours?"

"No, just priests and male teachers. The only women in our school were in the cafeteria, and the school nurse," Nad explains.

"What order of priests?" Cav asks.

"Norbertines. They were officially named the Order of Premonstratensians, centered in Wisconsin. Boy, was that odd. They were terrific teachers, but they looked and talked very differently from South Philly types. They had buzz cuts and light skin that couldn't get tan. They finished their words in i-n-g and said 'water' rather than 'wudder.'"

Everybody laughs again.

"Well, if they were from where I grew up, they would have said 'wahtah,'" Carl adds.

More smiles from the group. Doreen, still recovering from the street gang stories, wants to know how the boys mixed with the girls. She went to a caricature suburban high school in a typical New England town. Boys were sometimes a tedious distraction, often a perturbing irritant, but always a lurking presence. There were times when she wished her parents had sent her to an all-girl school.

"We had weekly dances at our high school. Girls from our sister school would come and girls from the public school or from any high school, too. But only the boys from our school could get in. The dance was DJ'd, and the music was great. Dancing was big back then. The school was almost four thousand boys, about a thousand in my class freshman year. We lost a couple of hundred along the way."

Nad remembers that almost all the guys from his neighborhood didn't make it through high school. Some of them didn't make it far into life for that matter.

"You seem to have done pretty well, Nad. How did you manage to get an education in that kind of setup?" Cav asks.

Cav's own experience was so different that he couldn't begin to imagine how it would have worked. In Lincoln, his high school class was much smaller, and everybody pretty much looked the same and acted the same as one another. Yes, Eon and he were outliers intellectually, and there were a few bad apples in the group, but there wasn't any serious thuggery. Some of the kids didn't do very well, but he couldn't remember anyone who had flunked out of school or died of violent causes.

"They grouped us homogeneously," Nad explains, "so that everybody got a chance to work to their own level. With a class of around a thousand, they divided us up into roughly twenty-five sections. I was in classes with the same crew pretty much all the way through. It worked pretty well. If you had a higher academic ability, you were given college-prep courses. The guys with more practical ability were directed toward courses that would help them get into trade schools or go right to work. My graduating class produced guys who had all kind of careers—clergy, doctors, lawyers, and even a couple of judges, teachers, businessmen, plumbers, electricians, welders, pipe fitters, crane operators, shipbuilders, musicians—the whole gamut, everything you could think of. Oh, and, of course, there was that occasional gangster here and there as well."

"Then what?" Doreen asks.

Her background is also different from Nad's. She grew up in a prototype New England suburb, and although she was close to Boston, she didn't really experience urban life until she was an adult.

"My father placed a high value on education. He couldn't afford to go to college and went to a trade school. He wanted his kids to get a college education. I applied to one college. We didn't have much money, so I couldn't waste it on college applications. There's a Jesuit college in Philly, Saint Joe's, probably a lot like the one you and Eon went to in Nebraska, Cav. Creighton, right?"

Nad was aware of Creighton long before he met Eon because of the Jesuit connection and because St. Joe's and Creighton played one another in basketball every year.

"Correct," Cav replies. "We knew about Saint Joe's because of the Jesuits and basketball. And we heard about Fordham and Georgetown and Xavier and Saint Louis, too. The Jesuits felt that they had a special role in education, that their teaching techniques and the subject matter they covered set them apart from other schools. As a graduate of a Jesuit institution, I totally agree. Plus Eon and I debated against you guys in college."

"Who won?"

"We got slaughtered as freshmen, were competitive as sophomores, and we dominated junior and senior years."

"I debated in high school. Hearing this makes we wish I'd continued in college. I would have met you and Eon sooner."

"That would have been awesome. I was pretty good, but Eon was exceptional," Cav explains. "She would've been an imposing litigator if she'd stayed the course with her legal career. She had it all—analytical ability and facility with complex fact situations. She was logical and articulate. And she knew how to reach any kind of audience."

"Now there's a surprise," Doreen adds. "So, what was it like at Saint Joe's, Nad?"

"When I started, it was an all-male school. The president of the college was pretty progressive, though, and by the time we graduated, the school was ready to go coed."

Nad always thought it was significant that he went through high school and college in all-male schools. It helped him that he learned to understand male-female environments when he was more mature.

"Ah, so you got to take courses in moral philosophy, epistemology, and Aristotelian logic. Right?" Cav adds.

"Absolutely. The old square of opposition, too. We also studied Bertrand Russell and analytic philosophy."

"I remember it well. And all those theology courses."

"We had some pretty interesting ones. The president taught a course called The Church Today, which was pretty progressive, and I took a seminar called 'Religious Themes in Contemporary Literature.' Challenging, thought-provoking courses."

"So then it was off to law school?" Cav asks.

"No. Not at first. I took two years off and taught. That was an interesting experience. I taught English in an all-girls private high school after I finished high school and college in all-male schools. It was an interesting adjustment."

His answer has a slight smile in it.

"How so?" Doreen asks.

"Well, for one, I had to change my vocabulary."

They all laugh.

"No, not that way. Back then, girls, women—well, I guess they were still girls—weren't given as much of an opportunity to get involved in sports. I usually spoke in sports metaphors. We might be discussing some short story, and we'd come to a part where a character would fail to take an action, and I would say something like, 'Right, he decided to punt there hoping to get some kind of field advantage.' They would look at me like I had just switched to Mandarin. So, I had to be careful about the analogies and the actual words that I used. It was very developmental for me."

"I know exactly what you mean," Carl adds. "Our girls aren't into sports, so I have to adjust how I talk to them, too. Overall, how'd you like it?"

"I really enjoyed the experience, and I've kept up some contact with a few of my former students. One of them is the managing partner of a good law firm in town. She told me that she went to law school partially because of me."

"Why'd you leave?" Cav asks.

Eon had told him that Nad was a natural teacher, that he really liked being in front of a class, and that he felt that he might have made a difference to a kid or two along the way. Cav is particularly interested to hear why someone would pursue the law profession after they had already started a career they found so satisfying.

"I've asked myself that a few times. I did really enjoy the teaching, and I think I might go back to it someday. There's something about helping people grow and develop. That's attractive to me, but I think I got sucked into thinking about material things. I began to figure out that I probably wouldn't be able to do the things I wanted to do, have the things I wanted to have if I continued to teach. I had in the back of my mind from my old debate days in high school that someday I would be a lawyer. I'm really glad I taught those two years. I learned a lot about myself and other people, and I saved some money. The time off helped me approach law school from a different perspective. I think I took more things in stride because I'd been out in the world a little bit.

"So, is that enough detail? Should I meet some more of the folks here before the memorial service begins?"

"We'll make sure you meet everybody," Doreen answers. "Please tell us some more. I'd like to hear more about law school and what led up to your meeting Eon."

"Law school was law school. Cav, you know what I mean, right?"

Cav accents his affirmative nod with a slight grunt.

"Was it unusual being out a few years between college and law school?" Doreen asks.

"I think being a couple of years older than the traditional students helped me. I learned a lot and avoided imploding. I had always been interested in medicine. It's something you pick up as a distance runner. You learn about anatomy and the digestive system, about stress fractures and plantar fasciitis. Plus, I have a cousin who had been premed and decided to work in the pharma industry after college. He talked about medicine quite a bit. So, I decided in law school that I wanted to be a litigator. I found the intersection of law and medicine interesting, so I gravitated toward medical malpractice. I decided to go on the defense side because I liked the security of a firm. I met Eon when I was well into my career. That about sums it up."

"Great. Thanks. But, what about you and Eon?" Cav asks. "Tell us about that, and, oh, I remember Eon saying that sometime after the Vineyard, you got married."

"That's right. After the Vineyard, I tried to make a go of things with her, but things fell apart. When I met her, I thought, this is it. I found the one. The search is over. I thought it would be just a matter of figuring out the geographical issues and spending some more time together, but I felt relatively sure we'd be together. I knew her pretty well already. We'd spent hours and hours talking. With me back in Philly and her in either Brewster or Boston, we talked and e-mailed every day, sometimes several times a day. The e-mails were always delightful, fun but intellectually challenging. She had this thing with words, so if you said something that had a couple of meanings, she would act as if you were using the words in the most obscure way possible and then take the conversation in that direction. Playful and endearing. I got up to see her in Brewster for two days the next weekend, and she came to Philly the weekend after that. Then there was a bit of a break. I had a big case in Phoenix that kept me out there for a few weeks. When I got back, she had a speaking engagement in Chicago. For a time there, our schedules didn't mesh at all. I kept trying to make plans to come up to see her, or have her come visit me in Philly, or to meet on the Vineyard, or on the Cape, or in Boston. She always said yes but seemed to have something going on all the time, so it never happened. And, then, without warning, about two or three months after the Vineyard, everything stopped. Boom. Cold turkey. Nothing. I couldn't get through to her either at her home or at her office. I left messages, but she never returned them. I sent e-mails. She didn't respond. I didn't know what I'd done wrong. I never found out, even though I asked. I was hoping that you might know something about this, Cav. Or you, Doreen."

"That would happen with her sometimes," Cav explains. "In high school she stopped talking to me for months. Eventually, she came around, and I later found out she thought the girl I asked to the prom was a bad choice. I had no idea what was happening until afterward. It's happened a few times since then, too, mostly over silly things but sometimes over real ones. You heard Doreen's story. If you were close with Elaine Olivia Neal, there would come a time when she would disappear from your life for some extended period of time. That's the way she was. She would come back into your life, but you could be guaranteed that at some point she would cut off contact for a while."

"After a while, I gave up," Nad continues. "I sent her a few hand-written letters, but she never wrote back. I tried for a year. I sent flowers. I sent music for her birthday. I almost drove to Brewster on one of my trips to the Vineyard, but at the last minute, when I was only a few miles from her door, I had second thoughts. I didn't want to barge in on her. I didn't know where her head was, and I didn't want to be intrusive, so I turned off. I didn't know what I might be walking into. I felt like I was wasting my time. I thought that maybe she had found somebody else and that I was just a passing thing for her. I was distraught and totally confused. I just gave up. I moved on. I met someone else. She was really terrific—a nice match for me. We had a quite a few things in common. We decided to get married."

As the words tumble out, Nad realizes that he's sounding a bit wistful, like he was settling. He can't think of a way to fix that. The vestiges of regret have seeped out. There is a short but awkward silence as he regathers himself.

"But then she called you back at some point, right, Nad?" Doreen asks.

"Absolutely correct. It was about a few years after the Vineyard and only a couple of weeks before my wedding. She sent me an e-mail like we had been talking every day. It was totally out of the blue. She even invited me to meet her in Boston that weekend. I was totally confused. I told her about the wedding. She congratulated me and said that if I was ever in the area, I should let her know and that we could have 'coffee or a bite to eat.' When I asked her where she'd been for the past few years, she said that she went to California for a while and that she spent time back in Nebraska with you, Cav. I asked her why she cut herself off from me. All she would say was that she was going through some things at work and that she had some family issues to sort out. She told me it was her, not me. I pressed her for more details. All she would say was that she was back in New England for good and living in Brewster like before. I told her that even though I was getting married that I would like to renew our relationship on a friendship basis. She was fine with that. We kept up contact by phone and e-mail. A few times when I was in the Boston area for work, we had dinner or met for coffee and a chat. She seemed very comfortable with that kind of relationship, and it worked for me, too. That was about it."

The further Nad gets into the story, the more uncomfortable he is becoming. He doesn't want to monopolize the conversation, and although he doesn't think of himself as a particularly private person, he's not clear on how much detail they want or how much he should give them.

"Let's go meet some of the other folks here." Nad's tone makes it sound more like a request than a statement.

"I know that you want to meet everyone else, but please indulge us for a few more minutes. We want to hear about the week on Martha's Vineyard, but first I want to ask you about something else. Last year, Eon started talking about you again. Was there some kind of change in your relationship with her?" Doreen asks.

"Well, over the past couple of years, things started to fall apart in my marriage. I tried to work things out—we both did, but we couldn't put it back together. I got divorced last year. Eon knew about that, and we talked about it quite a bit. I wondered whether she and I would have more contact once I got past the divorce. I was sorting things out when she got sick."

During his separation and divorce, Nad wanted to make sure that his feelings for Eon weren't affecting his family situation, so he pulled back from her and limited their contact to less frequent e-mails and phone calls. He also made it a point not to see her during that time. He wanted each situation to be separate. He made sure that his relationship with Eon was no more of a friendship than he had with other female friends and colleagues. She seemed very comfortable with that, too. Most of their conversations during that time centered on her teaching. She was always very much aware of what her students needed. She told him many times that some of these very bright medical students had big holes in their background, that some of them lacked the emotional intelligence she thought was necessary for someone to be a great doctor. She was also concerned that because so many of them had been so successful in everything they had done for such a long period of time that there was a real danger that arrogance had or would set in. She was very attentive to try to prevent this.

Their other big topic of conversation was the book she was coauthoring with a non–med school friend, a woman named Lena.

"Sorry," Cav adds, "there's only one more thing, and it's pretty relevant—that week on the Vineyard. Give us some more of the details about that, and then we'll let you off the hook. I'll circulate you around so you can meet some more of Eon's friends."

MARTHA'S VINEYARD

"Okay, but please make sure I have enough time to meet some of the other folks here, too. Eon mentioned some Irish friends. I don't know if they're here, but if they are, I'd like to meet them. And, she told me about a Russian mathematician and one of her students in medical school. I want to make sure I meet them and your family, Cav. I briefly met Karen in the hospice facility. I'd like to make sure I talk to her. And, I want to hear more about Eon and other parts of her life. Okay?"

He's not sure when they'll be leaving for the actual memorial service on the flats. He wants to make sure he doesn't run out of time. His question goes to all three of them. They all nod assent.

"Definitely," Carl promises.

"I really knew the Cape and Martha's Vineyard well. I went up there for vacation quite a few times, ran the Falmouth Road Race, went to Hyannis and Chatham, and spent a week or two on the island. I fell in love with the Vineyard, diverse beaches and towns with unique characteristics. After renting for a couple of years, I had a small house built just outside of Edgartown, kind of in the woods. Not long after

I started my practice of law, I got this itch to do some creative writing—short stories, poetry, some songs. Just for my own recreational purposes. I really liked my literature courses in college, and I thought writing fiction would be a good break from writing legal briefs and organizing facts for trials. I started going up to the Vineyard for long weekends to get at the writing, to play the guitar, and to do some sketching. It's really quiet there in the off-season, much easier to concentrate without the distractions of everyday life. One time up on the island, I saw a roadside sign for the Chilmark Writing Workshop, and then I saw some flyers about it, too. So I decided to sign up one year. I was pretty hesitant, not sure what to expect."

"I remember when Eon went up there," Doreen adds. "She told me about her family situation and how it haunted her. She said she couldn't escape the demons of her youth no matter how hard she tried. She tried therapy for a while. I think the therapy was hard for her."

"Therapy never worked for her," Cav interjects. "With her intelligence and her guardedness, it was almost impossible for any therapist to get through."

"You are sooo right," Doreen continues. "She gave it up after a while—said she didn't believe in it. 'That's what friends are for,' was her comment."

"She even had a hard time letting friends in. She didn't tell me about what went on until we were almost out of college. I wish I'd have known back when we were growing up in Lincoln. Maybe I could have helped."

Cav vividly recalls that conversation and how shocked he was that he didn't have a clue when it was going on. He was briefly frustrated with Eon for not telling him back when they were in high school. It made him feel helpless. His anger with Dr. and Mrs. Neal survived their deaths. He blamed them for Eon's several missteps with romantic relationships.

"Well, she came up with this idea," Doreen goes on. "She thought that if she went to a writers' workshop, she might be able to step back from she what she went through and write about it in the third person, and that might help her exorcise those demons. She didn't want to go to a workshop in Boston or on the Cape. She thought that would be too close to work and home. One day she told me she found a writing workshop on Martha's Vineyard that was run by a woman and that she was thinking of going to it. It took her a year or two to work up the courage, but she finally signed up."

"I think that quite a few of the folks who sign up for that workshop have the same idea," Nad adds. "They think that maybe they could unburden themselves. Most of the people in that workshop really opened up."

"I remember that she was excited but also apprehensive about going. She had a plan B." Doreen picks up the thread of the story. "She said she was going to leave her car on the mainland and bring her bike over instead. As she set off for the ferry, she told me that if she didn't like the workshop, she would just ride her ass off for the week. When she came home, all she talked about was you, Nad. She didn't tell me much about the week or the workshop."

"Ha, that sounds like her," Nad responds. "She was already giving herself an escape hatch. I felt the same way. I thought I'd try it for a day or two, and if I didn't like it, I'd just go to the beach instead. I wasn't interested in riding my ass off."

Everybody laughs.

"The workshop lasted a week. It was in midsummer. There were fifteen of us in the class. It was run by this dynamic, high-energy woman named Ariel—very nurturing, very supportive. She created a totally safe environment."

"Could you tell us about the other folks?" Cav asks.

"Sure, I've actually kept up an e-mail correspondence with just about everybody from the group. There were just two guys in the group, me and this really cool, good-looking guy in his late twenties. He worked construction up on the island and had the caricature rugged looks of a construction worker, the perfect disguise for a sensitive, introspective man who had a unique way of stringing words together, almost melodically. His writing had a real rhythm to it that was very apparent when he read out his work throughout the week. The women in the group ranged in age from nineteen to sixty. There were two students, two professors—Eon and this chemistry professor at Brown—two stay-at-home mothers, a professional photographer, a financial planner, two women who were a couple and owned a bed-and-breakfast together in New Hampshire, an actress, a waitress, and a massage therapist. For writing assignments they mostly wrote personal essays or poems. They were surprisingly open about what was on their minds—and in their hearts. I don't know how the other guy felt, but at first it made me uncomfortable. A couple of times I felt like I was watching the replay of a train wreck."

"How did you handle that?" Doreen asks.

"Well, I squirmed a little bit here and there, but Ariel did a great job of reassuring everybody that no one in the class was judging anyone else. She validated everyone, so I eventually I felt a lot more comfortable."

"It sounds like it was pretty intense and that it was a really diverse group," Carl interjects.

"Absolutely, ethnically diverse as well: three black women and three Irish women, including Eon. The other guy was born in Brazil. There was a woman of Austrian descent, and a Chinese woman, and one Italian, me. I didn't get background on the other folks. It was a great group, though, and I learned quite a bit about them as the week went on. We spent a lot of time together."

"It sounds like a terrific experience," Doreen adds. "How did you connect with Eon?"

"Well, the week was magical for me," Nad continues. "Ariel runs the workshop from her home. In warm, dry weather, she hosts the group in her backyard. She sets up sixteen chairs in a circle and greets the class with coffee, orange juice, and homemade sweet rolls. As I said, almost all of my classmates were women, but Eon stood out immediately. At the very beginning of day one, she caught my eye. You know how attractive she was. I was mesmerized by her deep-red ringlets splaying out every which way. She liked to stretch out her great legs as she slumped in her chair. And those eyes! They grabbed me immediately. And I studied them through the week—deep blue eyes, eyes with changing hues, sometimes beryl, sometimes cerulean. I tried not to stare, but she caught me looking at her a few times, so I smiled. She smiled back, but it was this restrained smile. I'd call it winsome. That smile added even more allure, a bit of mystery for me."

Cav, Doreen, and Carl again nod in assent.

"And, on day two, her writing caught my ear—reticent, reluctant, but poetic. The overnight assignment was on the subject 'Things That We See' or 'Seeing.' We had to fill in the blanks and write whatever we wanted. I wrote a little short story called 'Seeing Heather' about this guy who was in an accident while driving with his girlfriend, Heather, and is blinded when the windshield shatters in his face. Everybody else except Eon wrote personal essays. She wrote a short poem. She gave me a copy. I remember it clearly:

> The innocence of my childhood
> Passed long before I ever could
> Learn to live and live to love
> To learn to love and give my love
> To be the person I want to be
> And see the things I want to see.

"That's her," Cav interjects. "She had such strong opinions and feelings. And, she loved strongly and deeply, but she was always afraid that she couldn't love, not the way she thought she should. She could never acknowledge her great capacity for love. But, we saw it, didn't we, Doreen?"

"She was a totally loving friend. I'm sure her other friends here would say the same thing. And, she was capable of strong romantic loving feelings, too. Nad, in my conversations with her, I came to learn how much she loved you."

"Definitely," Cav adds.

"Well, she had me totally hooked in."

Nad feels much more comfortable talking about her than about himself.

"She tried to hide her vulnerability, but it pushed its way out. Her writing was so beautiful and personal. I felt pulled toward her, like there was a gravitational force I was helpless to resist—not that I wanted to. Between assignments that second day, I eased over to where she was standing and tried to insinuate myself into a conversation she was having with the Brown professor. I tried not to be obnoxious, but I wanted to make contact. I basically just stood there, smiled, and nodded my head. Grunted a few times, too, like I was part of their discussion. When the session ended, I went right up to her and asked if we could continue our conversation with a walk on the beach. She looked at me, laughed, and asked, 'What conversation?' I felt the temperature rise in my face and hoped that my tan hid the blush. After a few seconds, she let me off the hook. 'Just kidding,' she said. 'I liked your short story. Did that really happen to somebody you know? I wanted to ask you about it.'

"I told her no but that there were times I felt like I didn't measure up, like the guy in the story. She said she knew how that felt, too, and then said she hadn't been to any of the beaches on the island yet and did I have any suggestions. I told her about how I did much of my writing on the beach at Aquinnah. We agreed to drive to the Aquinnah beach to take a walk and maybe grab some sun time. She left her bike at the workshop, and we headed out. Have you folks ever been to that beach?"

The Aquinnah beach is more commonly known as Gay Head because of its multicolored clay cliffs. They spring up out of the sand

and light the scene with red, orange, and yellow tones that meld into darker tones of grays and blues. The head forms a glorious foreground to the Atlantic Ocean.

Cav, Doreen, and Carl shrug negatively.

"Seen pictures, though," Doreen acknowledges.

"Well, we drove with the top down and shouted to one another over Bob Seger's 'Against the Wind' playing on WMVY. You know, 'Caught like a wildfire, out of control.'"

"Yep! 'Wish I didn't know now what I didn't know then.'" Cav sings it out.

"'We were young and strong, we were runnin' against the wind.'" Carl and Doreen add their voices to Cav's.

"I forgot to tell her that some people bathe nude on a part of that beach. We parked in the remote lot and started the half-mile walk to the family beach on a trail just behind the cliffs. We made our way through that part stepping around the stones that cover much of the beach. There were lots of little kids digging holes and building castles. Preteens were boogie boarding through the waves. Some of the teenagers were acting cool, above it all; others tossed footballs and Frisbees; some played horseshoes. Adults were sleeping, reading, or fighting off the seagulls scavenging for food. You know how bold they are diving toward picnic baskets and swooping in to try to make off with French fries or pieces of sandwiches while people are having lunch. They even pry their way into closed bags to steal food. There were quite a few people actually in the water, which surprised Eon because there were no lifeguards or even lifeguard stands. We began sharing backgrounds, when we got to the nude part of the beach. All of a sudden, she came to a dead stop, squared to me, and in semiattack mode took a challenging stance. 'Where the hell are you taking me, Nick?' Boy, was I embarrassed! I told her that this was the 'clothing optional' part of the beach and that I was sorry I hadn't warned her about that. She just laughed and said, 'It'll take more than that!' We walked on, opting to stay clothed. That's when the Nad and the

Eon introductions came in. That we both used our initials as our names was only the first of many things we found out we had in common that day. We eventually walked up to the old World War Two bunker that had fallen off the cliffs into the water. We sat on rocks. We went into the water…without shedding our clothes. She loved thrashing around in the surf. It was rough that day, and it was easier to bob around on the waves. It was a struggle to try to just stand there. She was much more comfortable in the water than I was. At one point she snuck up on me and tossed me into a wave. I, of course, had to retaliate. We wound up playing like that for quite a while. Then, we talked and talked and talked. We were at the beach for almost four hours. We talked law, literature, and philosophy, all in small doses, as the conversation seemed to meander on its own. We got into our very first 'animated conversation' when I told her my legal specialty is medical malpractice defense. Eon was outspoken that doctors and hospitals should be defended but that sometimes they are wrong, and when they are, they should be accountable for their conduct. This got us into a discussion of the legal system and the ethics of advocacy. That initial conversation turned into a bit of a debate, but the argument was intellectual, not personal. She certainly earned my respect, and I think I earned hers as well."

He stops for a breath and to collect his thoughts.

"She was always quick to assess whether somebody could hold a real conversation with her," Cav injects. "If you couldn't, she'd either switch to superficial chatter or else be gone in a heartbeat."

"Eventually our conversation morphed toward music. It was starting to get dark, and we had this writing assignment due for the next day. We started talking about it: dinner at my house. I had lots of fond memories of childhood dinners. I grew up with my parents and grandparents. Often our aunts and uncles and cousins came to the house for dinner. I told Eon that I was really in the workshop to write fiction, and so instead of writing about my actual home, I was going to write a short story about a confrontation in a restaurant in South

Philadelphia, and I would call the story 'Casa Mia.' There would be a fight that would change the protagonist's life forever. She said that at her house, most dinners were pretty quiet. Most of her memories were not happy ones. Her mother almost never talked. Whatever conversation that took place was directed by her father, mostly talks about medicine and local activities. And, he would do most of the talking. She said there was little or no interest in hearing what the children had to say. It was clearly a patriarchal environment. She said the best dinners were when you were over, Cav. She said you came over a lot and that she had dinner at your place a couple of times a week, too. That's when she started to tell me about her home situation, but she just touched the surface in that first conversation. It was not until the next day that more of the story came out."

It surprises Cav that she brought Nad into her confidence so quickly.

"She was pretty turtled up about that subject. You should feel flattered that she trusted you enough to fill you in so soon after she met you. That speaks volumes," Cav says.

"Thanks. I felt the connection, too," Nad says. "Certainly, there was the physical attraction, but it went far beyond that. She seemed to listen with her whole being, like the rest of the world disappeared, like there was nothing more important to her than what you were saying right then. It was very impressive and very enticing. From the outset, I felt like I mattered to her. That opened me up to her."

Cav, Doreen, and Carl nod affirmatively.

"She told me she did a lot of dancing that week," Doreen adds. "What was that about?"

"I suggested that we go back to the house and listen to some music while we worked on our assignment. On the way, we picked up a pizza and a six-pack of Moosehead from Edgartown Pizza to help get the creative juices flowing. We liked a lot of the same music. She had seen Tom Waits in concert; I hadn't. I had seen Phil Ochs; she hadn't.

We had both seen Tom Rush, Jackson Browne, Joni Mitchell, and Bonnie Raitt. Back at the house, it was a challenge to get our writing done, but we managed. Mostly, we danced furiously to the Stones and Bruce and devoured the pizza and beer along the way. George Thorogood kept our spirits up and our legs moving. The week rolled on in much the same way—always together, talking, walking, eating, writing, sleeping, dancing. We didn't even pick her bike up again until the week ended."

"Sounds like quite an idyllic week." Doreen is delighted to be hearing these details.

"Well, it was. I remember only one awkward episode. She told me she had been seeing some guy back on the Cape but that it wasn't working out, that he was looking for a nursemaid to take care of him and his kid. That didn't sound right to me; Eon certainly didn't display any subservient tendencies that I could see. On the second night we were together, she asked for some privacy to make a phone call. I camped out in another room while she talked from the bedroom. The conversation sounded combative. I could hear muffled sounds. I couldn't make out what she was saying, but her tone seemed agitated. When she came downstairs, she looked flustered and a bit sad. I asked if everything was okay. She said yes but wouldn't elaborate. I never found out what that was about."

Doreen and Cav look at one another and simultaneously blurt, "Wayne."

"That's when she broke up with him," Doreen continues.

"I should give you a heads-up, Nad," Cav adds. "Wayne held that against you. Somewhere along the way, he found out she met you on the Vineyard and that you came up to the Cape for a few visits. He attributed their breakup to you. He thought you stole her away."

"Sounds somewhat delusional," Nad blurts out.

"He has a tendency that way," Cav explains. "Well, anyway, he confronted Eon after that weekend and said menacing things toward her and toward you. She kept him at bay, but I ran into him a few times over the years. He continued to hold a grudge. Just saying, in case he shows up tonight."

Nad, Doreen, and Carl look surprised.

"She never said anything about that to me. I'm sorry I invited him," Doreen says.

"It'll be okay," Cav assures her.

"Okay, thanks. I'll be on the lookout," Nad adds. "I didn't know anything about him. At the beginning of our first walk, I asked if she was seeing anyone, and all she said was 'not really.'"

Nad can't believe that anyone would initiate a confrontation at a memorial service, ten-plus years after the fact, but his street instincts kick in. He immediately becomes more attentive to his surroundings.

"We spent all our time together every day that week," Nad continues. "We were either at the workshop, on the beach, walking through one town or another, or back at the house. When I went out running, she came out with me on my bike. I do remember one funny incident later in the week. On the last day, we got a bit of a late start and got to the workshop late. We got out of my car holding identical coffee mugs from the Chilmark store and got razzed a bit for that. Ariel greeted us with a smiling, 'And where have you two been? Glad you could make it.' I blushed. Eon just threw back her ringlets, and, for the first time in public that week, she flashed an unrestrained smile, then glided into a slight curtsy to the polite applause from the other participants. We scrambled to read our assignments from the night before, which were on the subject of eavesdropping."

"Eon liked to cause little stirs. She had a mischievous streak," Doreen tosses in. "I've witnessed a few myself."

"Well, I left the workshop on cloud nine. I got the feeling she was happy, too."

Nad decides that this would be the end of his soliloquy. He simply shrugs and stops talking.

"Okay, Nad." Cav breaks the silence. "We promised to let you off the hook. If there's any more to this part of the story, we'll finish up after the service. It's time for you to meet more of the guests. I think you may have met Karen Langley briefly. Let me get you over to her."

Nad sighs in relief.

KAREN AND ELAINE

Karen Langley, a sculptor by passion and by profession, set up a studio immediately after graduating from the Massachusetts School of Art and Design. She started with the belief and resolution, shaky at times, that she would make it as an artist. Early on she understood that she would need a bridge from art school to becoming a self-sustaining, independent professional. Her dreams of having her art on display in collections at renowned museums and selling at high-end galleries were sobered by the reality of rent payments and peanut-butter-and-jelly-sandwich dinners. Having decided that a retail job would span that gap, she started out working sporadically at her art during the days while working part-time at a bookstore on Newbury Street at night to try to make ends meet. Many days she would just stare at the cold, hard stone waiting for some meaning, some warmth, some image to emerge. She tried to wield her tools with strength, determination, and vision, giving form and life where once only shapelessness prevailed. Many days she would just throw up her hands, throw in the towel, toss on a change of clothes, walk over to the bookstore, and try to be cheerful while attempting to sell the book of the month or whatever.

One August Friday evening, Dr. Elaine Olivia Neal left the Tufts University School of Medicine and decided to take a walk on Newbury Street before having dinner. She loved window-shopping, specializing in houses of creativity, artisans' boutiques where she could check out all manner of contemporary creations: paintings, sculpture, stained glass, wood carvings. She would wander into music stores and put on some headphones to sample the songs of somebody she'd never heard of. She particularly liked a bookstore-café on Newbury. Dr. Neal had a rule: never walk by a bookstore without stopping in for at least a few minutes.

That night, as she approached, she remembered that she'd been meaning to pick up a copy of Seamus Heaney's *Seeing Things*, but first she had to wander aimlessly, pulling out one book after another to read the summary and learn something about any of the authors she didn't already know. She gravitated toward fiction and poetry but would occasionally stop in the philosophy, psychology, or gardening sections as well. She was frequently on the lookout for some new anthology of short stories. In the fiction section, she would check out her favorite authors alphabetically, starting with Patrick Conroy through Richard Ford, to John Irving, to Anne Lamott to Alice Munro, finishing up with Annie Proulx, Joyce Carol Oates, and Richard Russo. She never found anything unexpected—she kept close track of these authors—but she checked anyway. She did the same thing in the poetry section—e e cummings, Emily Dickinson, Seamus Heaney, and Dylan Thomas.

After meandering through the aisles, she found a copy of *Seeing Things* and decided it was time to eat. With the book in her hand, she approached the register, staffed by a clearly distraught young woman. The woman was attractive—long, straight brown hair hanging loose, well down her back, a perfectly symmetrical face with Audrey

Hepburn cheekbones and a Katherine Hepburn smile. Her deflated eyes reminded Dr. Neal of her own. The woman wore a blue calico peasant dress and a bracelet made of many colored strings. A vision of Woodstock popped into Dr. Neal's head, but the music she imagined in the background was sad—no songs of joy and celebration. She sensed instantly that the young woman had only recently stopped crying. Dr. Neal froze to form an intention. Another of her rules was not to pry. But, for some reason, this time she just couldn't help herself. This "child of God" looked so sad that she couldn't just pay for the book and leave.

"Are you okay?" she asked as she arrived at the checkout counter.

Startled, the woman looked up and hesitated as if she might resume crying. Dr. Neal couldn't ignore those puffy eyes.

"What's wrong?" she asked softly.

"Is it that obvious?"

Looking up from the counter, Karen met the gaze of the strikingly pretty woman wearing a lightweight blue striped seersucker suit. Karen's first thought was that this woman must have come straight from work. Her attire was much more professional than she was used to seeing on a Friday night in August. Her second reaction was embarrassment, thinking, *Am I that transparent?* It irked her that she had been so self-absorbed that she lost consciousness of her deportment. Normally, she tried to leave her sadness at home or in the studio. This time she knew she had failed.

"I'm afraid so...Karen," Dr. Neal read off the name tag. "Yes, Karen, I'm afraid so. What is it? Can I help?"

Karen did a quick check around the store. None of her colleagues were close by. Neither were any other customers. She sensed a genuineness and warmth coming from this patron, so she decided to reply openly.

"I'm an artist. I've been trying to get started as a sculptor, and for the past few weeks, I've been totally stuck. I have a beautiful stone but no ideas, no vision, no inspiration. I'm paralyzed. I've never experienced this before."

"Do you want to talk about it?" Dr. Neal asked, smiling knowingly.

"Thanks, but I have to work the register for the next few hours."

"Okay, but let me make sure I understand. You feel stuck, paralyzed, unable to start your project? Do I have that right?"

Elaine had a plan that worked for her every time she felt that way. She hoped to get this young woman to buy into it.

"That's about it," Karen responded.

Just having someone reach out to her like this lifted Karen's spirits. She hadn't yet had the opportunity to make many friends in the city after her graduation.

"It happens to me all the time. I do some writing, and sometimes nothing wants to come out. I have the perfect cure," Elaine responded.

"I definitely need the perfect cure. What is it?" Karen started to smile.

"Tomorrow's Saturday," Elaine explained, "and it's supposed to be warm and sunny. Are you working?" She knew the plan was foolproof.

"Not during the day." Karen had no idea where this was going. "I work a short shift from five to ten tomorrow night, but I'm free until then."

"Okay," Dr. Neal replied. "Meet me tomorrow at noon in the lobby of…"

She named a nearby hotel and told Karen to wear sunglasses, be dressed in a bathing suit with a cover-up, and to carry a large straw basket with reading material and suntan lotion. Karen listened with amused confusion.

"We're going pool crashing. I do it from time to time. I vary where I go, and I try to show up at peak times. They never check to see if you're actually staying in the hotel. I've never seen them check women's IDs, and I've never been caught. If you look and act like you're supposed to be there, they'll think so too. What do you think?"

The candlepower in Karen's face shot up like mercury in Boston in summertime.

"Pool crashing, what a great idea! I'm definitely in. Oh, by the way, I'm Karen Langley." She extended her hand.

"I'm Elaine Neal. I think you're going to be my friend. Friends call me Eon—my middle name is Olivia. My mother was an Olivia de Havilland fan," she said with a smile, wondering whether Karen would recognize that name.

When Karen cocked her head and furrowed her brow, Eon clarified, "She was an actress."

"I'll look her up. That's sort of easy in a bookstore. I'll see you tomorrow at noon."

Karen became immediately distracted, wondering if they stocked an Olivia de Havilland biography. Karen checked the books and found one.

The next day, they rendezvoused in the lobby and dashed into the ladies' room to change out of their street clothes and into their beachwear. Armed with their straw bags and sunglasses, they sauntered into and through the lobby and onto the veranda by the pool. The ploy worked. The attendant smiled them by with a "Welcome, ladies. We're glad you can join us today."

They were not the first to arrive, but they were clearly the most striking. The few men at poolside shamelessly watched as they removed their cover-ups and lotioned themselves up for the day. Eon's long red hair falling out the back of her navy-blue sun visor sharply contrasted with her fair skin. Karen maintained her flower child look with a tie-dyed floppy hat. They pulled up chaise lounge chairs and sat next to one another at poolside for the next four hours, soaking in the sun, sipping margaritas, and sharing life stories.

Karen, several years younger than the professor, had graduated just a short time ago. Her relocation from home in Maine to school in Boston had been infinitely easier than her transition from school to the world. The oldest of seven children from up in logging country, Karen learned in high school that she could see things, beautiful things, trapped in stone. Her family was supportive, and though everyone in the Langley family stayed in Maine after high school to begin making their own ways, they knew she was different and needed to try a different path. They couldn't help her financially, but they provided the love and encouragement that got her into and through Massachusetts School of Art. During her stay there, she acquired the technical skills to free that beauty she saw. But now that she had graduated, she felt adrift. Without the structure of classes and guidance from faculty, she struggled to bring the perseverance and tenacity, the discipline and the whimsy to her work.

Karen shared those thoughts with Dr. Neal that first day, and Dr. Neal, on the spot, by her questions and comments, began to help Karen build the kind of mind-set she needed to become unstuck. Eon first asked Karen to recall what it was like for her when she first started to sculpt.

"What was the first thing you sculpted?"

"It was a unicorn," Karen replied.

"Did you know what it would become when you first started working on it?"

"Yes. We were given a piece of stone and told to go at it. We had worked with clay, and we were taught sculpting technique, but they just threw us into the deep end and told us to create something. We were given free rein," Karen explained.

"Where did the idea come from?"

"I'm part Scot. My mother's family is from Edinburgh. The royal coat of arms is the lion and the unicorn. I always liked the coat of arms, and who doesn't like unicorns?"

"Did you have even the slightest idea on how to sculpt a unicorn when you started?"

"Well, maybe the slightest but not much more," Karen answered. Actually, I didn't have a clue."

"Of course you didn't," Eon continued. "That's usually how it goes when you're starting out. When did its identity start to emerge?"

Eon was confident that she understood the creative process from her own forays into it.

"Once I started working on the stone," Karen answered.

"How did you feel about working on a stone for the first time with no idea what you were doing and no plan on what the outcome would be?"

"I was terrified. I didn't want to ruin it, and I didn't want to make a fool of myself in class."

Karen was starting to feel better already. It was sunny and warm, and her new friend exuded confidence. Karen felt cared for and important.

"How did it turn out?" Eon asked.

"It was okay. Not great but not horrible. When I finished it, I had a strong sense that I'd really accomplished something. I learned a lot."

"What did you learn?"

"I learned that, if I had an idea in mind, things would be okay, that I could find meaning in what I was doing as I went along, that things would become clearer, that I shouldn't be afraid, that I could be careful without being paralyzed. I calmed down. The calmness helped me create."

Things were crystalizing for Karen.

"Did the idea for the unicorn come from staring at the stone?"

"Not at all. I just grabbed on to something that was meaningful to me, and the idea came from that."

"*Voila!* That's how it works. Every once in a while, I write fiction or poetry. I find my voice as I work through the project. I don't try to define it at the beginning and then assemble the pieces. One of the things I like about this process is that it is so different from what I do in the rest of my life. When I'm writing a professional article for publication or preparing a lecture for one of my classes, those processes require analysis and organization. For me, the creative process is more fluid. I just need to get out of my own way. Sounds like staring at the stone might be exactly the wrong way to come up with an idea of what to sculpt. Maybe once you have the idea you can stare at the stone to find your beautiful unicorn, but maybe you have to be looking for it to find it. Do you still have that unicorn?"

"As a matter of fact, I do. We were allowed to keep our work. I know exactly where it is."

"Where?"

"In my apartment, on my nightstand."

Karen realized that she would look at the unicorn at least twice each day without actually seeing it.

"You may want to take it off of your nightstand and bring it into your studio. Every day before you start to work, look at it, really look at it. Look at what you created, and remember how that first time was. Then remind yourself that you're a better artist now than you were then, that it'll be okay. It'll calm you down and open you up. Reach into your imagination to find what's important to you, and then get the hell out of your way and let it happen."

"I'll do it," Karen replied with a smile in her voice.

"You'll be fine. Just get out of your own way."

The lesson was over. Eon reclined for some serious sunbathing.

At the end of the cross-examination/therapy session, Karen felt so motivated to sculpt that she wanted to call in sick so that she could go home and work rather than having to go sell books. Elaine persuaded her to stay the course, go to the store, and attack the project the next day.

"Sustain the motivation," she cajoled. "If you get stuck, give me a shout."

"I will. Oh, by the way, I found a book on Olivia de Havilland. She was quite an actress. Shakespeare and *Gone with the Wind*. Academy Award winner. Impressive. And she had a famous actress sister, Joan Fontaine, who also won an Academy Award. Did your mother want you to be an actress?" Karen wanted to get to know a little bit more about Eon's background.

Eon decided not to share her family saga with Karen just yet. "Well, we were expected to do quite a bit of acting in our family. We were expected to act normal. We were expected to act happy. You know, the way all parents want their kids to act."

As the day wound down and Karen got ready to leave for work, they exchanged contact info and pledged to stay in touch.

Karen could hardly contain herself at work that night. She knew that she wouldn't have the chance to go into the studio until the next day. She arose early, grabbed her unicorn, and set off. She decided to sculpt a lion to go with the unicorn and immediately saw it in the stone. The process was slow, but she lost herself in the work.

She stayed in contact with Eon. They continued their pool crashing whenever they could. They dined together often and frequented those houses of creativity on Newbury Street and elsewhere. Elaine wanted to learn to draw, so Karen tutored her on sketching. Elaine became a frequent overnight guest, first at Karen's apartment and then, after Karen married, at her home on those nights when Eon left Tufts too late and too tired to bus back to the Cape.

Their friendship became an inspiration for Karen. When Karen became a well-known sculptor whose work sold handsomely throughout the art centers of the world, she lavishly acknowledged that it was during her first conversations with her dear friend Dr. Elaine Olivia Neal that she first conceived the two works that jump-started her career. She began work on *The Mentor* about a year after that fortuitous night in the bookstore. *The Mentor*, a study in Italian marble, featured a woman walking with her arm around a younger woman, hand extended, obviously offering guidance and support. In *The Professor*, Karen depicted her dear friend at a lectern, arms gesturing in frozen animation. Both award-winning works would have been museum pieces had they not been privately purchased by a renowned collector.

ILLNESS

Just after New Year's Day, eight months before the memorial service, Nad was cruising through southern Connecticut, returning home from a weekend of writing on Martha's Vineyard, when his cell phone rang. He looked quickly at the caller ID: Elaine Olivia Neal. He hadn't seen Eon in more than a year. There were random messages in clusters here and there from time to time, nothing for several days, then a flurry of contacts—three, four, five in a day.

They'd spoken only briefly at the end of the summer, just before his divorce became final. After that conversation, he began to entertain thoughts of trying to reestablish a close relationship with her, but then the school year started, and she was very busy with her new classes and various other projects. He had his typical workload to juggle and no real blocks of available time. Springtime would soon arrive, and he thought that would be a good time to try to see if the old feelings survived. He didn't feel any urgency to reconnect. Plus, because the divorce was so recent, he felt very comfortable with not forcing the issue. He figured there'd be plenty of time. He wanted it to evolve naturally, if at all. He was pretty sure that it would. Things had developed that way before. He was more unsure of whether the ingredients that catalyzed the chemical reaction between them years ago retained enough vitality to set things in motion again. And, of course, the half-life of her disappearing act had left a residue on his memory. Well, anyway, he'd be game if she were. From their initial communications, he thought she'd be interested, too. He'd been looking forward to trying to get to see her in the spring, toward the end of the school year, and then more frequently, he hoped, if things went well, through the summer.

He sent her a token Christmas present, a brass sand crab reminiscent of the crabs they had seen from time to time on the Vineyard beaches. He enclosed a note: "Please don't take this as my description of your personality. Instead, that's what mine will be if we don't get together sometime soon. Merry Christmas. PS: the crab reminded me of our walks on the beach. Nad." She had sent him a present, too: the soundtrack from Joni Mitchell's surprise performance on November 6, 1995, at the Greenwich Village club the Fez, her first gig before a paying audience in New York in well over a decade. The note said simply, "I assume you were there for this performance—Merry/Happy. Eon." He remembered the show very well. "Night Ride Home" particularly grabbed him:

Once in a while
In a big blue moon
There comes a night like this
Like some surrealist
Invented this fourth of July

He would often think of this song when driving home from the Vineyard over July 4 weekend. He also loved "Amelia":

People will tell you where they've gone
They'll tell you where to go

But till you get there yourself, you never really know
Where some have found their paradise
Others just come to harm
Oh Amelia, it was just a false alarm

Joni still had much of her voice then. And, of course, her timeless poetry would never fade. He had tried to call Eon to thank her for the gift but couldn't get through. He was used to that. He assumed she was calling him back from that message.

"Nad?"

Even if he hadn't seen the caller ID, he would have known it was her from the first sound. But the reception was weak; he could barely hear her.

"Yes, Eon? It's great to hear from you. Happy New Year. How was your holiday? It's a little hard to hear you."

They both preferred face-to-face conversations

"I need to talk to you. Are you in the car?"

She had told him many times that she hated talking to him when he was driving. He heard a faint quiver in her voice.

"Yes. I'm on my way home from the Vineyard. I'm somewhere in Connecticut, south of Mystic, near New London."

"Could you please take me off the speakerphone? I can't deal with the noise now, and this is important."

This was very unlike her. In most of their conversations in the past, she seemed unaffected by things like the speakerphone and car noise, except, of course, in the warm months if he was driving eighty miles an hour with the top down. But this was January. The windows were up, and the road noise was down.

"I'll pull over. Just a minute."

Nad eased onto the shoulder. He needed to settle himself. The inside of the burgundy Porsche 911 Cabriolet was comfortable but small. The diminutive interior was a great venue for listening to music. It was like wearing an enormous set of earphones. Typically, he drove fast with the music pulsing; this always amped him up. He shut the engine down and paused. The way she had opened the conversation seemed ominous to him. He wondered whether she had met someone else or whether there was a problem at work. She often discussed work-related issues with him, just as much to hear herself talk through them as to get his advice. He was hoping it was a work issue.

"Okay, I'm set now. Are you okay?"

"I don't think so. I'm not feeling well."

Her voice was weak, slightly more than a whisper, not the strong, clear voice he was accustomed to hearing.

"What kind of not feeling well?"

He'd never known her to be prone to illness. In fact, he didn't remember her ever being sick during the entire time that he had known her, never a cold, sore throat, headache—nothing.

"I'm not sure. I've been having problems with my cat. She stopped using the litter box, and she's been peeing all over the house."

Eon was almost panting as she spoke. He could hear the short, quick breaths almost as clearly as he heard her words. He couldn't pick up the connection between the cat and her health. This didn't sound like her, he thought. She was always so logical, without gaps in her communication, never missing a step in the sequence when speaking or writing.

"I don't understand."

He remembered when she got the cat—a dark-black Bombay with luminescent eyes and an endearing personality. He thought at first that she introduced the cat to him as "Hypo."

He laughed. "Are we back in law school?" Law professors frequently taught through hypotheticals. She laughed, too.

"Not Hypo—Hypa."

He'd intentionally misconstrued her to say "hippo," and he asked whether she really wanted a pet hippopotamus and settled for a cat instead. That amused her. She clarified that she usually called the cat

Hypa, short for Hypatia of Alexandria. He looked at her like she had three heads.

"Come on, Nad," she cajoled. "You went to a Jesuit school, took philosophy—Hypatia of Alexandria, a Neoplatonist thinker widely recognized as the first known female philosopher."

"Of course," he responded. "What was I thinking?" He knew that she knew that he had no idea who Hypatia of Alexandria was.

Hypa, the cat, had seemed to him to be well domesticated, very affectionate, and almost totally silent. Maybe she was getting up in age and losing some of her control.

"Well, the cat's urine has been stinking up the house, so I called a service in to clean things up. They sprayed some chemicals, but the chemicals are making me sick."

She sounded weepy—totally out of character.

"How long has this been going on?"

It didn't seem right to him that a problem like this could make her sick. He thought that this didn't really sound all that serious. Although maybe the chemicals were the problem, he doubted it. The old wives' remedy of apple cider vinegar was harmless, and he couldn't imagine that a professional service would use chemicals that would be dangerous to customers. He wondered what else might be going on.

"For about six weeks. She just stopped using the litter box. I don't know why. She goes all over the house. I didn't notice it at first, but then the smell started to get to me."

At this point she was almost crying.

"What kind of sick are you?"

It was beginning to sound like more than a trivial problem. Either that or she was wildly inflating the situation—again, not typical of her.

"I'm having a hard time sleeping from the smell. It irritates my nose and throat, so it hurts to swallow. I'm having a hard time eating. I've lost my appetite, and when I do eat, I'm not keeping the food down. Between the sleeping and the eating and the nose and the throat, I'm feeling pretty weak and disoriented."

She had to pause for breath several times during this explanation. He could hear her gasping for air.

"What does the doctor say?"

She worked in a medical school, so he figured she had easy access to a whole arsenal of physicians, specialists in every field.

"I haven't gone. I'm thinking it's just the odor and the chemicals. I'm thinking that once the chemicals and the smell are out, everything will go back to normal."

She'd earlier expressed a reluctance to see doctors despite working in health care. He said it was yet another vestige of her dysfunctional relationship with her father.

"When will the smell be gone?"

This was making less and less sense to him.

"I don't know. They said they haven't corrected the problem yet."

Her thoughts appeared to lack any semblance of rationality.

"Where is Hypa?"

He hoped that she had at least resolved the apparent source of the problem.

"I've put her in the guest room. I keep her locked up in there with a couple of litter boxes. I go in only once every few days to clean them out."

She sounded like she believed this was a rational solution.

"Eon, I'm sorry to tell you this, but if Hypa's the problem, you have to remove her from the house. You can't let her keep doing this. And, you have to see a doctor. Something else might be going on. How much weight have you lost?"

"Ten to fifteen pounds."

He immediately assumed that this meant twenty to twenty-five pounds. She was always on the thin side of average. He calculated that this loss was too high a percentage of her body weight to be insignificant.

"Okay, how about getting out of the house for a while? You can go to the Vineyard house until the smell clears out. I'll mail you a key."

"Thanks, but it's more complicated than that. They told me that the urine has seeped into the foundation and that a part of the house has to be torn down so the foundation can be ripped out and replaced. If not, the smell of urine will stay for years."

She seemed in genuine crisis.

"Okay, what does that involve?"

The story was becoming even more contorted, and she seemed more and more convoluted. There had to be something more to this, but he couldn't pinpoint what it was.

"I'm not sure yet. I'm looking into it. I'll let you know when I find out. But, I may have to leave the house when the work is being done. And, it could take a while. I could stay with my friend Karen in Boston so it would be easier when I go back to work."

"Back to work? You're not working?"

This new information was an additional sign of how serious the situation was. Her dedication to her students was uncompromising.

"I've been feeling too weak to go in. I've taken some time off."

"How much time?"

"It's been a few weeks."

Now he knew it was very serious, but he still wasn't sure whether it was really physical or something even more complex.

"Eon, maybe you should get checked out right away. In the meantime, when I get home, I'll mail you a key to the Vineyard. Get yourself out of there and get better. And make a doctor's appointment. Please."

Both the bizarre story and her health concerned him. He wasn't sure which was worse. He hoped the physical situation might be a minor allergic reaction and that she was just having a hard time dealing with it because she was so unaccustomed to being sick. But this was totally unlike her.

"I will," she replied weakly.

"Please, call me soon! Will you?"

"I will. Thanks. I just needed to talk with you. Bye."

She hung up before he could return her good-bye.

A week later she e-mailed him that she had rented an apartment a mile away in Brewster but that the work would take longer because her house was historically certified and she needed special permission to get it done. He felt assured that she would start to feel better now that she was away from the chemicals. At least, he hoped so. When he asked about the cat, she said she was leaving the cat in the house and would go there every day or two to check on her. This made no sense at all to him. He suggested that she find a real solution. She said she would be fine and would be going back to work soon.

He waited a couple of weeks, called her at work, and left her a message there. When he didn't get a call back, he tried a few times more before contacting the school. He persuaded them into telling him that she was on a medical leave of absence. She had no cell phone, so he couldn't reach her, and because she wasn't home or at work, he couldn't e-mail her. He didn't have contact information for any of her other friends. He considered driving up, but he wasn't sure where to go. He would just have to wait.

In mid-February she called and said that she was feeling better but that she couldn't gain the weight back. In all, she had lost an alarming twenty-seven pounds. He did a quick calculation: more than 20 percent of her body weight. That wasn't good.

"What do the doctors say?"

"I haven't gone. I thought that leaving the house would solve things. I haven't been going to work, so I've been trying to rest."

"You have to see a doctor. And right away."

He wasn't quite shouting at her, but it was close.

"I know. I know. I'll call as soon as I get off the phone."

"Call me back once you've made the appointment Then, call me back after you've seen the doctor. Okay? Please!"

Now he was flat-out worried. This condition sounded very serious. He wondered about Crohn's disease or some other digestive condition. He almost hoped it would be something like that, something correctible.

"I will."

She saw a doctor the next week. A battery of tests was ordered, and she was awaiting results. She would call when they came in. He waited impatiently for the next e-mail or call. In mid-March, it came, again as he was returning from the Vineyard. He didn't recognize the number when it flashed on his phone. Only the 508 area code suggested that he should answer it.

"Nad?" The voice was soft and shaky.

"Yes, Eon?" He recognized the voice but not the affect. "How are you?" He waited. No response. "Eon, Eon, can you hear me?"

"Yes."

She was barely audible. He pulled off the road, closed all the windows, and shut the engine off.

"Eon, I can hardly hear you."

"Sorry, Nad. This is about as loud as I can get. I'm really sick."

For the next several minutes, he strained to hear her. The test results showed rectal cancer. She was meeting with the doctors the next week. They would be laying out the options. She would keep him posted. In the meantime, she didn't want him to come up. She would let him know when she had more information. She was moving back into the house, but she wanted him to have two phone numbers—the Singers', an elderly couple who lived across the street, and Doreen Lyle's, a good friend. She would be in touch soon. She hung up abruptly.

During and after that call, an avalanche of thoughts and feelings swept him away. He knew that rectal cancer was frequently fatal, especially if undetected early on. How the Hypa story fit into this perplexed him. How had this happened so quickly? She always seemed so healthy. Why hadn't she seen a doctor right away? Had she been in denial? He felt her slipping away. For several minutes he sat quietly in the car now chilling in the January cold, traffic whizzing by at eighty miles an hour. He and the car shuddered when relentless tractor-trailers threatened to lift them off the shoulder.

During the next week or so, he called both numbers but reached no one. Both phones rang continuously with no pickup and no answering machines. He feared he had copied them down wrong. He tried her home phone. No answer there either, he repeatedly left messages for her to call him back.

Finally, toward the end of March, she e-mailed him. The options weren't good: surgery, chemotherapy, radiation with no guarantee that anything would work. She was getting another opinion the next week. She would write or call. He e-mailed her the numbers she had given him. She verified them. He tried them again to no avail.

In early April, she called. The conversation was brief.

"I've decided to go into hospice. Doreen is taking me in next week. She'll call you with details. Don't come up now. I'll let you know when I'm settled in, and I'll make sure you know how to reach me. I'd like to hear from you every few days if you can call."

She tried to end the conversation there. He barely had time to ask her for their phone numbers again. This time the numbers she gave were different from the ones she had previously verified.

Once he got off the phone with her, he called Doreen and left a call-back message. When they connected, he learned that Doreen and her husband had been making regular visits to Eon's home to care for her. She'd been growing weaker every day. They went over to try to get her to eat. They'd been helping her pay her bills. She was too weak to write out checks. They helped keep her and the house clean. They helped make the arrangements in a hospice center in Brewster and were about to have her admitted. Doreen told him that the cancer had spread very quickly and that treatment was no longer an option. She'd gone to a doctor's visit with Eon, and the physician said that with this form of cancer, unless it was caught very early on, almost at onset, there was a very low likelihood that treatment would be effective. It was like wildfire.

"Was any of this triggered by the chemicals in the house?" Nad asked.

"What chemicals?" Doreen asked back.

"The chemicals that were used to clean up after the cat."

"I'm a bit confused. Why would Eon be using chemicals to clean up after the cat?"

Nick then retold the story.

"This is very odd. The cat is fine. Hypa has been staying with Carl and me for the past few months. She's fine. I never heard any of this, and the house seems fine to me, too."

The call ended in deep sadness.

A week or so later, Doreen called back with the name and address of the hospice facility.

"She started asking for you yesterday. It might be good for you to come up if you can. Nick, make it as soon as possible."

KAREN AND NAD AT HOSPICE

Nad immediately arranged for his ex-wife to watch their five-year-old son. He packed clothes for a couple of days, not knowing what to expect, and drove as fast as conditions and traffic would allow. The trip seemed interminable. Rather than playing his normal driving music—"Radar Love," "Expressway to Your Heart," "Thunder Road," "The Road and the Sky," "Light My Fire," "Sympathy for the Devil," and a whole host of other upbeat tunes—he programmed a playlist of New Age artists: Enya, Alex de Grassi, George Winston, Scott Cossu, William Ackerman, David Lanz, Chris Spheeris. He mixed in some Michael Franks for variety. He needed something soothing in the background but paid almost no attention to the music. It kept him company without intruding, like when good friends sit with you when you're struggling. It was comforting just to have them nearby.

During the ride, he replayed his week with her at the writers' workshop, trying to remember as many details as he could—that first interaction in Chilmark when he saw her across the grass at the start of the initial session, his awkward approach, her coy but welcoming reception. He recalled the walks and the talks. There were many in that short time, mostly at Gay Head, Menemsha, or South Beach but some on the streets of Edgartown, Oak Bluffs, and Vineyard Haven. Each of the town walks involved ice cream. He remembered the wild dancing in his tiny living room. On the beach she persuaded him to make several forays into the water; he thought of their tossing one another around in the waves. She was more comfortable there than he was. The many drives around the island with the top down, salty air in their hair, and some pile-driving rhythm vibrating through them—"Free Bird," "Stairway to Heaven," "Jessica." They were all joyous. He held back the memories of their nights together for as long as he could. More than once during the ride, he had to wipe his eyes.

He made the trip nonstop, except for one quick fuel break. Two or three times it crossed his mind that he might not make it in time. He accelerated up north on I-95 to I-195 onto Route 28 and over the Bourne Bridge. Each time he crossed the canal, he stole a look at a sign sponsored by the Good Samaritans of the Cape and Islands advertising their suicide-prevention hotline. As he read it, he wondered what would bring someone to the point of scaling the fence and plunging the 135 feet to the Cape Cod Canal below. He had read somewhere that in a twenty-year period, more than fifty people had ended their lives by jumping off the Bourne Bridge and that evidently the Golden Gate led the world, with more than twelve hundred suicides. He recalled his conversation with Eon about the ethics of assisting a suicide when someone was close to death and either about to be or already in great pain. Typically, the discussion was animated and insightful. He tried to block thoughts of suicide, assisted or not, and replace them with something more positive. He summoned up the memory of their last day together on the Gay Head beach where they worked on their final assignment for the workshop: eavesdropping. He wrote a poem inspired by her. She wrote a hilarious vignette based on the gay couple sitting on the blanket next to them.

Finally, he rolled to a stop. Freshwater ponds almost surrounded the one-story red brick building nestled in the woods near the Brewster State Forest. Canadian geese left ample evidence of their presence throughout the parking lot. He looked over and saw a few on the nearest pond. The musky smell of earth and water wafted as he got out of his car, turned toward the foyer, and took a deep breath. He detected the slight scent of salt in the air. He wasn't sure what he would see and how he would react. Doreen had cautioned that Eon was very frail and, at times, heavily medicated. The entryway was all glass and sharp angles, but plants of various sizes and plush sea-blue carpeting added some needed warmth. The wall hangings were decidedly nautical and Cape-like in every way—paintings or photographs of beaches, lighthouses, lobster traps, lifeguard stands, whales, dolphins, and seagulls. He picked out scenes from Chatham, Provincetown, Hyannis, Wellfleet, and Falmouth. Woods Hole was represented and the Vineyard, too.

A receptionist with blue-gray hair sat at the desk inside the doorway pretending to be working on the computer. Her perfectly white, perfectly straight false teeth gave her smile a decidedly horselike look. She greeted him with a warm, grandmotherly, "Can I help you, young man?"

He smiled internally at the "young man" comment. In a very nurturing tone, she gave him precise directions to the room. Under other circumstances he might have considered her somewhat saccharin, but at this point, he welcomed that affect. He tried to walk softly through the hard tiled hallway, but to him, his footfalls sounded like a snare drum. He couldn't help but think first of Samuel Beckett's *Footfalls*, where May paced outside her dying mother's room, and then of Conrad Aiken's "Silent Snow, Secret Snow," even though it was spring. He wished he had a dreamworld he could retreat to, and he longed for rubber-soled shoes. He noticed there was no trace of hospital smell and was grateful. Hospital smells depressed and infuriated him. The inside air was more like what he experienced outside. He considered this a small victory.

He slowed down as he approached her room and hesitated at the door to allow the scene to come at him slowly so that he could make minor adjustments, adapt to what he might encounter within. The first thing he saw was a woman in a denim skirt, a mint-colored smocked chiffon peasant blouse with deep-blue and yellow embroidery on the back. The pattern struck him as Native American. She had a red bandana around her neck. He could see only her right profile. He noticed the large hoop earring that appeared to be a miniature dream catcher. She sat barefoot on the side of the bed; her brown leather sandals lay in tumbled disarray on the floor just under her feet. With her left hand, she was stroking the arm she supported gently with her right arm. There was only one bed in the room, and he couldn't tell at first whether or not it was Eon. The woman whispered soothing, tender words, but she blocked his line of sight. She was talking softly.

"Would you like some water? I brought some music for us to listen to. Here, I'll put it on. You look beautiful. Your eyes are so bright and blue. If you can hear me, just blink or nod."

Nad looked at a whiteboard on the wall, with black Magic Marker writing: "Elaine." His eyes went directly from the whiteboard to the patient dressed in a traditional hospital smock.

The patient blinked and whispered, "Help me sit up…please." Her words were barely audible.

"Yes, sweetheart. Let me help you."

Nad could now see her clearly. A slight vestige of the flash in those blue eyes managed to escape. She was skeletal. When she smiled, he saw a remaining trace of that winsome smile. A wave of warmth washed over him.

He entered the room as quietly as he could. Karen noticed him only when Eon looked past her to acknowledge his arrival.

"Nad," Eon whispered.

She mustered as eager a smile as she could and started to open her arms to him but lacked the strength to hold them out. They instantly crashed to her sides. He approached gently, cautiously, and carefully leaned down to embrace her. She winced, and a short but discernible grunt seeped out. He pulled back. She smiled, but her eyes welled up and failed to hold her tears. Nad stood paralyzed by the side of the bed. Karen grabbed for his arm and started to direct him toward the hallway.

"We'll be right back," Karen told her.

"I'm Karen Langley. Eon and I have been friends for many years. You must be Nick...Nad."

"Yes, I'm pleased to meet you but sorry that it's under these circumstances. You're the famous sculptor, right?"

"Well, thanks to our girl inside there, I do sculpt. Eon spoke of you quite a bit and always affectionately."

"And you, as well. How long have you been here, and what can you tell me?"

"A Doreen Lyle called me a few days ago. Do you know her?" Karen asked.

"Doreen called me, too. I've never met her."

"Me neither. I guess Eon told her about us. I'd been traveling in Europe for the past few months. The last time I saw Eon was back in the fall, before my trip. Everything seemed fine then. We even spoke about taking a trip together next summer. We wanted to go to Australia and New Zealand together. She was very excited about it and said she'd start making a plan. I've been here for about an hour, but she was mostly asleep until just a few minutes before you walked in."

"So, this was all news to you."

Nad tried to imagine Karen's shock when she found out. He had at least a little warning.

"Total shock. I spoke to the nursing staff. She's heavily sedated and drifts in and out of consciousness. When she's awake, she can communicate, sometimes with words, sometimes with nods or blinks, sometimes with gestures. She knows I'm here. She tires easily and slips off to sleep without much warning. She hasn't been out of bed for a couple of days. She asked me to try to get her out of bed a few times, but she didn't make it. She seems to like having someone with her."

The façade of cheerfulness Karen had displayed in the room fell away. Her tone was ominous.

"It's difficult to see. I'm not sure how to act."

On the ride up, Nad thought about how he would react if she was in really bad shape. He wanted to bring the right kind of presence to her bedside. He knew this would be a challenge.

"Just think of all the good things. When she's lucid, she's the same person. She knows what's happening, and she knows that we know. Be yourself with her. That's what she wants. That's what she needs."

Karen's wisdom shored him up. He felt like he'd be okay if he could get through the first few minutes.

"Thank you. Let's go back in."

Karen led the way. Together, they found Eon more alert and ready to talk. Eon asked Karen about the music and specifically asked for some Bruce and Santana and Bonnie. It seemed to revive her even more. She talked slowly but more audibly. She chatted almost lightly about dancing and concerts and pool crashing and writing work-shops and some of her favorite students. The rally lasted almost thirty minutes, but then she dozed off.

"I'll leave you two to have some private time," Karen said and gave Nad a hug. She left quietly.

Nad remained to keep vigil, hoping he would be able to talk to her one last time.

REINTRODUCTION: KAREN AND NAD

Nad feels very self-conscious having talked about himself for so long. He's pleased that he will finally get to meet some of Eon's other friends, so when Cav asks if he's ready to talk to Karen, Nad responds quickly so that he can be reintroduced.

"When I went to visit Eon in the hospice center, Karen was there sitting with Eon when I arrived," Nad explains. "I'm looking forward to talking to her again. We had only a brief time together, and we were focused on Eon. I didn't get a chance to find out anything about her."

"Let me get you over to her. She mentioned that you two met there. I'm sorry I didn't see you there, too. I flew in a few days earlier and left before you arrived."

Cav escorts Nad over to Karen.

"I think you two know one another," he says.

"Yes, hello, Nad. I'm so glad we had the chance to see her that day, just barely in time."

Karen hugs him tightly.

"Me, too. It was pretty clear that she was failing quickly."

Nad's hug matches hers in intensity and duration.

There is no mistaking that Karen is every bit the artist. She totally looks the part. Her dress is loose fitting with a scalloped hemline, ruffled at the top and pleated below the waist. The pattern is floral; the tiny flowers that appear to be pink and red tea roses imbue a vibrancy to her look that perfectly complements her affect. On her right index finger, she wears a large ring that matches the roses in color, size, and shape. It is a large silver piece Karen herself designed. The fingers of her left hand are bare except for the simple wedding ring that looks like it has been shaped from a teaspoon. Nad hadn't noticed that when he met her at Eon's bedside. On this occasion, she clearly is in a more positive frame of mind than when he saw her a few months earlier.

"Yes, Nad, you were the last one to see her. I hope that our visit was comforting to her."

Karen isn't sure Nad knows he was the last friend to visit Eon and watches for a reaction.

"I wasn't aware of that, but, yes, thank you. I'm grateful I could spend that last time with her."

"Let's go sit. I'd like to introduce you to my husband, too."

She whisks him off to a table and beckons to a man off to the side of the beverage table that Nad hadn't noticed before.

"That last day in her room we were totally focused on her," Karen says. "I didn't get the chance to find out anything about you. Eon mentioned you to me many times, but she always wrapped you in mystery. She acted like you two were very close, but she said she didn't see you often. To me you became her mysterious lawyer man from Philadelphia."

"Not so mysterious."

At this point, her husband has made his way over. With his Superman glasses, short cropped hair, yellow oxford shirt with a button-down collar and rolled-up sleeves, and plaid shorts, he has nothing of Karen's artsy look. Yet, somehow, they look just right together.

"Justin, this is Nad, Eon's very close friend from Philadelphia."

"Pleased to meet you, Justin."

"Same here. Karen told me she met you in Eon's hospice room, and Eon had talked about you from time to time when she would stay over at our house in Boston. You know, she was our maid of honor when we got married."

"No, I didn't know that, but I'm not surprised. She had a way about her. If she was close to you, she became almost woven into your life. At least that's how it was with me," Nad replies.

"I totally agree. Our lives were entwined with hers," Justin says.

"That's one of the reasons I was confused about why I never got to meet any of her friends. You two were so close to her, but I understand you didn't meet many of her other friends either. Do either of you have a theory on that?"

"No, we didn't. We did things with her but never with her and other friends. What do you think, Justin?"

"I agree that it was very strange that none of us met one another before," Justin answers, "but she wasn't at all reluctant to talk to us about her other friends. I felt I knew Doreen and Carl, and Cav and Joy, and you, too, Nad. She talked about everybody like we were a community of friends, but she never let the community actually form. I wonder whether she was afraid that some kind of conflict might arise. I do think she was very conflict averse. She always wanted everybody to get along, for things to be right, for there to be harmony."

"That makes sense. I think you're onto something. Do you guys know anything about her home life in Lincoln?"

Nad isn't sure who all knows about the family dysfunction and the abuse. His question stops the conversation dead in its tracks. Karen and Justin look at one another for guidance on whether or not to share what they know. Nad jumps right back in.

"Your expression tells me that—"

"Eon told us how close she was to you," Karen interrupts, "how much you meant to her, so I assume you knew what went on in her family when she was growing up. I'm sorry we froze there for a minute. I just needed to process for a few seconds to come to the realization that you know all about that. Sorry. Yes."

"That's okay. I didn't know whether you knew either. That's why I asked that way. Justin, I think that maybe she was okay with small groups of two or three close friends, where she could make sure there was no potential conflict, and shied away from making the groups bigger, where chances were higher for disagreements. She could handle microgatherings, but she was afraid of anything bigger."

"I think you're right," Justin replies.

"But, back to you, Nad. As I said, she portrayed you as mysterious. Could you tell us something about yourself and your relationship with her?"

"I don't think of myself as mysterious or even guarded in any way. What did she do or say that made me seem mysterious?"

He has heard this a few too many times already today not to try to understand it better.

"Well, I asked her to describe you, and all she would say was that you're very Italian looking, Mediterranean, dark wavy hair, thin and fit. All she would say about your work was that you're a lawyer. She made references about you swooping into her life for a week on Martha's Vineyard, and then you seemed to disappear, only to pop up now and again. She was just vague and evasive about you, and Eon was almost never vague. She was always precise and detailed. When you asked her to describe someone, you'd normally get enough information to make a pretty good sketch just from her words. And when you asked her what someone was like, you'd usually get such detail that you could almost do a psychological study of them. But, not about you. Everything was different when it came to you."

Karen's comments are giving him more insight into the "mystery" issue than anyone else had. He summarizes what he had told the others about himself and his relationship with their friend.

"Let me turn the tables on you, Karen. I know about the public Karen Langley from what has been written about you and your work. But what about you?"

Karen tells him about how Eon rescued her from her artistic paralysis early in her career, about the pool crashing, and about a variety of their other escapades together.

"She was my dearest friend. The dearest friend anyone could hope to have. She was my maid of honor and my son's godmother. I was closer to her than to any other woman in my life."

Karen's speech becomes halting. She pauses to allow her emotions to quell.

"Oh, and, by the way, before I forget again, on that Sunday at the hospice center, she was asking for you just before you came in. I thought you should know that. She kept saying, 'Nad? Nad? Where are you? I need to tell you something.' But she then became somewhat disoriented. She was talking about how Cav and Joy, Doreen and Carl, Justin and I, and you and she had all been going out and doing things together and how she was so happy to have such a close group who all got along so well. It was so strange, especially in light of the conversation we just had about her keeping us all apart."

"Well, she finally brought us all together," Nad says, "and I'm happy about that. I'm finally getting to meet the people who were important to her."

"We're starting to run out of daylight," Cav interjects. "I still have a few people to introduce you to before we head over to the flats for the service. Let's go find Evangeline."

EVANGELINE DIXON

Evangeline Dixon grew up on the streets of East Saint Louis, the middle child of five—two older sisters and two younger half sisters. Most of the time there was no man of the house. Her mother, Anne, struggled to keep the family going—safe, secure, and together—in an often turbulent, relentless environment. To Anne's credit, when Evangeline was very young, seven or eight, she recognized that Evangeline seemed different in nature and degree from the other kids in the neighborhood, even her own siblings. Anne saw a potential in Evangeline—a potential to reach heights, to have an impact far beyond what she saw in the others. This was not just a mother's skewed perception of her child. Anne Dixon didn't feel that way about her other children, although she loved them all equally. The differences in Evangeline were striking and unmistakable. She learned everything quickly: language, mathematics, science, social skills, sports, music—everything. Plus, she was exceedingly polite and had an effervescence about her that drew everyone in. Before she was pretty, she was cute, but she was always charming and charismatic. Everyone liked and admired her.

Often, having one child stand out so prominently in a family causes disputes—disruption, dissension, and dysfunction. But, not in this case. Early on she became the center of the family. Her older sisters, rather than becoming jealous, also recognized how exceptional she was and tried to pave a smooth road for her through school. Her accomplishments became a source of family pride. Evangeline's achievements reflected positively on the entire family. Evangeline gave them hope. It didn't hurt that she did more than her share of work around the house—cooking, cleaning, laundry, ironing. She had inexhaustible energy. In those early years, her younger half sisters idolized her, and her older sisters protected her.

Evangeline sailed through grade school and high school as a straight-A student. She learned the piano on her own and could play every kind of music, from ragtime to classical—Aaron Copland, Claude Debussy, Scott Joplin, Sergei Rachmaninoff, Igor Stravinsky. She had a natural talent for the liberal arts. She wrote beautifully in lyrical prose with penetrating insights. In English classes she could delayer and uncover meanings in the stories and poetry that brought revelations to her classmates and her teachers. She retained many of the details from her history classes, but more importantly, she saw the patterns and trends from past events and related them to many aspects of the current world. She excelled in foreign languages as well. To cap it all off, her extraordinary acumen in the sciences made her a totally well-rounded student, the female version of a true Renaissance man.

It was in high school that she first became interested in medicine. She witnessed close-up how difficult it was for inner-city families to gain access to quality health care. The battle to provide the basic necessities of life—food, shelter, and clothing—relegated health considerations to number four, at best, on the priority scale. Diets were bad. There was either no time for or no inclination to exercise. The availability of preventative, diagnostic, and treatment services were far too limited to meet the community's needs. And so, Evangeline made this her life's mission. She vowed to chip away at this shortfall by becoming a physician and then returning, hopefully to her own community, to try to narrow the gap between needs and services, to help provide to the next generation what her generation simply couldn't access.

In high school, she began volunteering at both the regional and the Catholic hospitals in her community. After a short time, she graduated from traditional candy striper duties to shadowing nurses, who soon began to feel very confident in delegating some of their responsibilities to this talented, willing teenager. She helped bathe and change patients. She took temperatures and blood pressures. She got the nurses to teach her how to change bandages and even IV bags. She watched and learned endotracheal intubations. Although they wouldn't let her actually perform any, she was confident she would be able to if called on in an emergency. She could and did set up EKGs and learned to draw inferences from the results. Her conclusions were always right on target. The staff taught her how to read medical charts and explained what medications were being used for certain conditions. She learned something from everybody: the nutritionists, X-ray technicians, phlebotomists, physical therapists, pharmacists, emergency room nurses, operating room staff, and the birth and delivery teams. She was anything but shy about asking questions, and, rather than seeming pushy or obnoxious about it, she asked in a way that seemed so innocent and sincere that everyone took time to explain and show her whatever she wanted to learn. Soon the doctors also noticed her abilities, and they, too, would take time instructing her. Her medical education began in those teenage years, and it was a practical, hands-on education.

As her high school time edged toward graduation, she began assessing the premed programs at various schools. She looked at all the top schools—Boston University, Cornell, Creighton, Dartmouth, Johns Hopkins. Her family didn't have the money for a shotgun application approach, so she decided to focus on Saint Louis University because of its reputation as a top-ten premed program and because it was just on the other side of the river. She considered the proximity to home a blessing and a curse. She wanted to be immersed in the college experience but wasn't sure how things would work out with her family if she were to go away. She hoped that the river would create the right degree of separation. To many in East Saint Louis, Saint Louis itself was an intergalactic voyage away. But she knew she could be home quickly in any emergency. She decided to apply only to Saint Louis, and she held her breath waiting to hear. Not only was she accepted for admission, but based on a combination of academic merit and financial need, she was also awarded a full scholarship that covered tuition, room and board, and expenses. She would be able to pursue her dream.

At the beginning of her college career, she found it difficult to focus on her studies, knowing as she did how much her family was struggling without her, even though she was still close by. The family dynamic suffered in her absence. Whenever her workload permitted, she went home on weekends to help out however she could. Balancing her family's needs with her academic demands and a desire to experience college posed a challenge, but Evangeline had the vision, mission, tenacity, and talent to pull it off. She continued to excel both academically and socially. The harshness of life back home did nothing to suppress her spirit.

In college she began to realize that there were some real deficiencies in her high school education; it seemed like many of her classmates were familiar with concepts, principles, and theories that she didn't know about. But she didn't allow those gaps to preclude her from mastering the subject matter of each course she took. Her grades put her near the very top of the class, and she managed to find time to play piano for the school choral group and to sing for them as well. Evangeline earned the respect of the faculty, the administration, and her peers. Even in college everyone liked her.

Between her freshman and sophomore years, she moved back into the house in East Saint Louis and worked part-time in both of the hospitals where she had been a volunteer. Her practical education continued, but she learned that she had to be more careful about taking on tasks that only those with professional training should take on. She still asked countless questions, but she refrained from asking to try things that might expose her and the hospitals to scrutiny or liability. At the end of her first summer, they invited her back for the next summer as well.

But during that summer, a few difficulties began to develop at home. For years her mother had worked two jobs barely making ends meet. Just before Evangeline came home for the summer, one of those jobs was eliminated, and the family income plummeted. The primary breadwinner was only partially employed for more than half the summer. When she did find work, it was more strenuous and paid less. As the summer wore on, Anne Dixon began to show the strain of providing for a household of six. She was constantly exhausted and become susceptible to various minor illnesses that sapped her strength even more. Evangeline considered dropping out of school to look for a full-time job, but her mother forbade it. She told Evangeline that it would kill her if her daughter didn't use her gifts to further herself and help the family that way. Evangeline contributed most of her modest income to the family. Still, the going was extremely tough. To further complicate matters, one of Evangeline's older sisters, Carla, fell in with the wrong crowd, started staying out late or not coming home at all. This was the first time anything like this had happened in the family.

Anne tried to assert herself but lacked the physical and emotional strength to do so. One night after work, Evangeline came home and found her sister catatonic from a drug overdose. Calling on knowledge she had garnered at the hospitals, she quickly filled the bathtub with cold water, carried Carla up the steps, immersed her, and continued to add ice to the water. She sat tub-side stroking Carla and talking to her. Eventually, Carla rallied, but this event set an entirely new dynamic in motion, one that threatened Evangeline's return to school. Over the next few days, Evangeline had multiple conversations with her mother, with Carla, and with her other older sister, Janelle. The outcome was that Carla promised to lean on Janelle for support and guidance, so Evangeline didn't insist that Carla go into a rehabilitation program. Janelle rose to the occasion and began to show real leadership and responsibility. With Evangeline's guidance, Janelle began to watch over Carla and provide the support necessary to hold the family together. Anne was relieved. The younger half sisters seemed unaffected. Evangeline's confidence in Janelle allowed her to return to school relatively worry-free, although she continued to be concerned about her mother's exhaustion. Everything seemed back on track for the beginning of her sophomore year.

The year at college was even better for Evangeline than the first. Her confidence soared as she continued to excel in every area of school. She lacked a romantic interest, but she figured that a relationship would develop when the time was right and she found the right partner. She dated some, but no one set her on fire. She would know without question when she found the right one.

The next summer brought her back to East Saint Louis and the same two hospitals. She continued her rotation through both facilities. By the time the second summer was over, she had spent time in several areas of the hospital: accidents and emergency, cardiology, chaplaincy, imaging, elderly services, endoscopy, nephrology, neurology, obstetrics, pharmacy, and a few other departments. Doctors, nurses, and staff from both hospitals knew that this extraordinary young woman was from the community and had great promise. They each did what they could to further her growth and development with a practical introduction into the medical profession. Their efforts weren't wasted: Evangeline took it all in.

On the home front, things didn't go quite as smoothly. The drama from last summer settled down, and Janelle kept close but nurturing watch on Carla, who was now working full-time in a steady job she could handle without too much stress. Her colleagues at work liked her and were a positive, responsible influence on her. That part of the family was fragile but stable. Anne continued to fight through periodic sicknesses that appeared to be minor and unrelated. She missed work far too often, and when she didn't work, she didn't get paid. The situation was exacerbated when both of Evangeline's younger half sisters got pregnant at about the same time, seeming to be in contest over who could mess up their lives more and faster. At first, they tried to remain in high school, but both experienced severe morning sickness followed by episodes of paralyzing depression. They dropped out of school just before Christmas of Evangeline's sophomore year, and it was only Anne's unwavering mandate that kept Evangeline from coming home and getting a job to help out. By the time that second summer rolled around, there were two infants in the already cramped quarters, and the already stressful arrangement became chaotic.

Evangeline talked to her mother several times about quitting school and reestablishing her presence in the home. She thought it would help things along. Anne shut her down each time. In fact, toward the end of the summer, Anne had a heart-to-heart mother-to-daughter talk with her middle child. She demanded that Evangeline keep her vision focused on the long-term goal of becoming a doctor and returning to the community. She made Evangeline promise that she would not allow the family situation to derail her in any way, assuring her that they would find a way to get through this. Janelle and now Carla were stabilizing influences. Anne said she would allow Evangeline to return for weekends from time to time during the school year but that it would be better if for the next summer, Evangeline could find a summer job farther away so that her growth and development could continue with the negative influences of the family situation swirling around more remotely. They would stay in touch by phone, and in a real emergency, she could come home. Evangeline agreed, buoyed by her mother's apparent return to good health.

At the beginning of her third year of college, Evangeline approached her organic chemistry professor about possible internships outside of the general Saint Louis area for the next summer. After a few discussions, Professor Marjorie Taylor suggested that the New England area might be a good place to look. Evangeline balked. The geography wouldn't work; she couldn't be that far from her family. Again, her mother intervened. There was no way her daughter would miss out on the best opportunities. They would find a way to go on without her for a few months. Professor Taylor and Evangeline worked with the placement office and identified three excellent possibilities in Boston. The placement office helped arrange for her to interview for internships at Massachusetts General, Brigham and Women's Hospital, and Tufts Medical Center. She received offers from all three, but only the Tufts program offered a two-year internship and would help with transportation and housing. It became an easy choice. And so, at the end of her sophomore year, after a short stay in East Saint Louis, Evangeline, with her family's blessing, packed up enough clothes to get her through the summer and headed off to Boston.

The transition proved to be more difficult and more exciting than even her entry into college. The sights and sounds in Boston were unlike anything else she had experienced back home. She found the activity level off the charts. The college communities poured their members onto the streets of Boston. Undergraduate and graduate students, professors were everywhere. Everyone went out at night— some to restaurants, bars, and coffeehouses. Others just walked around. She saw people out running every morning when she went to work and every night when she came home. The public parks teemed with parents walking with their children, artists setting up their easels, and young adults tossing their Frisbees. Street minstrels played guitars or saxophones or trumpets or fiddles, trying to cover James Taylor or Neil Young, Cannonball Adderley, Louis Armstrong, or Charlie Daniels. There were more opportunities to go to the theater than she ever knew possible.

She tried to immerse herself in the environment. Tufts set up the internship as a formal, organized program to ensure that the participants would receive a proper orientation, an appropriate exposure to the hospital setting, and the opportunity to learn and engage in meaningful work in the hospital. Evangeline met a score of new friends through the program, which functioned under the oversight of a Tufts Medical School professor. There were five other interns in the program from various places in the country. The other interns and the professor became the nucleus of her world that summer. They went to movies, plays, concerts, and baseball games. They explored museums, beaches, and state parks. That professor, who taught health-care policy and medical ethics, organized all the social activities and chaperoned the interns for each outing. Evangeline found Dr. Neal engaging, personable, available, fun loving, extremely well educated, and very, very smart. In fact, she had never met anyone quite like Dr. Neal. And to top it off, Dr. Neal played the piano!

When Evangeline was at work or with the group for an activity, she was energized, motivated, and happy. But those activities didn't occupy all of her time. It was a totally different story when she was alone. This was the first time that Evangeline had spent any meaningful time out of the Saint Louis area, away from her family. When surrounded by others, everything was fine. But in the evenings, through the nights, and in the early mornings, a wave of sadness would wash over her. She felt alone and guilty about not being at home where she was needed. This was the first time she had ever felt anything other than hope and excitement about her life. At those times, she felt like she was a different person. Depression had affected her younger half sisters. They staggered and stumbled through their days—and those were the good days. On the bad days, they were frozen, seemingly incapable of movement or maybe even of thought. Evangeline worried that she might fall victim to the same syndrome. She spiraled into a downward vortex. Although she consciously tried to break her fall, the harder she focused on it, the worse she felt.

None of her colleagues had any clue that Evangeline was suffering so. With them she was bright, engaging, enthusiastic, and avid about all that was going on. In every respect she was the very center of the intern group. She was the charismatic leader, and along with Dr. Neal, she was a primary planner and organizer for group activities.

By midsummer, the worry and depression were threatening to consume her. She seriously considered abandoning the program and returning home. After a few days of processing, she came up with the idea of talking things over with Dr. Neal. Maybe that would help.

It did.

INTRODUCTION: EVANGELINE
AND NAD

Cav guides Nad over to a willowy African American woman who stands a notch over six feet tall. Perfect skin accentuates her movie star features. She is made even more striking by her cascading black curls, large, comforting eyes, and electrified smile. At first sight, Nad thinks, *Well, there's an Olympic high jumper if I've ever seen one.*

He is, of course, totally wrong. Evangeline is naturally thin and keeps fit playing tennis and doing Pilates. In the winter she goes to spin classes and swims at the Saint Louis YMCA. It all works. She radiates health and fitness, but she is by no means an Olympic high jumper.

Rather, she's a physician and clearly the youngest adult Nad sees there in Brewster this evening. It takes him a minute or two to surmise that she was one of Eon's students.

"I'm pleased to meet you, Mr. DiDominico. Professor Neal mentioned to me that she had a lawyer friend in Philadelphia. She called you 'Nad,' and that stuck with me because, having an unusual name myself, I'm very conscious of other names that are different. I had never heard that name before."

Nad is just what Evangeline expected. Professor Neal told her that her friend was a distance runner. He has that gaunt runner's look, and he moves around like he's at peace with who he is—comfortable in his own skin. He's wearing a button-front magenta collared shirt with the words "Menemsha Blues" embroidered on the left breast. With that shirt, his khaki cargo shorts, and tan Merrell ventilator moc slip-ons, he seems quite beach ready. She thinks he's very Italian looking, and it pops into her mind that he and Professor Neal would have made a great-looking couple. The professor's light complexion and red curls would make a striking contrast to his deeply tanned Mediterranean skin and dark curly hair now cut short and neat. She muses that if he let loose, he could grow an Afro if they were still in style. Maybe he had one when he was younger. Knowing what she did about Professor Neal from firsthand experience, and what she had heard about Nad from her, Evangeline decides that those two would likely have been very happy as a couple. She wonders why they hadn't been together. It bothered Evangeline that her professor hadn't had a suitable romantic partner, but from what she had told Evangeline, Nad was her go-to guy.

"Nice to meet you, too, Evangeline. Nad is an acronym, my initials. I'm named after my father, Nicholas Amedeo DiDominico. I was Nick, Nicky, or Little Nick all through my early years, but because my father's nickname was Nad, I began introducing myself that way from high school on. Only my mother calls me Nicholas. I'm a bit surprised that Professor Neal would have mentioned me, though."

He revises his original thought about her and decides that she looks more like she should be strolling down a fashion runway with a cluster of photographers vying for close-ups. She is dressed appropriately for the occasion but also looks very chic. Her cream-colored crepe wraparound skirt allows her infinite legs to peek through when she shifts her weight. Even with sandals on her feet, her legs look like a model's. A loose-fitting turquoise blouse accentuates smooth, boney shoulders that flow into seemingly endless slender arms and long, elegant fingers, pianist's fingers, just like Eon's. Her cheekbones sweep upward, focusing attention on her almond eyes set in perfect skin that is dark brown with what appears to be a reddish-orange tinge. Russet, he thinks, but isn't sure whether that is the right hue. As she stands there in front of him, it appears that she's leaning back on her hips with this self-assured aura that seems to say, "I've already proven it to myself. I've paid my dues. I've come through a trial by fire, and I've survived, even flourished." Everything about her is beyond distinctive. He's eager to hear more about her relationship with his friend.

"Once we were talking about my name and how the original Evangeline from the poem wound up in Philadelphia. That's the first time you came up. I know you were special to Professor Neal. She told me you liked music and that you play the guitar but that you can't sing a lick. She said you write stories and that you're an attorney, medical malpractice defense, which for some reason she seemed to find amusing." Evangeline feels very natural talking with him, almost like she knows him through Professor Neal.

He's charmed and thinks that if he had a daughter, he'd like her to be just like Evangeline. "Well, Evangeline is a beautiful name. And I know the poem. Both Professor Neal and I were English majors in our undergraduate days. She was very literary. I'm not at all surprised that she would bring up Evangeline Bellefontaine and Longfellow. With your being a doctor, she probably also made the connection about how Longfellow's Evangeline wound up in Philadelphia caring for the sick at a Sisters of Mercy hospital. You said she found it amusing that I was a medical malpractice attorney. Did she say why?"

Evangeline laughs and is eager to share.

"Thank you. I know it's an unusual name, but I love it. I don't know whether my mother knew anything about the famous Evangeline, but I'm glad she gave me the name. She never called me Eva and never allowed anyone in the family to use a shortened version. I'm no Sister of Mercy, but I do what I can. Because of the support and guidance Professor Neal gave me during college and medical school, I'm now in a position to take care of sick people in East Saint Louis."

She smiles. Everyone listening to the story chuckles.

"About your medical malpractice question, she believed that med school, for the most part, prepared physicians to do great work, but that sometimes some doctors just didn't get it. They'd become arrogant and aloof and take things for granted. And, sometimes they would become too ambitious, take on too much. Then they'd make mistakes, sometimes serious mistakes. She said you were there to bail them out when that happened. The way she taught medical ethics, the underpinning of her approach was that physicians had an ethical obligation to make sure they were properly prepared and that their ethical obligation extended to the treatments they gave and the way that they administered those treatments. She said that you were there to rescue her failures. That made the two of you a team. She thought that was funny."

"Well, that's the way she analyzed things. She would always come up with something you wouldn't normally think of. Could you tell me some about her and you, how you met and so on?"

Nad is thrilled that he can get another perspective on Eon. He wants to hear more about her and how she related to this sophisticated, engaging, intelligent woman.

"I first met her when I was doing an internship at Tufts Medical Center in the summers when I was in college. She was overseeing the intern program, and she took us everywhere; she was our caretaker, making sure the experience was beneficial to us and to the hospital. She also made sure we had a good time outside of work. She arranged a whole calendar of activities for us. At one point, I was feeling pretty depressed about being away from my family. There was a lot going on back home in East Saint Louis at the time. I had an older sister who was struggling to fend off a drug addiction. I had two younger sisters who became teenage mothers. My mother was the linchpin of the family. She was a strong and courageous woman. She tried to keep us from making her mistakes. She kept saying those mistakes were hers, and we couldn't have them. She worked hard and became very exhausted; she started getting sick all the time. Professor Neal helped me hold things together. I was about to quit the internship and go back home, but she echoed my mother's words that I had to stay the course and follow through on my plan to become a doctor, for my own sake, for mother's sake, and for the rest of my family. I went through a rough time then. If it weren't for Professor Neal, I think my life would likely have taken an unwanted detour, and maybe I wouldn't have been able to get back on course."

The subject clearly brings a vortex of emotion to her. She speaks haltingly and is clearly trying to keep from crying.

"Professor Neal had that kind of effect on many people," Doreen says. "She kept me focused and directed many times in all aspects of my life."

"Me, too," Cav adds.

These two interventions give Evangeline time to recover. Cav gives her a brief supportive hug.

"She clearly meant a lot to you," Nad says. "We all share your grief."

"Thank you. I'm okay. She got me through that internship."

"She sometimes mentioned her students to me but never by name for some reason," Nad says. "She told me about one of them who must have been you. You were special to her. She said you inspired her."

Nad wants to make sure Evangeline hears that. Everyone's emotions are high. His words brighten her considerably.

"She mentored me from that internship in college through medical school and residency and into my practice. From the very first time I met her that summer, she talked about having a long vision. She said that she had read an article about a Formula One race car driver who said when he was racing, he would focus his vision as far as he could see. When he did that, everything closer in took care of itself. That stuck with me. She helped me with my decision on med school. When it was time to pick, I chose Tufts mostly because of her. I was fortunate enough to have a few choices of really good schools. We had quite a few conversations about where I should go. She never advocated for Tufts. Instead, she tried to help me come up with a framework to make my decision. She talked about all the factors I should consider—the quality of the faculty, the specialty I wanted to go into, geography, how the demographics of the school related to where I wanted to practice. We talked about everything. In the final analysis, I chose Tufts because of Professor Neal."

Evangeline is smiling with the memories.

"Looking back on it, how do you feel about your decision?" Nad asks.

"I definitely made the right choice. The education was great there, but that probably would have happened no matter where I went. The big difference was Professor Neal. I doubt that there would have been others like her anywhere. The first course I took with her was medical ethics. I looked up to her as a person because of the way she looked after me and other students. But, in that course, I learned she was also a brilliant professor. Her intelligence was challenging to deal with, but she was so warm and inclusive that the challenge was never threatening or demeaning. It was more motivating and inspiring. Her goal was always to create an environment that was conducive to learning. Her style was to guide us so that we could identify our own insights. Of course, she covered the subject matter, but more than that, she fostered autonomy. She enabled us to master the principles and then go beyond that to refine and elevate our own values. I wanted to do well in her courses, not so much because the grades themselves mattered, but more so because I wanted to match up, earn her respect. Over my stay there, we became friends."

"She told me that she was so impressed that you could escape," Nad says. "My word, not hers, that you could escape a tough environment and excel at so many things."

"Thank you, again. I didn't so much escape from my home as much as go out on an expedition from it. I told you about what happened to my sisters during my internship. My mother had trouble keeping everything together. Finances were hard for them, and I was living in this great environment in Boston. I felt guilty about that. They were home and struggling, and I was having the time of my life in Boston, learning exciting things during the day, spending time with nice, quality, supportive people in the evening. Professor Neal helped me deal with that guilt by reminding me that I was an inspiration for the family and that they were living through me. I sent back as much money as I could and also little presents from time to time. But as much as Professor Neal helped me during the internship, she helped me even more when I was in med school."

Evangeline explains how her mother's fragile health situation took a turn for the worse during Evangeline's second year of medical school. She suffered a series of strokes that put her in the hospital for weeks at a time, leaving her a shell of herself. She could walk and understand what you were saying, but her speech became unintelligible. She had trouble with her gag reflex and had to be fed very carefully. Evangeline made frequent trips back to East Saint Louis, taking the bus most times to keep expenses down. She used the travel time to study and catch up on her sleep, but she couldn't spend too much time away from school. When she was in Boston, she worried about not being in East Saint Louis. When she was in East Saint Louis, she worried about not being in Boston. Professor Neal was her confidant and support system. She helped keep Evangeline's spirits up and made sure she stayed focused on her mission. The situation deteriorated further when one day, on top of the strokes, Anne Dixon had a heart attack. She lingered only long enough for Evangeline to get home. This time she flew. The whole family was at her bedside when she passed.

"When my mother passed away, if I'd have been at any other medical school, I would definitely *not* be a doctor today. Professor Neal was very instrumental in helping me get a leave of absence for three months to get everything in order. Not that there was much of an estate, but my mother did have the foresight to have a small life insurance policy, which we maneuvered around so that my sisters could be somewhat taken care of. Even though she was sickly, my mother was a very strong presence in the family. The Dixon family was strongly matriarchal. With my mother gone, I felt it was my role to step in immediately, so during that time, I made the decision not to go back. Professor Neal convinced me that if I dropped out, I'd run into a blind alley back home, that my life would be unfulfilled. She convinced me that the best way to pay tribute to my mother was to continue on and fulfill her dream, our dream, by finishing my education and returning to East Saint Louis as a doctor. She kept reinforcing to me, just as my mother had always done, that I was a source of pride to my family and that if I failed, they'd feel they had failed, too. Over and over she told me that I could help my family more by staying the course and getting my MD. She kept me zeroed in on my goal. She was teacher, mentor, parent, sister, and friend."

Evangeline's comments set Nad's thoughts in motion. He knew how much the dysfunction in Eon's family upset her. It angered and frustrated her. When they talked, she always told him how fortunate he was to have such a great relationship with his parents and siblings. She even told him that those relationships made him more attractive to her. She wanted that kind of family feeling too. In those first weeks when their emotions were ablaze and they couldn't contain themselves from thinking and talking about a future together, Eon told him more than once how eager she was to meet his relatives and experience family warmth and acceptance. He regretted that he'd never had the chance to put them all together. She would have loved them, and they would have loved her right back. Nad wonders whether Eon was experiencing that family cohesiveness vicariously through Evangeline, whether Evangeline's family had become a surrogate.

"It sounds like Dr. Neal considered you family," Nad says.

"She used to use the phrase 'chosen family.' I know that for some reason she wasn't close to her biological family. She never told me exactly what the story was, but she more than hinted that there were issues there. She did tell me that her father was a well-respected doctor but that she didn't like the way he treated her mother and other women. She warned me that if I ever ran into him at a convention that it would be better if I avoided him and that I certainly shouldn't let him know that I knew her. She told me that her mother was a traditional stay-at-home professional wife and mother and that from time to time she fought off the boredom of her life and the way she was treated by her husband by seeking refuge in Chardonnay. It came up when I talked to her about my sister's substance addiction."

Cav, Doreen, and Nad just nod silently. Evangeline continues by explaining that Professor Neal never talked about seeing her family, so Evangeline had concluded that she didn't. She had told Evangeline that she was stuck with them by the accident of birth, but that her real sense of family came from those she picked as family members; "chosen family" was her real family.

"I respected that, and I was fortunate—I chose my biological family and Dr. Neal both as family, even though they never met one another. I miss her already."

Evangeline glazes over and goes into her bag for tissues. Nad, Cav, and Doreen wait for Evangeline to regain her composure.

"I also want you to know how much influence she had on my professional development. Sometimes I don't talk about that so much because of what she did for me personally. I don't want to shortchange her gifts as a professor. Most of the teachers I've had in my life were very, very good. They cared about their students and wanted to teach as best as they could. But, with the professor, there was something different. She wanted to do more than teach. She wanted to make sure you knew how to learn. She often spoke about the concept of mastery. She instilled in me, in us, that it is important to learn not only the bare essentials but to delve into things more deeply, to understand the history, the context, the nuances, the evolution of principle, to try to immerse yourself in the subject. I knew that she disdained politics and politicians, so I was surprised when she quoted a government official, someone named Reich who had been the secretary of labor. It was a simple quote, easy to remember. It went 'Figure out for yourself what you want to be really good at, know that you never really satisfy yourself that you've made it, and accept that that's okay.' She said if you followed that advice, you would become a master of you vocation."

"Mastery was a big theme in her life," Cav adds. "She was always an excellent student, but even back in high school, she'd say that the grades were only an indication of whether she was mastering the subject."

"That reminds me of another quote that she would trot out once in a while. I know Professor Neal wasn't much of a basketball fan, but coming from the inner city, I was exposed to basketball at a young age. I was tall, so I played some in the neighborhood. Loved it. I knew that she didn't, so I was surprised when one day she quoted Dr. J, Julius Erving. She said she'd read some about his view of professionalism that said, 'Being a professional is doing the things you love to do on days you don't feel like doing them.' She'd pepper her classes with things like this that would stick with me because of the combination of their simplicity, their incisiveness, and the unusualness of the source. I'll miss her for the rest of my life."

"We know," Cav says. "We're all with you in that. We miss her, too. Dr. Neal was very proud of you. We talked on the phone all the time when I was in Lincoln, and we had long talks up here in Brewster during our summer vacations. She knew from the beginning you'd be a great doctor, but she was even more impressed that you followed through with your commitment to go back to your community and serve there. She told me she was inspired by your passion to change the world you came from. Over the years, many students would tell her that they wanted to give back to their communities, but only rarely could they keep from getting derailed. You never got derailed. You were on a mission, and she was very aware that you were following through, living your mission every day. That mattered to her."

"Thank you, Mr. Cavendish. And thank you, too, Mr. DiDominico, for doing all that you did to make Dr. Neal happy. She always spoke of you with deep respect and affection."

Evangeline steps forward and gives Nad a hug. After a moment, Cav speaks up.

"Time for the next introduction, Nad."

PADRAIG COUGHLIN

You didn't have to hear him speak or know his name. By just seeing him, you knew immediately that Padraig H. Coughlin was as Irish as they come. He looked the part exactly—red curly hair, ruddy complexion on a bright roundish face haphazardly adorned with translucent whiskers, clear blue eyes, and a sunbeam smile. Standing five feet, eight inches tall, he wore his 165 pounds well. He was fit and athletic. When he spoke in his melodic baritone brogue, your only remaining question about his heritage was whether he was from Dublin or Cork, Waterford or Wexford. Cork would be the correct answer.

The Coughlin family lived in Brandon Parish, and so, Padraig went to Hamilton High School, where, for some reason he claimed he didn't totally understand, he took an occasional good-natured ribbing for sharing his first name with that of Padraig Hamilton, son of the school founder, Sean Hamilton. The headmaster position was handed down from father, Sean, to son, Padraig. Padraig Coughlin's classmates thought it was amusing to tease him mildly about his first name, as if "Padraig" were an unusual name in the community, which it wasn't. Several Padraigs occupied the parish. But, Coughlin seemed to be the only one who got the nickname "Headmaster" Padraig. They were certain that his middle initial stood for "Hamilton." They were wrong; it stood for "Hagan." It didn't really matter much; the nickname created no real problems for Padraig. It was always used good-naturedly, and Padraig was well-meaning, well-liked, and well-friended. He actually took a bit of pride in the moniker, feeling he had a special standing in the school. That sentiment was validated when he was elected class president in his final year.

At Hamilton, Padraig's academic interests took fairly polar routes: he enjoyed the hard sciences like biology, chemistry, and physics, but his Introduction to Philosophy class sent his head reeling, and he started reading the philosophers as voraciously as any teenager could. Neither of Padraig's interests delighted his father, who wanted Padraig to study business and finance. After all, Hamilton High School had the reputation of being the place where Ireland's chief executives went to school. Seamus, Padraig's father, wanted his son to build on his own career as a bank teller, take it to the next level, and become a mover and shaker in the financial world. Padraig had no interest at all in those matters. He liked learning about scientific principles and philosophical theories, and he like to play all manner of sports—soccer, athletics, rugby among them. To his credit, the old man supported his son's interests rather than trying to pressure him.

When Padraig was closing in on graduation from Hamilton, he decided to put the science interest on the back burner. He figured he could pursue those subjects after college and maybe use them as the basis for an actual career of some sort. He reasoned that if he didn't immerse himself in the study of philosophy as an undergraduate, he would never acquire the basic knowledge to build on.

UCD School of Philosophy was fewer than two hundred miles from Cork, far enough away from home for Padraig to be independent but close enough to make the transition fairly easy. But he didn't pick UCD because of its geography. It was listed in the top one hundred philosophy departments in the world and was recognized as one of the top ten schools for graduate studies in twentieth-century Continental philosophy in an English-speaking country. Because he was pretty sure he didn't want to study philosophy in graduate school, it was important to him to have access to top-shelf graduate courses as an undergraduate. At his interview during the application process, Padraig was assured that if he demonstrated the ability to handle the subject matter, he would be permitted to take some graduate courses while he was matriculating as an undergraduate. At this early stage in his development, he wasn't sure what branch of philosophy he wanted to study. The range of courses offered at UCD gave him many choices. The school had expertise in contemporary European, analytic, and classical philosophy, philosophy of law, political philosophy, and cognitive science. Members of the faculty were widely published in esteemed academic journals. He thought that he might be able to establish connections with the editors of *The International Journal of Philosophical Studies* and the postgraduate philosophy journal *Perspectives*, both of which emanated from the UCD School of Philosophy.

Before making his final decision, he spent a few random days hanging around the school, wandering here and there, and sneaking into classes. He even happened to be there when a workshop/conference was taking place, so he sat in on a presentation by Avram Noam Chomsky, the American linguist, logician, and analytic philosopher from MIT. Padraig had heard about him and read a little bit of his work. Padraig thought he might have some interest in the philosophy of language, but he wasn't sure.

It was very exciting that Chomsky was speaking at UCD. In his presentation, he steered clear of his controversial views on politics and anarchism, focusing instead on his linguistic theory that the principles underlying the structure of language are biologically determined in the human mind and therefore genetically transmitted. Chomsky forcefully stated that all humans share the same linguistic structure regardless of social-cultural differences. These lofty thoughts provoked Padraig's thinking. It was one thing to read books on various theories, but it was an entirely different thing to hear someone talk about their theories and to have a chance to ask them questions and engage in debate with them.

Hearing Chomsky speak about generative and universal grammar inspired Padraig. He had begun thinking about the nexus between language and philosophy and about various attributes that unite humans regardless of where they were born and how they were raised. He first began to put these thoughts together when he dabbled in anthropology and learned a bit about how different cultures speak about their children. This led him to theorize on how they think about their children, how they parent their children, how they protect them, and try to provide them with the right opportunities and the means to develop independence. He saw strong similarities that seemed to be unrelated to time and place; they were cross-cultural. These thoughts drew him into thinking about how people from different cultures communicate with one another. He wondered whether there was something universal about communication. Padraig concluded that Chomsky's theory supported his own developing view about the universality of parenthood and communication.

All these thoughts fascinated him. He found Chomsky interesting and entertaining. He said some very quotable things, like, "If you don't like what someone has to say, argue with them," and "Either you repeat the same conventional doctrines everybody is saying, or else you say something true, and it will sound like it's from Neptune." Padraig frequently felt that many of the things he thought and said placed him firmly on Neptune. It was validating to hear someone acknowledge his feelings. Padraig was in; that visit clinched the deal. And so, after Hamilton, he ventured off to University College Dublin to study philosophy.

At UCD, he became especially interested in the readings of the Irish philosophers. He started with George Edward Hughes, usually regarded as Scottish. Padraig discovered that Hughes was actually born in Ireland but left for Scotland with his family in his early years. Padraig was confident that Ireland could legitimately claim him. Hughes wrote extensively on ethics, the philosophy of religion, medieval philosophical logic, and modal logic. Padraig read and easily understood Aristotelian logic and the square of opposition. Modal logic, however, was in a different echelon. In soccer terms, Aristotelian logic was youth competition; modal logic was World Cup level. And so, it surprised Padraig that he understood *A New Introduction to Modal Logic*, which Hughes coauthored with one of his former students, Max Cresswell. Their original *An Introduction to Modal Logic* was widely considered an important treatise in the field. The Hughes-Cresswell principles were new and exciting and had a significant impact on computer programming. He had read about classical propositional and predicate logic briefly at Hamilton, but these fairly new modal logic theories went well beyond those. He was impressed that Hughes and Cresswell were instrumental in describing forty-two normal and twenty-five non-normal logics.

Padraig wrapped himself up in these studies. He took to the studies of expressions like "it is necessary that" and "it is possible that" to qualify the truth of a judgment. He delved into deontic logic examining judgments qualified by the phrases "it is obligatory that" or "it is permitted that" or "it is forbidden that." Temporal logic brought him into the realm of thinking about propositions qualified by the phrases "it will always be the case that," "it will be the case that," "it has always been the case that," and "it was the case that." And, he studied the aspect of modal logic called doxastic logic, which involved statements beginning with "*x* believes that." It all seemed like an elaborate game to him, like solving a Rubik's Cube, which he could routinely do in just over thirty seconds. He liked playing logic games, and he played them very well.

Padraig was so taken with Hughes and Cresswell's work on modal logic that he set out to learn more about what Hughes was thinking and saying. It was then that he stumbled on "Motive and Duty," which was published when Hughes was only twenty-six years old. Reading this work impacted young Padraig in two significant ways. First, it brought him squarely into the world of ethics. Padraig pondered Hughes's opening statement:

> I wish to discuss the view that our duty is in every case simply to do a certain *act*, and never either to have a certain motive or to act from a certain motive or to do a certain act from a certain motive.

Padraig found it interesting to think about the difference between behavior and motive and that if your duty was to do an act and you then did it, you fulfilled your ethical duty. Hughes postulated that in such a setting, the actor acted irreproachably. Why he did it, said Hughes, was ethically irrelevant. Padraig really delved into the principles set out in "Motive and Duty" and decided that ethics would be a subject for him to pursue and explore in greater depth. Second, the fact that the paper was published when Hughes was only twenty-six gave Padraig hope that maybe he, too, could be published at a young age.

His course work also exposed Padraig to the thinking of Desmond Clarke, who brought together philosophy and the theories of science through analyzing the works of René Descartes. Padraig was intrigued by Descartes's scientific thinking and his view that human mental abilities can be explained, in significant part, by reference to the brain and other physiological systems. He agreed that human thought cannot be explained by reference to the physical properties of the brain—it goes beyond that. When Padraig eventually began his career in physical therapy, he was careful to pay attention to his patients' mental states as well as their physical conditions. He did so, in part, because he understood the differences and the connection between them.

Padraig also read Clarke's works on human rights with particular interest. Clarke wrote about three works from the seventeenth century that articulated establishing gender equality—Marie le Jars de Gournay's treatise "The Equality of Men and Women" written in 1622, Anne Maria van Schurman's dissertation on women's education written in 1641, and Francois Poulain de la Barre's "Physical and Moral Discourse concerning the Equality of Both Sexes" written in 1632. Padraig subscribed to the principles espoused by Clarke.

The works of Terence Irwin exposed Padraig to ancient Greek philosophy and the history of Western moral philosophy, medieval, and modern times. Irwin's *Plato's Moral Theory* was published when Irwin was thirty years old, and Irwin gained additional stature by translating and commenting on Aristotle's works in *Aristotle's Nicomachean Ethics* and *Aristotle's First Principles.* Padraig appreciated the contributions of both Plato and Aristotle to contemporary philosophy. He understood that just as there couldn't be an Internet without Guglielmo Marconi's thinking, so, too, there would be no contemporary philosophy without Aristotle and Plato.

Reading George Chatterton-Hill's writings on evolution and sociology presented a breakthrough opportunity for Padraig. He found himself disagreeing with Chatterton-Hill's thesis that mankind has a ceaseless urge for expansion that conflicts with the idea of equality for all and that society will always develop a superior group or class that will always oppress the inferior masses, who eventually revolt and form a ruling class, therefore creating a new cycle of oppression-revolution. Studying Chatterton-Hill was important to Padraig because it was the first time he could summon the temerity to dispute the theories of a well-established philosopher. Padraig's professor was impressed by his incisive, analytical assault on Chatterton-Hill's thesis and told him that with additional work on the paper, it might someday be publishable.

Another of Padraig's professors was Gerard Casey, who introduced him to the philosophy of law. He felt Casey's libertarian and philosophically anarchistic tendencies were too radical for him. And, although Casey was a forceful and relentless thinker, Padraig's exposure to him confirmed that he would never study the philosophy of law—other branches of philosophy were more rigorous and challenging.

In those years at UCD, Padraig also read some of the works of William Desmond on ontology, metaphysics, ethics, and religion. Desmond had formulated an entirely new and complete metaphysical/ontological philosophical system based on the potencies and senses of being. Desmond's system captivated Padraig. The more he read of Desmond, the more he felt he himself had some things to add to the field. As he neared graduation, he started to crystalize his thoughts so that someday, after he began his "practical" career, he could pull a document from his archives and begin writing his own treatise.

In the meantime, reality was setting in, and he felt it was time to make a career choice. He liked sports; he liked science; he liked autonomy. After a bit of churning, he decided to parlay all of his deep philosophical knowledge and thinking with his love of science and sport to pursue the study of kinesiology and physical and massage therapy. He reasoned that this would allow him to pay the bills but also have the free time, if he wanted, to pursue his interests in philosophy. He'd not yet had any of his works on philosophy published, but he had a strong desire to see his thinking printed in a well-recognized philosophical journal. He needed only the time and perhaps the guidance of published scholar.

Padraig decided to stay at UCD and study for an advanced degree in physiotherapy from the College of Human Sciences. Every day, he thanked his lucky stars that he made that decision, because not only did he acquire the necessary knowledge and skills to become one of the premier sports therapists in Ireland, but more importantly, it was there that he met Sonia O'Shay. Just a few years later, Ms. O'Shay became Sonia Coughlin. While studying together, they formed a true symbiotic partnership built on love and respect. And, they came up with a plan to revolutionize the treatment of sports-related injuries in Ireland.

They built the Coughlin Institute, which quickly became a renowned treatment/therapy center for local, regional, and even world-class athletes. The walls of the institute were covered with photos of athletes of all kinds, including rowers, runners, archers, equestrians, swimmers, and wrestlers. Some of the photos were action shots; others featured the athletes wearing their Olympic, World Championship, or Commonwealth Games medals of all three colors. Together, Padraig and Sonia repaired boxers, sprinters, soccer players, Ping-Pong players, marathoners, javelin throwers, and basketball players. Sonia was a gifted therapist who also liked to keep everything running smoothly on the marketing and business side of the endeavor. Padraig became a world expert on active release therapy techniques, myofascial release, and a variety of acupuncture methodologies: traditional Chinese, French energetic, Korean, auricular, and myofascial-based acupuncture.

Even with his growing reputation as a physical therapist, Padraig never abandoned his roots in philosophy and was particularly enthralled with Desmond's metaphysical/ontological philosophical system based on the seven potencies and the four senses of being. He continued reading on these subjects that he began as an undergraduate at UCD and even took a turn at writing a paper, which he hoped to be publishable despite his lack of scholarly credentials. His thesis was on Desmond's second potency, the aesthetic. Padraig tried to elucidate how Desmond's concept of aesthetic goes far beyond Kant's purified realm of the aesthetic.

His two passions fused when he began using athletics as the subject matter for illustrations while he espoused on human sensual communication and interaction with the world. He exposed his patients to many of his philosophical theories. The athletes would leave the institute smiling in confusion after they went to Padraig Coughlin for a problem with a rotator cuff, a labrum, or an iliotibial band, got the treatment protocols they needed to put them back in action, but in the process heard about how the exceeding power and force of being is intimated aesthetically to you through the sublime. It didn't matter to Padraig that the athletes largely had no understanding of what he was talking about and didn't care. Generally, they used these conversations, or more appropriately, these monologues, as sedatives. Padraig fixed them up; that was all that mattered to them. Only middle-distance runners got something of a reprieve. Occasionally, he could make an actual connection with them by revealing that these principles were articulated by Dr. William Desmond, who happened to be a professor at Villanova University in the United States, where noted middle-distance champions Ron Delany, Eamonn Coghlan ("No relation—different spelling," he was always quick to point out), Marcus O'Sullivan, and Sonia O'Sullivan (no relation to one another) began their careers.

Padraig loved his own Sonia dearly, and they had much in common, but she lacked the interest and the background to discuss these topics with him, so he often just talked to himself about them, or he would ramble on to his captive athletes while he put them through various protocols to rehabilitate a soleus, a vastus lateralis, or a piriformis. Even with all the philosophical chatter, Padraig was charming and engaging. It was a win-win situation for everyone.

Padraig Coughlin was not only smart; he was also clever. He would often agree to make presentations on physical therapy at times and places where a philosophical symposium was also taking place. Some of the presentations were local, like at UCD, where he was often a guest lecturer in physical therapy, not in philosophy. Other sessions were held in such European countries as Spain, France, Germany, Austria, and Croatia. He occasionally went down under to Australia and New Zealand, where he spoke in Wellington at the Kinesiology Association of New Zealand Symposium. He could cover almost any subject in the field: applied kinesiology, clinical kinesiology, neural organization techniques, and metabolics. Sonia rarely made the trips with him, particularly if he found a philosophy convention that he could dovetail into the trip. It worked out well for both of them. She liked running the institute for a few weeks at a time on her own, and he got to spread the word about the operation globally and keep in touch with his avocation.

Many of his trips brought him to the United States. He did a quick one-week guest lecture series at the University of Michigan School of Kinesiology in Ann Arbor. He linked that with a trip to East Lansing to attend the International Plato Society Meeting. He gave presentations at the Indiana University School of Public Health for the Department of Kinesiology and also managed to attend a conference there on Aristotelian logic and metaphysics.

It was on his trip to San Francisco that he happened to meet Dr. Elaine Olivia Neal for the first time. The trip was planned well in advance. He was flying from Heathrow through Boston to California to speak at a conference put on by the University of California, Berkeley. He would speak on biomechanics and get to see a few different parts of California. He was flying into San Francisco earlier than necessary so that he could attend a philosophy conference there. After his presentation, he would stay a bit longer, drive part of the Pacific Highway, visit Carmel and Calistoga, tour the Napa Valley, and visit the redwood forest and Muir Woods before his talk. He was very excited about the trip. He even decided to stay over in Boston for a few days to see Fenway Park, walk through the city, loiter in Harvard Square, and go for a run along the Charles River. When he left Ireland, he had no clue that he would make a new friend along the way.

ELAINE AND PADRAIG

Seven years before the memorial service, Dr. Neal boarded the plane in Boston en route to San Francisco. This would be her fourth trip to the Golden State and her second to the Bay Area. The first visit was eight years earlier when she flew to San Diego with her then–guy friend, Jason, for a five-day weekend. She was experimenting with having a relationship then. She'd heard San Diego was idyllic and decided to take the risk of checking it out with him. It was late May, right after her semester ended. Her objectives were to chill, see the sights, and try to understand if she could have any kind of a thing with this guy.

The trip went as anticipated—perfect weather, beautiful sights, nice folks. She particularly liked running and walking in Balboa Park and watching the cyclists race in the velodrome. She had never seen a bicycle-racing track before. The steep banked turns looked like they would be fun to ride on. She wondered how fast she would have to pedal to stay up on the bank. The strategic nature of each race fascinated her—in some, the cyclists would ride at a recreational pace until the penultimate lap and then go like hell for two laps; in other events they would throw in periodic midrace surges to string out the field. She and Jason went to the zoo, the maritime and art museums, Little Italy, Presidio Park, Seaport Village, Old Town, and Coronado.

The sightseeing was delightful; the relationship wasn't. After three days, she discovered she couldn't be around him for more than three days. It took only that long for her to realize that their circadian rhythms just didn't match. She liked to get up early and start living the day. He liked to laze around and get started only after burning hours of daylight. She would prefer dinner with wine at sixish. He couldn't eat before nineish. She liked the room warm; he liked it cold. She closed the bathroom door; he left it open. She liked to make love by candlelight; he wanted total darkness. It would never work. She considered aborting the trip right then and there but decided that that would be rude and unkind. Exercising restraint, she chose not to be that way. She could endure a few more days. She told him as soon as they arrived back in Boston and was surprised that he was surprised. Oh well! At least she tried.

Her second trip to California, two years after the first, was to Los Angles for a conference. She wanted to stay at the Four Seasons in Beverly Hills so that she could stroll on Rodeo Drive. She lucked out; the conference booked her into the Beverly Hills hotel, which was very enjoyable but perhaps a bit too highbrow for her tastes—"lots of pretty people there, reading *Rolling Stone*, reading *Vogue*." She remembered thinking the lines from the Joni Mitchell song as she walked in to register. She was optimistic that she would be able to window-shop and see all the unneeded, unaffordable elegant wares on display, but she had only a few small slivers of free time, so she never got to see Disneyland or Universal Studios or Rodeo Drive or anything else. All of her time was spent either preparing for her presentation, making her presentation, attending other presentations, or working on various position papers on health-care policies that she was writing for one group or another whose ideologies meshed with hers. She wasn't one to leave her work unfinished no matter how strongly the decked-out windows on Rodeo Drive, sparkling with all manner of dazzling jewelry and vehicle-priced apparel, called to her.

The third trip was just three years before this one, only a few months after she met Nad. It, too, was to this very Bay Area. That visit was prolonged and had a clear purpose. A few months after the Vineyard trip, she took a last-minute sabbatical to sort out some important life issues. Her contact with Nad challenged many of the rules she had developed for herself. After several experiments, she had come to the realization that it would be very difficult for her to have any kind of a meaningful relationship with a man and that she probably wasn't well suited to being a mother. Meeting Nad called those guidelines into question. She needed some time to try to figure out if she could find a way to overcome the debilitating effects of her abusive childhood and have a real, viable romantic relationship with him. She knew he wanted children, but because of what happened to her in Lincoln, she firmly believed that she was ill suited for parent-hood. As confident as she was in all other aspects of her life, she was terrified of making mistakes as a parent, mistakes that would cause irreversible damage to her progeny. She didn't feel competent to be in charge of another's life. She knew that she loved Nad, but she was terrified of making that commitment. After struggling with these thoughts, she decided that maybe someday that might happen but that she wasn't ready now. It was a hard choice. She decided to move on from him, and because she was shaky in her resolve, she decided to do it without telling him. She wasn't sure she'd be able to stick to her decision if she talked it out with him, and she was firm that she wanted to stick with her decision. She wasn't comfortable with cutting off contact so abruptly, but that was the only way it would work for her. After making that decision, she felt free enough to enjoy her pro-longed stay in the Bay Area. She didn't leave until the next June. After a stop-off in Lincoln to visit Cav and Joy, she headed back to Boston.

Before she left, she did some guest lecturing. She taught a mini-course on ethics in the media, a foreign subject for her. Immersing herself in the subject matter, she mastered it in short order and facilitated a thought-provoking seminar. Although she was frequently exhausted, she had some time to explore, visiting Fisherman's Wharf, Ghirardelli Square, Golden Gate Park, the bridge itself, and, of course, Haight-Ashbury. She walked through Muir Woods, drove parts of the Pacific Highway, and spent a few nights in Carmel. She took a refreshing mud bath in Calistoga—more tepid than hot. She spent ample time on the Berkeley campus. She very much enjoyed her stay.

The Bay Area was so alluring that she resolved to return. She had set up this current trip so that she would have a little time before and quite a bit more after her presentation to do some revisiting. In the meantime, she had a six-hour flight to negotiate. She always dressed casually to fly when she could. To the extent that she ever "built" her wardrobe, it would always be from the feet up. Her Naya Palomi sandals were expensive but very, very comfortable. That they were also somewhat stylish was an added but unnecessary feature; she always chose function over form but didn't object to fashionable attire if it felt good. Today, she wore basic jeans slung low on her hips, and a white tee shirt with a picture of a cave on the front under the words "Plato's Place" in black block letters. The back read, "Your Cave or Mine?"

At the time she didn't know that years later she would be given another philosophy tee shirt with the words "Plato and a Platypus Walk into a Bar" printed on the front and with a picture of Plato and a platypus sitting at a bar, each with an adult beverage in front of them. She would be given that shirt by the authors Thomas Cathcart and Daniel Klein, who were writing a book of the same name. It would be orange to match the book cover. She would meet them at a gathering at Harvard and find them very bright and amusing. They would tell her they knew of her reputation in the field and ask if they could run some of their ideas about the content by her and get her feedback. They would ask her to read the galleys, and they would have a tee shirt made up just for her. She would wish she had thought to write a book explaining basic philosophical principles through jokes. She would make only a few very minor suggestions. Overall, she would find that the book ranged from amusing to hilarious, more often toward the hilarious side. But that would come years later. For now, it was just her Plato's cave shirt. Most importantly, it was made of very comfortable, soft brushed cotton.

She made her way to seat 11E, the middle seat between two men, and noticed immediately that their presentations couldn't be more different. The window seat, 11F, housed a significantly round man with loose, thick ankles that spilled over the sides of his hard leather slip-on shoes. They looked like bedroom slippers. Regrettably, he was sockless. She couldn't help thinking that he probably always wore slip-ons because he wouldn't be able to bend past his girth to tie shoe-laces if required. A thin mustache-like border of dark-brown hairs lay under the shiny backside of his formidable head—a dome that veritably begged to have a smiley face drawn on it with a yellow high-lighter. She had a yellow highlighter in her purse. Maybe she would have occasion to use it.

The slender aisle-seat occupant, 11D, smiled a full openmouthed smile as she turned to enter the row. He jumped right up and slipped out of her way after making sure that his carry-on bag was not in her path. His khakis were relatively unwrinkled, and his blue but-ton-down oxford shirt was roughly three shades lighter than his eyes, which danced lightly around the plane as she ducked into her seat. She noted that he wore Reebok running shoes, so she speculated that he might be involved in sports in some way. His hair was more typically carrot than her auburn shoulder-length waves and boasted tight, wiry curls. On her way by, she caught the scent of something— probably shampoo or scented soap, Irish Spring?—minty and clean smelling. It was refreshing.

As she made her way to her seat, 11F turned, looked up, and gruff-ly muttered, "Oh, are you in here, too?" with an exasperated look.

She looked down to the 11E seat cushion, which could be used as a flotation device in the unlikely event of a water landing, where he had thrown a bruised cordovan soft-sided briefcase.

"Yes, I am. Excuse me, please," she said neutrally.

"Ugh," he grunted in reply and yanked his briefcase from the seat, almost hitting her and 11D in the process. He then turned dramatically toward the window, presenting her with an up-front view of the back of his turquoise polyester shirt embroidered with a large wine bottle silhouette and the words "Napa Valley—the Wine Country." She smiled on the inside thinking that this guy would likely be quite a treat for the next several hours. Well, she had her books, her iPod, and her Bose noise-cancelling headphones if she needed them.

It would take only an hour or so into the flight for 11F's sweat to mix with his polyester shirt and for the offensive malodorous emanation to force her to breathe mostly through her mouth. She would then have to do some fighting to fend off hyperventilation. But that would come later.

For now, she settled in and pulled out her half-read copy of *Nobody's Fool* and a well-worn edition of Kant's *The Metaphysics of Morals*, in the original German. She figured she would bounce around from book to book. Quietly, she began to read. Soon after takeoff, 11F jerked down the window shade, cutting off her light. She thought nothing of it, reaching up to turn on her overhead.

When the light flashed up, he jumped, glared at her, and said, "I'm trying to sleep."

"You go right ahead," she said smiling back. "I won't be reading aloud, unless you would like me to."

He didn't smile. Instead, he grimaced and turned back toward the window. She again considered the yellow highlighter.

11D witnessed this exchange amusedly, and she made casual eye contact with him as she turned away from 11F. When 11D noticed her shirt and her reading material, he couldn't restrain himself.

"Plato's cave, I see. And Kant! Grand, very grand!"

He didn't notice the Richard Russo novel. His thick accent gave him away.

"From Ireland?" she replied.

"Yes," he answered.

"I'm of Irish descent. Have you read Kant?"

She was surprised to have *The Metaphysics of Morals* be a conversation starter.

"Oh yes, Kant, many of his tings, including dat one you have dere many times. Brilliant. Brilliant."

And so the conversation began.

When Padraig found out that 11E was a PhD philosophy professor, he was both elated and a bit embarrassed. He noticed that she was reading Kant in the original German and quickly confessed that he had read only translations, notably the Mary J. Gregor translation of and comments on *The Metaphysics of Morals*. Elaine commended him on his choice, validating that Gregor was a foremost authority on the work.

In the ensuing conversational hours, Padraig revealed an uncanny understanding of Gregor's explanation of Kant's terms *Rechtslehre* and *Tugendlehre* and spoke cogently on Kant's *Doctrine of Right*, dealing with the rights that people have or can acquire, and his *Doctrine of Virtue* dealing with the virtues that they should acquire. Padraig went on to speak passionately on the system of law Kant formulated to protect individual rights. The dialogue went smoothly.

Elaine contributed insights on Kant's *Groundwork of the Metaphysics of Morals* and *Critique of Practical Reason*, pointing out nuances that she had picked up from reading the originals, nuances he wouldn't have been able to glean from the translations. He was thrilled.

In the meantime, 11F twisted and turned like a rat in a maze, thrashing about and more than occasionally intruding into Elaine's personal space. Engaged as she was in delightful conversation with Padraig, for the most part, she ignored 11F without even realizing she was doing so. The flight attendant became a regular visitor to their row as 11F frequently summoned her by way of the call button, asking alternatively for water, aspirin, a pillow, a blanket, or whatever else popped into his mind. The attendant professionally indulged him, but both Elaine and Padraig saw her roll her eyes after the fourth visit. When he wasn't tossing about, 11F was climbing over them every twenty-five minutes or so to use the restroom. He scattered various items from his carry-on bag around and under his seat and under 10F. He abruptly pushed his seat back down as far as he could, knocking a beverage from the 12F tray table. For the most part, as Elaine expected from first impression, he proved to be a basic pain in the ass for the entire flight.

Elaine and Padraig, of course, couldn't talk about Kant without bringing up Martin Heidegger's critique of Kant. That brought them to *Being and Time* and Heidegger's influence on philosophy, theology, art, architecture, artificial intelligence, cultural anthropology, design, literary and social theory, psychiatry, and psychotherapy. They agreed with the way he talked about the relationship between experience and caring.

"I tink all of us humans experience most tings best of all when we are caring about dose tings and de people dat are involved wit dose tings," Padraig tossed in.

Both he and Elaine paid homage to Heidegger's thinking and contributions to contemporary thought but excoriated him for his early affiliation with Nazism. Elaine gave Heidegger a bit of a reprieve because she heard that he privately acknowledged that affiliation as the biggest stupidity of his life. Padraig threw in that Heidegger claimed to have been influenced by Augustine of Hippo and Soren Kierkegaard and had written penetratingly on Friedrich Nietzsche. These comments opened a whole new thread to the conversation as they discussed the bishop of Hippo Regius, now Algeria, and how he founded a school of rhetoric in Carthage. They spoke of Augustine's view that human beings are the perfect unity of two substances: body and soul. They discussed his concept of original sin. This conversation was particularly spirited; Padraig, as a devout Catholic, and Elaine, as a convinced atheist, took totally divergent views on original sin. His was the religious view that man spent his life overcoming the effects of original sin, and she took the view that there was no such thing as sin—only morality and immorality. While the conversation was animated, it remained mutually respectful, and Elaine was impressed with the power and clarity of Padraig's thinking, even though she lacked the faith that underpinned his beliefs.

From time to time, they noticed that 11F was eavesdropping. At one point, Padraig tried to bring him into the conversation, but, at that point, 11F twitched and, acting like he had been asleep, merely asked, "Did you say something to me?"

Padraig let him off the hook by replying, "Oh, sorry, I t'ought ya might have someting to add."

11F rolled back over toward the window, and Elaine and Padraig continued their talk.

The conversation took various turns. She asked him how he got started with his study of philosophy. He took this opportunity to make sure she knew that he had only an undergraduate degree in philosophy but that he continued his study on his own after graduation.

"From listening to you, that must've been a very robust undergrad program," she said.

He told her about UCD and his first visit, where he heard Noam Chomsky speak, and how Chomsky's theories on generative and universal grammar tied into his observation that, in their role as parents, people seemed to speak about, think about, and interact with their children in some universal way. She said that from her experiences she hoped that wasn't true but that they should save this conversation for some other time. There was an awkward pause. Elaine filled the void by telling him that she was very interested in language and that she was helping a young Russian math genius who could grasp even the most subtle, esoteric math principles with relative ease but was struggling mightily with English syntax.

"I'm sure my friend wished there was just one universal language and that it more closely resembled Russian than English," Elaine told him.

They veered off Chomsky as Padraig leveraged their common Irish identities to reference George Edward Hughes and "Motive and Duty." Again, Elaine personalized the discussion by revealing that she felt it was her duty to act in a certain ways and that she didn't examine her motives but was confident that she was acting ethically even though others might not know or understand why she was acting that way. When he pressed her for examples, she told him that this conversation and the Chomsky one would probably go well together. To tide him over, she tossed in that she wasn't pleased with the way she was parented and that because of that, she had decided not to be a parent. He let it go at that, and they moved to Kierkegaard and Friedrich Nietzsche.

The trip was passing quickly but not before Padraig had the chance to tell Elaine about his physical therapy practice in Ireland and about Sonia, his wonderful wife and business partner. Elaine's ears perked when he told her how much Sonia liked to play the piano and that she loved many of the Irish singers—Mary and Frances Black, Maura O'Connell, Dolores Keane, Paul Brady. These were all artists that Elaine listened to often. And Sonia liked to dance. They agreed that she and Sonia would probably hit it off. He hoped that Elaine would visit them sometime. She, in turn, said she would love to show them around Boston and Cape Cod. They exchanged contact information, looked over at 11F and smiled, and then resumed their conversation.

Before they landed, Elaine told him about Tufts Medical School, her life on the Cape, and her writing. He asked about her husband. She felt comfortable enough with Padraig to spit out that she hadn't figured out that part of her life yet, maybe never would, that maybe she was too independent.

He balked at her explanation. Rather than deflecting, she engaged.

"Did you ever see the movie *Top Gun*?" she asked.

"Ah, yes. Tom Cruise," Padraig answered. "Maverick and Goose."

"Well, sometimes I feel like Maverick after he got caught in jet wash and his jet engines flamed out. Do you remember what happened?"

"Yes. Yes. Maverick ejects, but Goose doesn't make it."

Padraig turned his whole body toward her as best he could in 11D. He curled up the right side of his face and closed his right eye, tilting his head toward his right shoulder.

"Well, do you remember what happened after that?"

"Sure. Sure. Maverick lost all his spark. His personal jets flamed out too."

Padraig relaxed his face to a more normal expression, and his eyes twinkled ever brighter.

"Correct, Padraig. He lost his desire to get involved. He thought he would destroy anyone he was close to, so he stayed away from everyone. He wouldn't engage."

"Brilliant. Brilliant. But, I'm sure ya remember whut happens next, eh?"

Padraig loved the movie. He had watched it well over a dozen times. The music amped him up. The "She's Lost that Loving Feeling" bar scene made him laugh out loud each time, and he often felt the need for speed.

"What do you mean?"

She did a quick brain scan and couldn't access the next scenes from her memory.

"Ah! Maverick gets back in da game. It was but a temporary witdral. He got back in. Remember dat?"

"Well, maybe I should use another example. I can't use the other Tom Cruise movie *Days of Thunder* because the same thing happens there. But you know, I saw a special on a few boxers whose opponents died in the ring or afterward as a result of the fight. Boxers like Ezzard Charles and Emile Griffith. Have you heard of them?"

"Yes. Yes."

"Well, I've heard it said that when that happens, they often become afraid of throwing a blow that might land. It changed them. I might have become like that."

She made the comment as casually as she could, but her restrained, thin-lipped, tight smile betrayed her. He knew this was serious.

The conversation stopped for an awkward moment. She felt she had made a connection with this charming man during the flight, a closeness that surprised her. She felt the awkwardness of the moment but quickly figured a way out.

"I'm not lucky like you, Padraig. You recognized your soul mate when you found her. I may have missed the boat on that one."

He touched her arm lightly, leaned toward her, and spoke in slightly more than a whisper.

"I hoop yur day will coom, and sun."

They both recognized that the moment decidedly needed a new subject matter. Elaine made the transition.

"Thank you, Padraig. But, we haven't really talked about why you're making this trip. Do you have relatives or friends in San Francisco?"

Padraig explained that he was part of a presentation team for a seminar in kinesiology at the Stanford School of Medicine put on by the Sports Medicine Program. She, in turn, told him that she was presenting at a symposium at Berkeley cohosted by the Departments of Philosophy and Classics. She got confused when he started to laugh.

"What part of that is funny?" she asked.

"I'll be in yur addyance," he answered. "I've packaged my trip to give my presentation and attend da philosophy symposium at Berkeley."

He went on to explain what he hoped to learn from those presentations. They were both thrilled to learn that they would cross paths again very shortly. Padraig knew he would learn something from the professor. For her part, she was extremely impressed that her new friend, this accomplished physical therapist with only undergraduate exposure to philosophy, was more erudite and incisive than many of the credentialed professors she had come across. She complimented him again on his knowledge and insights. He blushed and eked out a "Tank ya" as 11F thrashed again in his seat and belted out a resounding burp. They laughed again and thanked each other for making the trip with 11F a tolerable one.

INTRODUCTIONS: PADRAIG, SONIA, AND NAD

As the sun continues its slow descent, Cav and Doreen make their way through the tent, escorting Nad over to a very animated couple who are chatting up a storm in thick Irish brogues. It's still very hot, and most of the crowd is gathered under the shade of the tent, which Nad notices is more occupied than when he first arrived. There's probably less than an hour before they will have to head over to the flats for the memorial service. He hopes that he will be able to speak to everyone before the night ends.

A checklist of Eon's friends that he has talked to so far cycles through his thoughts—Cav, Doreen and Carl, Karen and Justin, and Evangeline. Hearing about their lives and how they connected with Eon's helped fill in several of the blanks about her. He knew many bits and pieces, but these conversations are helping to pull things together. A feeling of regret over having missed an opportunity to share more of his life with her swirls through him as Cav and Doreen whisk him over to the couple as quickly as they can. They want to make sure he meets Padraig and Sonia and hopefully Lena Gelfond before they leave for the flats. He smiles to a few other visitors they bypass on the way.

"Padraig and Sonia Coughlin," Cav introduces, "this is Nad, a friend of Eon's from Philadelphia. Nad, Padraig and Sonia Coughlin—the Irish connection. The Coughlins came the furthest of anyone else to get here. They flew into Boston from Ireland yesterday, and they drove over to the Cape this morning."

"Ah, the Philadelphia lawyer," Padraig says as he extends his hand. "I've heard so much about you. Eon spoke of your writing and how much she liked it…and you. She called you a beacon for her life."

Padraig exudes a boundless energy that matches the lilt in his speech. Nad finds himself blushing yet again. It seems to him that everyone else knows more about him than he knows about them.

"Thank you. She was very important to me, too. I was hoping that we'd be able to make up for lost time, but then her illness set in. We talked quite a bit, but I didn't see her all that often, and when I did, it was only for short snips of time. I knew that Eon had friends in Ireland, but she never told me how she knew you."

Padraig quickly explains that he met Elaine on an airplane years ago when they both were traveling to San Francisco. Their alliance against the demanding, obnoxious traveler sitting with them was all that got them through the trip. They self-medicated with an intense discussion of weighty philosophical principles and frequent doses of vodka as palliatives to severe turbulence and the "sour man in da window seat." In discussing various philosophical principles during the flight and thereafter at the conference, they forged an enduring friendship.

"Wow, I'm very impressed that you made the trip all the way from Ireland."

Nad now remembers that, in one of their many phone conversations after they reconnected, Eon had told him about the trip to San

Francisco and the creep in the window seat. He'd forgotten that it was on that trip that she met Padraig.

"Eon was very special to us," Sonia says. "On that flight she got to know Padraig well, and then she and I became close friends, too. She had sooch a strung Irish identity. She loved Irish sweaters and Irish beers. I was very impressed wit' her knowledge of the Irish beers. Her favorite stouts were Beamish, Murphy's, O'Hara's, and Porterhouse. I like a pint or two mehself, so we had that in common. I was delighted that she introduced me to Kilkenny Irish Cream Ale. We shared a few wit' her, didn't we, Paddy?"

Padraig nods an ear-to-ear smile

"We liked many of the same Irish singers," Sonia continues. "We played piano and sang together, too."

"Well, I'm pleased to meet you both, but I'm sorry it's under these circumstances," Nad replies.

He notices that Sonia's accent is much less pronounced than Padraig's and wonders why.

"Doreen and I just met Sonia and Padraig today, too," Cav explains. "It's another example of our girl building silos in her life. She'd maneuver around among them but wouldn't allow any crossover. Maybe we can change that. Wouldn't it be great if we got together each year for a remembrance—you know, keep her memory alive through one another?"

Everyone agrees.

"Will you get an opportunity to stay on the Cape for a while?" Nad asks.

"Just a wee bit, two more days," Padraig says. "But, we've been here before. Sonia and I twice visited Eon in Brewster. We stayed wit' her for about a week each time. She showed us the sights here and in Boston, too."

"One of the highlights for us was when she took us to some of the towns on the Cape—Provincetown, Chatham, and Falmouth, I remember," Sonia adds. "In Falmouth, we felt right at home at Liam Maguire's

Irish Pub. Eon knew the singer dere, Danny Quinn, and he invited us up on the stage, and we sang some songs with him. Danny knew the Clancy Brothers and Tommy Makem. We felt we were in a home away from home when we were wit' her. I remember we sang 'The Water Is Wide.' I can still hear our voices blending together." She pauses to allow the memory of their singing play through her thoughts.

The water is wide, I can't cross over, and neither have I wings to fly.
Build me a boat that can carry two and both shall row, my love and I.
There is a ship and she sails the sea. She's loaded deep, as deep can be.
But not so deep as the love I'm in, I know not how I sink or swim.
Oh love is handsome and love is fine, the sweetest flower when first it's new.
But love grows old and waxes cold and fades away like summer dew.
Build me a boat that can carry two and both shall row, my love and I,
And both shall row, my love and I.

From Sonia's expression, the others realize that she has drifted off to replay that memory. They wait politely until she's ready to speak again.

"She told me I sounded like Mary Black." Sonia's voice cracks noticeably. "She also loved the Donagh Long song 'You'll Never Be the Sun.' She heard Dolores Keane sing it. She taught it to me, and we sang it together in Maguire's. She loved that song."

"I know that song, too," Nad says. "There're many versions—Nanci Griffith, Emmylou Harris. Eon and I agreed that the Dolores Keane version was our favorite. We talked about the kind of love and respect at the basis of that song. I thought that she and I might have felt that way about one another. Sonia, do you remember the words?"

"Yes, I do," Sonia replies.

"Would you be willing to sing it for us?"

Nad hopes that this isn't too unusual a request. The others quickly encourage her as well.

After a brief hesitation, she sings softly:

You'll never be the sun turning in the sky,
And you won't be the moon above us on the moonlit night,
And you won't be the stars in heaven although they burn so
bright,
But even on the deepest ocean, you will be the light.
You may not always shine as you go barefoot over stones.
You might be so long together, or you might walk alone.
And you'll find that love comes easy,
Or that love is always right,
So even when the storm clouds gather, you will be the light.
And if you lose a part inside when love turns round on you,
Leaving the past behind is knowing you'll do like you always
do,
Holding you blind,
Keeping you true.

You'll never be the sun turning in the sky,
And you won't be the moon above us on the moonlit night,
And you won't be the stars in heaven although they burn so
bright,
But even on the deepest ocean, you will be the light.
You will be the light.
You will be the light.

She finishes to applause, appropriately subdued for the circumstances.

"That was beautiful," Nad says.

He noticed that Sonia sang with no traces of Irish brogue at all. That's probably why, when speaking, her accent is so mild.

"In one of our calls, Eon mentioned that she had some friends from Ireland visiting her on the Cape. That must've been that trip."

"Ah, yes, yes. She also set up a trip to Ireland to visit some relatives, but she stayed with us almost the whole time," Padraig explains.

He tells how she really came to Dublin so that they could talk about philosophy and the writing he was doing and so that he could work on an abductor she had injured in a bike fall. Sonia chimes in that it was on that trip that she really got to know Eon well.

"We shared music and took several long walks. When we were walking, she told me about her childhood and how her family was worse than a mess. She used the word 'fraud.' She t'ought her family life was a lie and that her father was a fraud. She told me her father had no conscience, no morals. She saw this enormous flaw in him. To the outside world, he appeared to be such a great person, a great doctor. But in the home, he was a monster. She wondered about the morally of that, the etics of it. She told me that's how she began to have an interest in etics. She described herself as having an almost obsessive interest in how someone as intelligent as he was, who seemed to be so religious, and who was so well respected in the community could act the way he did in his own house with his own family. She said he took advantage of his power as the patriarch of dere family. It made her oppositional to authority, she said. With her, power and position made her suspicious. Only after you showed her your morality, your etics, would she decide whether or not to trust you. And she confided in me that it prevented her from forming truly close relationships for many years.

"I'll never forget one of the things she told me that sent a shiver through me. We were talking about art. She loved the Postimpressionists—Cézanne, Odilon Redon, Rousseau, Gauguin, Charles Angrand. She particularly loved how Cézanne brought beauty to the commonplace, the things of everyday life. When she was talking about Cézanne, she stopped in midstride and said, 'You know, Sonia, I love staring at Cézanne's work, but I can't help wondering about how lonely he must have been. I was reading about him and saw that he was quoted as saying, "I allow no one to touch me." I felt that way for many years.'

"She went on to tell me that, starting in high school but reaching its peak in college and beyond, she couldn't stand to be touched by another person. Doctors' visits, dentist visits, handshakes, many of the normal things of life sent her into panic mode. She couldn't hug anyone. The t'ought of being touched was so alarming, for a while she tried to wall herself off from the world. She tried to get past the terror and forced herself to do some dating, made herself go out with a few different men, but she never felt comfortable wit' them. She said she took a trip to California with someone, and that didn't work out. She was seeing someone on the Cape for a while, but she couldn't ever get past her aversion to being touched."

Sonia stops to assess whether she was going too far with sharing. She decides that she owes it to Eon to go on so that Nad can have a greater understanding about where he fit in.

"Nad, during that same walk, she opened up to me about you. She said that the only break in her repulsion to being touched was when she met you on Martha's Vineyard. Miraculously, in the span of a few hours, the aversion vanished, she said. She used the word 'miraculously.' She said that dere was something about you that she trusted, that she respected, and she told me that she made a big mistake by pulling herself away from you."

Sonia goes on to explain that Eon asked her not to share the conversation with Padraig because she felt self-conscious about how she had felt and how she had reacted. She wanted to confide in Sonia, woman to woman, because she wanted someone to know how she felt.

"I think we had just the right closeness between us. We talked openly woman da woman, but I wasn't part of her everyday life."

Sonia feels at liberty to talk about this now that Eon has passed.

"Nad, I want you to know that Eon recognized how much you changed her life. She was grateful for dat change. She said you would always be her light, like in the song."

Cav, knowing what he does about the Neal family, is not surprised. Doreen and Padraig stand there slack-jawed, as this is the first time they have heard about Eon's aversion.

Nad has been listening in humbled silence with conflicting emotions. It feels good to know that she really loved him, but it's also frustrating that they never had a life together. He's still confused about what happened, why she disappeared so quickly without warning and without explanation. Once again, there's an awkward silence. Cavendish saves the moment.

"Thank you, Sonia, Padraig. I have to do at least one more introduction before we head over to the flats. Nad, I have to introduce you to Lena before we go. You can meet the others after, but you have to meet Lena before."

Cavendish drags him away.

LENA GELFOND

Lena Gelfond sat at her usual spot in Area Four on Technology Square, Cambridge, Massachusetts, the coffee shop where she parked herself almost every day. She was partial to cappuccino, but from time to time, she would substitute a latte for variety. Espresso put her over the top, and just plain coffee lacked the power to ignite her. She typically gravitated to the two large overstuffed black leather chairs in the corner next to a window. It pleased her that even though they were in Cambridge, some of the wall hangings sported scenes in Boston. On the wall across the room, two well-framed thirteen-by-nineteen photographs, one of Beacon Hill and the other of Boston Common, cued up with her line of sight. More than once she found herself staring off into those scenes. She liked them, Boston in the springtime—bright sunshine and blooming flowers, a variety of walkers walking a variety of dogs, strollers dressed in more than rainbow colors, everyone hopeful that the day they were living would be a good one. She wondered if anyone in those pictures ever saw themselves on the wall of Area Four or if they even realized they were being photographed.

The pictures cheered her up on the many days when she sat on one of the black chairs frustrated by some cryptic words in one of her textbooks. She chose the black chairs because of their comfort and because, when she sat in one, other coffee drinkers mostly shied away from the other chair to avoid appearing to encroach on her space. And, these particular chairs reminded her of her father—he had similar leather chairs in his office back home. She began to think of and treat the area as her office. It was helpful that the owners had placed a small, round, three-legged mahogany-stained mini-table between the chairs over by an air duct. The table was large enough to hold two cups and two small pastry dishes. Lena stretched its limits by using it as her desk. She stacked her books or placed her computer on it. The handy electrical outlet on the wall between the chairs enabled her to plug in if she had to.

She had only recently circled the seasons for the first time in Massachusetts. In the year she had been camping out in Area Four, she found only two drawbacks to her office spot: in those transitional times between seasons, when the air conditioner or heater were unnecessarily cranking, it could be inappropriately cold or hot there; and everyone entering the main seating area in Area Four had to pass the chairs to find a place to sit. She found herself often and easily distracted by the traffic. Each time, she renewed her resolve to be more disciplined, more focused, more locked in, knowing that in a few minutes, she would fall short once again. She liked to watch people, especially now that she was in a new locale where everything was stimulating and impossible to ignore. She found herself smiling to many of the patrons; some of them even smiled back, especially the young men—students, like her. She regretted that none of them ever gathered the courage to come over to talk to her, but she made it a point to keep smiling. These two flaws in her chosen positioning were outweighed by the comfort of the chairs, the light beaming in from the window or, after dark, dripping down from the overhead incandescent, and the pleasant reality that she could observe as much of the comings and goings as she wanted to on any given day.

On this day, she hadn't noticed that her well-worn, overloaded deep-green backpack had toppled from the other chair onto the dark-gray linoleum floor with the marbleized pattern—a floor that over the years had welcomed countless splashes and spills of java and other slick, messy, staining substances. She tried to be attentive, to tread carefully over the slippery floor, assuming that one day the time would come for her to splat herself on a wet spot. Each time she entered the shop, she consciously hoped that this would not be the day. Had she been aware that the backpack had fallen, she would have retrieved it.

Today, Lena wore her customary uniform for this time of year: the black, tight-fitting jeans would have made her look taller than her actual diminutive five-two height, when standing, which she wasn't; the black, formfitting cotton turtleneck would have made her look even younger than her age, twenty-five last month, had it not been covered by a loose-fitting royal-blue midweight wool sweater, which it was. And so, sitting there, she looked like a five-two, twenty-five-year-old, attractive Russian woman—exactly on target. Her short-cropped platinum-blond hair framed a pleasant, slightly angular face, which at this moment featured pursed unglossed lips and gray squinting eyes. Describing her as pixieish would be right on target.

She was looking more than slightly befuddled as she tried to balance, almost successfully, an English-Russian dictionary on her knees while attempting to plow through a mathematics textbook that was written in English. If only the authors would have just set out the pertinent principles in numbers and formulae, she would have had no problem following along, she thought in Russian. But, no, they decided to use too many words to explain; what were they thinking?

She mumbled, "Chort Vozmi," expecting that anyone who heard her wouldn't understand her frustrated utterance. She was correct.

As she continued to fumble around, her ever-present concern that her difficulty with English might put her doctoral candidacy at risk lurked on the bubble between her conscious and subconscious thoughts. She questioned whether she had made the right choice in coming to the United States to pursue her education. In Russia she felt the pressure of her pedigree: the daughter of a well-known mathematician and the granddaughter of an iconic figure in Russian mathematics. Her math acumen seemed congenital. She understood number theory intuitively, almost like she had been force-fed it with the baby food that sustained her in those early years. As an undergraduate student back home, she was precocious in her writing and thinking: early on she took the concept of transcendental numbers to another level and began garnering accolades.

But, with her insights came a set of expectations. In the homeland, both her father and particularly her grandfather were so well-known and respected that it was presumed that she would be a supernova of Russian mathematics. She began to feel enveloped by expectations. Pressure morphed into stress, and the early stages of emotional and intellectual paralysis started to set in. Fortunately, her parents picked up on this. They saw her struggle to get out of bed each day, to eat, to sleep, to smile, to talk. They watched her attack her work like an anorectic attacks exercise: compulsively, without sufficient rest or recreation, obsessively expending enormous energy—hundreds of sit-ups and miles run with only an apple and a piece of cheese for dinner.

Lena herself didn't know she was trapped. She knew she was dissatisfied, unhappy, anxious, and prone to bursts of energy when she seemed to be powered by plutonium followed by catatonic periods of time when she felt like a dormant volcano, building up pressure below her hardened, immovable surface. Until her parents intervened, she didn't realize how much she needed help. They were typical parents in wanting her to be healthy and happy. Her mother and father were completely supportive, but her father voluntarily shouldered a tad bit more of the responsibility, feeling as he did that some of his accomplishments were contributing to her condition. Together, as a family, they recognized how important it was for Lena to be on her own, to find her own place in the world. Her parents were open to her finding that place anywhere, doing anything that brought her peace and satisfaction. As they spoke, Lena made it clear that she wanted to find her own place in the world of mathematics. She loved to think in principles and formulae, just maybe not in Russia.

So, with her parents' support and blessings, Lena Gelfond decided to relocate to the United States to study for her master's and doctoral degrees, with no clear intention on what she would do or where she would do it, once her formal education concluded. She applied to all the top mathematics programs: MIT, Harvard, Princeton, Stanford, Cal-Berkeley, and University of Chicago. They all eagerly welcomed her with generous financial support. After a whirlwind family trip to all six schools, she made her decision. It was off to America, to Cambridge, and the Massachusetts Institute of Technology.

The professors at MIT knew who her father was, but they were quite accustomed to dealing with brilliant students, some of whom were children of the famous and brilliant; it didn't really faze them. As renowned scholars, they weren't intimidated by whatever cachet accompanied those families. They were there for the students, not for the parents. They understood their role in this pedagogical arrangement—challenge these students, tease the brilliance out of them, being careful not to rip them apart in the process. For the professors, it was all about the thinking. They zoned in on their individual students and focused on nurturing their development, helping them become unencumbered by whatever burdens their last names or anything else brought. They knew how to broaden perspectives, allowing their students' own identities to emerge.

Lena was no different from others in this respect. She was different, however, in two ways: language was an impediment—even the other foreign students were well beyond her in their mastery of English; and, her mathematical brilliance exceeded most of what they were accustomed to observing, even at MIT. In this new environment, she was beginning to live up to those supernova expectations without being confronted minute by minute by the reality that she was indeed her father's daughter. But the language issue continued to frustrate her; even with her extraordinary facility for mathematics, her acumen for the English language was low. She had mastered German and various offshoots of Russian, but English, French, and Spanish were more aspirational for her. She struggled mightily with them, especially with English.

On this particular day, absorbed in her balancing act, she didn't notice the professionally dressed woman—maybe a professor or a doctor or a lawyer or a businesswoman—casually walk into the coffee shop and order a triple espresso. She didn't notice that the woman was noticing her; she was too preoccupied muttering in Russian to her notebook and pencil and to her textbook and dictionary.

The woman watched Lena peripherally while the barista prepared the explosive drink she craved every few days. On other days, she would bounce around the menu, selecting whatever first popped to mind, but every third or so was triple-espresso day. As she observed the young woman struggling over on the black leather chair, she remembered that on her frequent visits to Area Four, she had seen this student sitting in the same spot every time she came in, usually dressed mostly in black with some splash of color somehow added to her wardrobe. It caught her attention that the woman always seemed to be deciphering something in an overly cumbersome, intimidating mathematics textbook. More than once, she considered approaching the student, hoping to begin a conversation. She had a keen interest in the philosophical aspects of mathematics. Although she concentrated on ethics, she had the intellectual bandwidth to read some of the seminal works in the philosophy of mathematics when she was earning her master of philosophy degree. She managed time effectively, enabling her to stray outside her core area of study. She knew she would be fully immersed in ethical theories while doing her work, so she indulged herself by learning about set, modal, recursive, and proof theory and constructive mathematics.

Today, the woman couldn't help herself; she had time, and she felt compelled to intervene. Triple espresso in hand, she began her approach to the student. She was focused on saying something to open a conversation without startling or offending her.

She was about to say, "Maybe you need a bigger desk," when she was almost tackled by the unseen backpack sitting on the floor that seemed to pounce on her ankles. As she began to stumble, she took a few quick cha-cha-type steps, then swooned to a tango-like dip, and somehow managed to stay vertical without spilling a single drop of espresso. Her free hand came to rest on the top of one of the leather chairs.

She was in the process of righting herself when the young woman instinctively jumped up to try to help. The student kicked the table. Books flew every which way; the large chair that had prevented the triple espresso and its owner from hitting the floor spun sideways. The backpack, now dislodged from the ankles it was attacking, flew across the floor and came to rest in the vestiges of a past stain. A much more audible, more of a screech of "Chort vozmi!" filled the room. Everyone stopped to look, but only the woman with the espresso knew that "Devil take" was the Russian equivalent of "Damn it." The two women caught each other's eyes, and both started to laugh. Neither the cappuccino nor the triple espresso hit the floor, but the scene looked very much like a spoof of a cheesy sitcom episode.

"Da, chort vozmi! I thought you might need some help, but I may be the one who needs it more."

The woman announced the last part in English. She spoke Russian, but it was, at best, her third language behind English and German. The young woman seemed to understand; they both laughed again. The young woman struggled to articulate an apology as she grabbed to retrieve her backpack and move it out of the way before it attacked someone else.

"Izvinite—how to say…sorry! So sorry! S Vami vsye normaljno? You are okay? No harm? Ti govorishj po-roosski? Speaks Russki?" The words carried a heavy accent.

Elaine was still not sure how much English the young woman spoke so she decided to use both languages.

"Da. Yes. Vy predpochitayete govorit' na russkom? Do you want to speak in Russian?"

"Nyet," the young woman answered. "Needs English practice, please."

Elaine realized she had to slow down her speech, exaggerate her pronunciation, and use simpler words and sentence structure.

"Okay. We can practice your English. I'm okay, fine. I did not spill a drop, and nothing is harmed. Da. I have seen you here before with your textbooks, but today you looked a little flummoxed, so I thought I would come over. Do you need help?"

"Flummoxed? I don't know 'flummoxed.'"

The young woman smiled a large, open smile, thrilled that someone had come over to talk to her.

"'Flummoxed' means, well…puzzled, at a loss, confused."

"Ah, da, yes, confused. Very confused. This language, English, no sense to it. Words means different things, and sounds and looks are not alike. To go and two people and too many. All the tos means different. And they're going there with their friends. All the theres. All the same but all different. And you write with pen, but pigs live there, and crooks go there, also. Not so much a like for English language. Da, yes, flummoxed. Very flummoxed."

"Well, maybe I can help. May I sit down with you? You are new to America? Correct?"

"Da, yes, from Russia. Little more than year here. All those heres too. I am here, and I can hear you, and I have yellow hair. Sound same to me but means different."

Lena threw her hands in the air. They both laughed again.

"I agree." Elaine spoke very slowly, carefully exaggerating each sound. "There are many things in English that don't make sense, and many words are said the same way, but they mean totally different things. You can wait around and do nothing but eat and gain lots of weight. You can come back and turn your back. You can see the sea from the beach. It goes on and on. English is my first language, and I still have trouble with it."

Lena smiled in agreement as Elaine continued.

"It seems you are studying mathematics. Do you go to school here?"

"Da, MIT. For master's, then to get doctor degree in mathematics. You look like professor to me. You teach MIT?"

Lena felt great that she finally had met someone in the coffee shop that was willing to talk slowly with her so that she could practice her English. She felt like she was actually having a conversation.

"I'm a professor but not at MIT. I teach at Tufts Medical School. I teach medical ethics and health-care policy, but I'm very interested in mathematics, especially the philosophy of mathematics. Alfred North Whitehead and Bertrand Russell. I'm sure you have studied them. Do you have time to talk some more, or are you on a deadline?"

Elaine was hoping to learn some more about the young woman and, more specifically, about her studies.

"Yes, talk. No deadline. I have read *Principia Mathematica*. My grandfather taught it to my father, and my father taught it to me. I'm Lena, Lena Gelfond. Nice meet you, Professor…" Lena was broadly smiling.

"Elaine Neal. Same here, Lena. Gelfond? Have you ever heard of Aleksandr Osipovich Gelfond?"

Elaine hoped that this conversation might last another espresso or two. She settled in when she noticed that Lena was blushing.

For her part, Lena experienced an unfamiliar feeling. Back home, when someone linked her to her widely renowned grandfather, she would turtle up, shut down, and withdraw, but right now, she felt only pride and comfort.

"Da, my grandfather. Very smartest man. I never meeted him. I borned after he died."

"Yes, he was a very smart man. I'm sorry you didn't get the chance to grow up with him around."

"Thank you. My father was mathematics, too. He carried family tradition. I trying to learn." Lena's blush faded.

"Great. So, tell me about your studies."

Elaine kept the conversation going. Over the next hour or so, Lena talked about how hard the work was at MIT, especially explaining her plight with the English language. She grasped the formulae easily and could derive principles without much trouble as well, but the discussions in class and the reading in English slowed her down. Oddly, she was improving with the class discussions because the professors used the blackboards to scrawl out ideas in a universal mathematical language, but the textbooks continued to be a major challenge. Elaine volunteered to help with translations, not only to help Lena but also to gain more intimate knowledge of a subject matter that fascinated her. She was always looking for opportunities to learn, to widen and deepen her horizons. If she could do that while also helping a student, so much the better—her desire to learn perfectly complementing her desire to teach.

Lena told her about her work back home and agreed to discuss number theory, the philosophy of numbers, and transcendental numbers. They would work together to translate from Russian to English the papers that Lena had written back home during her undergraduate days. Elaine was well aware of the kinds of papers that would be publishable in American university and professional journals. She wasn't quite sure that Lena's work was of that caliber, but from this initial conversation, and from her pedigree, she thought it was likely.

Thus, the collaboration began over a fallen backpack and a couple of cappuccinos and espressos in Area Four. For the next year, Lena and Elaine met three times for ninety minutes most weeks. They spent some time going over Lena's issues with understanding her textbooks, and any comments made in lectures that she didn't quite grasp, and sometimes translating her previous works. But they also spent time just talking, getting to know one another. Lena told Elaine about life in Russia. Elaine talked about American practices and culture. They discussed art and music. Lena's English quickly improved. Lena earned her master's degree and began work on her doctorate.

Elaine's Russian was decently fluent, but her German was even stronger. These strengths helped facilitate the process. When Elaine had difficulty grasping a concept that Lena explained in broken English or Russian, they would often switch to German, and that seemed to work every time. With Elaine's support and encouragement, Lena's English improved so dramatically that she was able defend her thesis in English with no problem. She earned her PhD with abundant praise.

Lena was aware of the importance of producing written work both from her father's proclivity to publish and from being around other scholars at home and now at MIT. After helping Lena put into English the complex concepts and principles that drove her doctoral thesis, Elaine helped her work on articles for publication.

During that year, they had several conversations about the history of mathematics and logic. Because of her father, Lena's knowledge of the background and history of mathematical theory was deep and broad. Everyone knew about the contributions of the Greeks. But Lena knew about George Boole and Augustus De Morgan, who elucidated systematic treatments of logic that build on the thinking of such algebraists as George Peacock so that they could extend Aristotle's traditional doctrines of logic into a framework facilitating the study of the foundations of mathematics. Elaine's natural thirst for knowledge made her very interested in this history. She firmly believed that without knowledge of the history of a subject, you could never really master it.

MIT was eager to keep this brilliant woman close by, so it was arranged that Dr. Gelfond would teach one course per semester and continue to write groundbreaking mathematical treatises. Elaine continued to provide support.

INTRODUCTIONS: LENA AND NAD

Cav brings Nad and Lena together.

"Nad, this is Dr. Lena Gelfond, another friend of Eon's. She's from Russia and the world of mathematics. Dr. Gelfond is a professor at MIT. Dr. Gelfond, this is Nad, Eon's lawyer friend from Philadelphia. They met on Martha's Vineyard."

"Ah, the writer. Eon showed me some of your short stories. I enjoy your writing. Eon had me reading many things in English. She said that if I read your stories, I could understand better about growing up in big cities in America and about how people get along. She said some were 'rite of passage' stories. I had never heard that term before, but I know about it now. Other stories, she called 'relationship stories.' I liked them all."

Nad never published any of his writing or even made it generally available. He showed his stories to selected family and friends, and, from time to time, he would read his poems or stories at literary open mics at coffeehouses or the like in the Philadelphia area or on the Vineyard. He perceived that the act of writing differed substantially from the act of publishing: one was difficult, challenging, emotionally rewarding, and edifying; the other was boring, tedious, draining, and too much like work. He already had a job. He wrote for pleasure and to see if he could do it and because every once in a while, he seized on something he wanted to say, even if it was just to hear himself think out loud, so to speak. He had no idea that Eon had showed his stories to anyone. He wonders whether she shared his stories with anyone else.

"Thank you, but I would say I write some, more than calling myself a writer. But yes, thank you. Eon wasn't good at sharing names, but I do know about you, the Russian math genius from the coffee shop in Cambridge. When she told me some of your story and I asked her your name, she said names sometimes just confused things. She said that in her mind, she called you 'Midge,' from 'MG' for 'Math Genius,' but that wasn't your real name. So, Lena, it's very nice to meet you and to know your actual name."

It seems that Eon went out of her way not to provide him with names of many of her friends—she talked about their backgrounds and their attributes and their talents and their proclivities, and often of her relationships with them, but she preferred to skirt actually handing over their names.

"Genius, I don't know." Lena laughs. "She never called me 'Midge' to my face. Very funny. She had that sense of humor. But, da, yes, mathematics, easy for me, in my blood from grandfather and father. English, not so much."

"Your English sounds very good to me, Midge…Lena. You have learned well."

The accent is still strong and clear, but he has absolutely no problem conversing with her.

"Eon helped me so much. She let me practice my English with her."

Lena was proud of the progress she had made under Elaine's tutelage over the years.

"All that practice paid off. I know that you worked closely with Eon and that she respected and cared for you very much. That was very clear from the way she spoke about you. I'd like to hear more about your work together, if we have time, Cav."

Nad looks to Cav, who nods in approval. During the next few minutes, Lena explains that after making behind-the-scenes contributions on language and organization for a few books and several articles that Lena had written, Eon had finally agreed to co-write a book with Lena on number theory. Lena was providing the technical content, and Elaine was making the book readable. They wanted to reach a wider audience, hoping that it could be used as a textbook for younger aspiring mathematicians who might have been turned off by the more stilted, almost indecipherable books on the subject that presumed too much a priori knowledge. They were both excited about it. Eon had been a teacher for many years, and under Eon's guidance, Lena's teaching passion and effectiveness had grown geometrically. It bothered Lena that Eon wouldn't agree to be more recognized for the contributions she made to Lena's work. Lena dedicated her first book to her father and her second book to both Eon and her mother. In her other works, she was always careful to give Eon top billing as one of her editors and advisors in the acknowledgments, but she wanted Eon to accept the designation as coauthor as well. Eon always declined, saying that it was Lena who did the architectural work, put down the foundation, and built the house, and that all she did was splash on some paint, put down some carpets, and hang some curtains. Anybody, she used to say, could do that. Lena always disagreed.

In her charming Russian accent, Lena extols Elaine's uncanny grasp of esoteric subject matters and nuances in mathematics and her acumen for reducing complex thoughts to words that even Lena could easily understand, despite the reality that English was really Lena's third language. A strong symbiosis and mutual admiration connected them. They had only recently completed the first draft of the new book when Eon was stricken. Their work together came to a stop.

Lena then tells Nad, Cav, and Doreen about her interactions with Eon toward the end. She may have been the first one to begin noticing symptoms. All through their collaborations, Eon had been diligent, reliable, resourceful, creative, and funny. But, late last year, things began to change. Lena noticed first that Eon's sense of humor seemed to be dwindling. Normally when they met, their interaction was light and laced with funny remarks from Eon, usually based on language or some idiosyncrasy in one of the math principles they were working on. Those remarks started to become less and less a part of their interaction. Then Lena started to feel that Eon was exhausted or at least tired much of the time, and her radiance faded. She always thought of Eon as spewing energy and spirit and intellectual curiosity. Eon began struggling to meet deadlines. Lena didn't think too much of it at first, but the change was palpable enough to catch her attention. Maybe the onset of the school year was proving to be more difficult for whatever reason. Eon had pointed out that her department had a new head who liked to have more meetings than his predecessor and that a large part of the burden of his orientation to the position had fallen to her. Part of her responsibility during the orientation process was to make sure important parts of unrecorded institutional history and practices were passed along to him so that he could more knowingly decide what components of the existing culture to retain or even build on and what parts to retool or replace or eliminate. It was stressful for Eon because she was serving as the new department head's link between the past and the future. She talked to Lena about this role and these changes enough times for Lena to know that they were weighing heavily on her.

At first Lena thought that these things were at the heart of the exhaustion. But then Eon began to have a hard time understanding some of the principles Lena was explaining. This had never been the case before. No matter how complex the issue, once Lena was able to negotiate the language obstacles, Eon would pick up the concept, including all the subtleties. Lena first thought it was her own fault, that she was not finding the right words to communicate. She was always prone to frustration when she couldn't get her thoughts across as clearly as she wanted, so she often replayed interactions in her head. But, as she thought over some of the conversations, she realized that she was communicating the same way she always had and that the ideas she was trying to get across were no more sophisticated or elusive than other ideas that Eon had grasped quickly. The next clue was that even after Eon assimilated the concept, she began having a hard time producing succinct, clear text to elucidate it. Lena began having a hard time understanding what Eon was writing. This, too, was a new phenomenon.

The final clue came after Lena had not seen Eon for about two weeks. Their schedules hadn't meshed. Eon looked pale and shrunken, and only a couple of weeks earlier, Lena thought she had looked fine.

Lena's first comment was not a greeting but a concerned "Are you okay?"

"Not so sure," was Eon's reply.

Eon told Lena that she wasn't feeling well, that she had lost her appetite, and that her weight kept plummeting. She also confided that she was having trouble concentrating. Focus was an issue. Energy was low. Eating was a chore. She slept fitfully and only for short periods of time. Eon told her she was just exhausted from work and that maybe she had a low-grade virus. She said she'd know in a week or so, and if she hadn't come out of it by then, she'd get checked for Lyme disease or an iron or vitamin D deficiency. Lena pleaded with Eon to go to a doctor right away. Eon's references to the other possible conditions made Lena think that maybe Eon did have a good grasp of what was happening, so she relented. It was difficult not to back off with Eon because she was so knowledgeable about so many things and because she always seemed to be in control, especially when things seemed to be swirling around. Eon assured her that this minor illness would pass; Lena deferred. It didn't; it worsened.

"I should have pressed harder. I should have insisted. Maybe the outcome would have been different if they found the cancer sooner. Maybe they would have been able to treat it. I'm sorry that I didn't step in."

Nad, Cav, and Doreen nod with understanding. Cav speaks up.

"Lena, none of us are to blame on this. Eon was headstrong and often not controllable, and from what I've heard, once these symptoms began to manifest, the likelihood that any treatments for this type of cancer would be successful is very, very low. It was better that you remained close and supported her. There was nothing more any of us could have done."

They exchange soundless, supportive looks. Doreen breaks the silence. She announces that although there are a few more key people for Nad to meet, it's time to load up for the quick drive to the flats. Nad will have to wait until later to meet the striking woman about Elaine's age and two young girls who look to be either fraternal twins or friends—too close in age to be just sisters. They gather to depart for the flats.

TO THE FLATS

This Saturday fights hard to stay alive. Everything glows. The sun rails through the sky spewing white heat. The guests move slowly from the tent to the parking area as if paced by a lugubrious dirge, New Orleans style. No one can muster the vigor or the eagerness to hurry. Heat and sadness sap energy. Scattered cars and vans that have been absorbing the day's intensity inertly await their passengers. As if entranced, the guests approach the vehicles and get shocked back to consciousness by simmering door handles that repel their unwary hands. Baking leather seats tingle the backs of their bare legs. Groups of four to six come together almost haphazardly.

Nad, Karen and Justin, Doreen and Carl, and Lena form a cluster with Cav and slip into Cav's perfectly restored vintage Volkswagen minibus, authentic in classic dove blue and silver white. With its customary bench seating, the bus easily seats eight, but they're all pleased to have the extra room—no air-conditioning in this baby. Nad is glad he's not driving; he half expects flames to spew from the steering wheel. Plus, the trip and the emotions of the occasion are making him weary. He hopes that a few minutes of relaxation will restore him. He wants his participation in the evening's events to be as full as possible.

He settles into his seat in the middle of the bench behind the two front seat consoles. He leans forward toward the gearshift that grows out of the floor. Cav occupies the driver's seat on his left, and Lena has shotgun on his right. He wants to keep the conversation casual as Cav fiddles with the key. The ignition flows power to the starter, which twirls the crankshaft. The fuel pump adds gasoline for the carburetor to dispense into each cylinder so that when the distributer parcels out spark to each plug, the engine springs to life. In his youth, Nad spent years around cars working with his father. He knows that the engine is air-cooled. From listening to it rev, he figures it is a four cylinder—maybe fourteen hundred to fifteen hundred cubic centimeters. It's firing on all cylinders but lacks the smooth, steady purr of a six. They are ready to roll.

"Cav, this bus is perfect. Looks to be about a sixty-three to sixty-five. How close am I?"

"Thanks. You're in the right zone. Pick one," Cav says.

"I'd say sixty-five, but I'm not quite sure why."

"Yes. Perfect. Good job. 1965. I'm the second owner. I bought it from a guy who drove it pretty hard. It was quite a mess when I picked it up. I've had it awhile."

Cav is always in the mood to talk about cars, especially his bus.

"Do you keep it here on the Cape?" Nad asks.

"No, sir. I drive it from Lincoln every year. It's part of our adventure. I can cruise safely and comfortably at sixty-five to seventy miles an hour. We drive with the windows open when we can—natural ventilation. Even with the volume turned all the way up, you can't hear an intelligible thing on the radio with the windows open—just random noise, like in the early days of broadcasting. But we don't care. The girls are either singing or playing games. They even seem to manage to find a way to sleep through the noise."

Both Cav and Nad are now smiling. Cars are a common interest. They are both pleased to find another point of contact. Each of them wants to like the other because of their love and respect for Eon. A bond seems to be forming without being forced. Lena seems pleasantly engaged in listening to the conversation as well.

"I don't know a single thing about cars, but this looks like fun, very old-fashion machine," Lena says.

"Yes, it is. Definitely old-fashioned," Cav says.

"I'm impressed that you take it on that kind of trip," Nad adds. "Many owners of restored cars let them just sit. They're afraid to take their toys out of the box and play with them. Who did the work?"

Nad knows many people who keep restored cars up on blocks and under cloth covers. He himself subscribes to the view that with most "things," you buy them to use them and to get pleasure from or to have them make your life easier. He admires restored vehicles, but he's more a new-car guy. He also gravitates toward German cars— Porsches in particular. He admires Porsche's high performance and style, plus he feels that his Porsche is the kind of car he could drive every day, regardless of conditions. He had started out with normally aspirated 911 Cabriolets and eventually stepped up to the turbo cab. He picks up a new one every five or so years. He respects cars and takes very good care of them, but drives them hard, the way he thinks they should be driven. You display trophies and artwork.

"I did almost all of it myself. I enjoy it. It's a great diversion from the law. My work is very adversarial. Like with you, quite a bit of what I do is litigation. I don't have to tell you how unpleasant that can be."

"Amen to that. What parts of the restore were easy, and what parts were hard?"

Nad figures this conversation will be a good time passer, and he wants to continue the bridge building with Cav.

"The electrical work on these old ones is pretty simple. No computers to deal with. Just straightforward wiring. New points and condenser for the distributer. With contemporary models, it's circuit boards and computer chips. That stuff is beyond me. The engine rebuild went really well. I had to have the cylinders bored out and sleeved. I was able to do the work on the head myself—valve job and gaskets. The biggest problem was locating the needed parts, but there are quite of few of these guys on junk heaps, and many of the parts are fungible over several model years."

Cav checks in the rearview mirror to peek at Nad's reaction. He's not sure how much Nad actually knows about cars. That Nad's expression reveals comprehension reassures him. Nad smiles and nods understanding and interest, so Cav rambles on.

"I had to learn how to do the bodywork and how to replace some of the glass. Lots of glass here—thirteen windows. I'm proud to say they're all watertight. I think I might be able to get her to float. Maybe I should look into installing a propeller," Cav jokes. "Well, anyway, it was fun."

Everyone in the bus listens attentively to the conversation. Only Cav and Nad participate. The passengers smile and nod, unseen, from time to time, happy to have a distraction from the heat and the task at hand. There will be ample time for reflection as the evening unwinds.

"It really does look great. And, we're moving, so you did it right. Did you have to rebuild the transmission, too?"

Nad could talk on and on about cars.

"No. The transmission was fine. I don't know if someone else rebuilt it, but I didn't touch it other than to drop it out to replace the clutch. You seem to know a lot about cars. What's the connection?" Cav asks.

"My father was a machinist and a mechanic. I started working on cars when I was nine or ten. Rebuilt my first engine when I was twelve. The paint looks good, too. Did you have to have it painted, or was it just a big-time cleanup job?"

"No. It's the original color, but there was so much bodywork I had to do, I had to repaint the whole bus. It was a challenge finding the pigments to blend into the original color, but I did. I'd never painted anything like this before, so I had to learn how to use the spray gun. The prep work was tedious but pretty easy. It was the actual painting that caused me heartburn."

Cav is on a roll. It also feels good to have the car talk as a diversion from the looming task. A tacit understanding has emerged that the conversation needs to be weightless as they navigate toward the Brewster Flats. There will be plenty of time later on for more serious conversation.

"Terrific job. How did you keep all the dust out of the paint job?"

Nad knows something about car painting because he had worked with his father to help a friend set up a paint booth—an enclosed, ventilated clean room for car spraying. Even small amounts of dust can ruin a paint job.

"I represent a family back in Lincoln that has an auto-body repair business. The father and I have become friends over the years. I did most of the restoration work in his shop. He has a spray booth. He taught me. I practiced in there, and then when I passed his test, I let it rip. I was terrified the whole time. I was very afraid of uneven coverage. And if you're not careful, the paint can run, or you can leave paint spots. He stayed with me the whole time—kept me on track."

Cav makes a mental note that Nad seems to know quite a bit about cars and is delighted to have such a knowledgeable person to go back and forth with. He wonders whether Nad ever listensed to *Car Talk* with Tom and Ray Magliozzi, Click and Clack, the Tappet Brothers, on NPR, but he forgets to ask.

"That makes it even more impressive that you drive up here every year from Lincoln," Nad says.

"It's a car, well, a bus, a microbus or a minibus, really. That's how I think of it. You know, a 'child-of-God mobile.' Built to roll. It's not a museum piece. It's supposed to be driven. If I need to do more restoration work down the road, I will, but for now, it's what we take to come up here every year."

"Not a bad choice," Nad says.

He feels an additional level of simpatico with Cav and settles back in his bench seat between Carl and Justin. Doreen and Karen sit on the bench behind them, hands folded on their laps, staring straight ahead.

The suspended sun seems to hover over the ocean, now a red blaze tickling the horizon. Solemn silence punctuates the remainder of the drive to the flats. Each mourner reflects on random moments spent with their departed friend.

Nad remembers that first weekend in Brewster after the Vineyard week. When he pulled off Tubman Road, up the gravel driveway to her house, he noticed what appeared to be a paddock and a bright-white stable with matching half doors trimmed in phthalo green. The trim matched the stable roof, and the stable took its color pattern from the house, a very old, stately classic Cape. He thought he heard neighing, snorting, and snuffling. It was that weekend that he learned for the first time that Eon had been an equestrian back in Nebraska and that she still rode often. He remembered coasting to stop next to where her old orange Peugeot 504 rested in the shade. He previously had ribbed her about that car but also greatly admired that she had kept it for so long and in such great shape. The austerity and awkward classiness of the vehicle seemed consummately appropriate.

"But, orange?" he teased.

"Yes, orange. Burnt orange. Not pumpkin or alloy orange and certainly not that hideous Princeton orange. Burnt orange. A mature, elegant burnt orange!" Her non-defensive rebuttal ended with her flicking her head up and back, Katharine Hepburn style. They simultaneously let out deep belly laughs.

On that trip, before he knocked on her door, he poked his head through the open top half of one of the stable doors. In the two stalls, fraternal stallions—half Trakehner, half Thoroughbred—were rummaging for hay. To him, they were indistinguishable—almost-walnut flanks with four high black socks and black manes, tails, and ears. He found out that they didn't belong to her; she boarded them, and, along with their owner, she kept them worked. She tried to get him to ride that weekend, but he soon learned that Philadelphia street games, even a game with the apparently appropriate name "buck-buck," had done nothing to develop his inner cowboy. They took a few bike rides instead.

Eon took him to the Brewster Ladies' Library, founded in 1852, for a book signing. The exterior building impressed him with its twin peaked roof over red shingles and a lovely trellis teeming with blossoming flowers. The inside was even more impressive, particularly the main study room, with a hand-carved wood mantel surrounding a deep set, still-working fireplace.

"I like to come to this room to write. I pretend I'm at the Raffles in Singapore with Ruuudyard and Jooooseph." She exaggerated both names.

"Ah, your friends Mr. Kipling and Mr. Conrad," he parried.

"I've never been there, but I like to imagine that the bar where they hung out was old and elegant like this room. I get a warm feeling here. I sometimes smuggle in a flask of rum to help my creative juices flow," she confided.

"Yes, the Writers Bar. I've been there. This room is more stately and warmer, but the Writers Bar has a feeling of elegance, too. Maybe later we can grab a Singapore Sling. The first one came out of the Long Bar at Raffles."

Nad had visited Singapore to take the deposition of an opposing medical expert in a big case he was trying. The expert was in Singapore for a prolonged stay, and Nad's client insisted that the deposition be taken sooner than later. The expert offered to schedule the deposition in Singapore, never thinking for even a second that that would be acceptable. Nad's client insisted, and so he sucked it up, and he and his client made the trip together. They built in ample time for sightseeing.

"You're on," Eon said.

That night Eon and Nad had Singapore Slings at the Brewster Fish House. It made him even more euphoric. The next day, she took him swimming in the freshwaters of Crystal Lake off Monument Road in Orleans. There was only one spot left in the intentionally undersized parking lot when they arrived. On that visit, they also meandered down Beach Road to walk in the surf on Nauset Beach. She told him she liked to walk that beach at sunrise but that she liked the Brewster Flats for sunset walks. She would take him there the next time he was up, she promised. That walk never happened.

His reverie slides into some of their other times together and their frequently stimulating, often absurd conversations. He thinks back to their walk through the multicolored lanterns hanging on the gingerbread houses on Illumination Night in Oak Bluffs that first week on the Vineyard, holding hands in the glow of their new romance, talking about how illumination nights in the inner city might help promote a sense of community, galvanize neighborhoods into more cohesive units, and lead to reduced violence and other street crimes. He remembers one of their ridiculous conversations walking through Valley Green in Fairmount Park in Philadelphia, trying to describe a femtosecond by analogy to real-time events.

"It's about as long as it takes for a mosquito to bite you," he said to her.

"No! No! Much shorter! More like the amount of time between when a New York traffic light turns green and the guy in the next car in line honks his horn," she countered.

"Or maybe it's about the amount of time it takes to hit the previous-channel button on the remote when a commercial comes on," he argued.

"No, I got it. It's about as long as it takes from the time you bungee jump from a hundred-foot bridge until you tell yourself what an idiot you are," she countered.

This conversation went on while they strolled a mile by the creek as the watched local kids plunge into Devil's Pool. The memories keep rolling through.

Karen fondly remembers how Eon made sure her career actually got started and how Eon advised, supported, and mentored her. She also thinks back on the many fun times they shared, especially the pool crashing. From time to time, Eon would stay in Boston on the weekends as a change of pace from the Cape, especially if Karen was going to be around for pool crashing. One time, they almost got caught. It was at the Colonnade Back Bay on a hot July 4 weekend. They craved a sundeck with a refreshing, sparkling swim. From off on the side, they watched to see if anyone was checking for room keys. An attendant stood at the entrance like a palace guard, humorless, woodenly checking the credentials of every would-be bather.

"We're done for," Karen volunteered. "We have no keys, no chance."

"Maybe not." Eon took the challenge. "Let's just be patient. On my signal, we'll launch," Karen remembered Eon saying. As a couple was entering the cabana area, Eon saw that two men were sitting on the far end of the pool. "Here we go," she signaled.

As the attendant leaned in to check the couple's room keys, Eon bustled through, saying, "The men have the keys," as she waved to the two guys. The attendant didn't notice that the men looked confused when they waved back; he just motioned the women through. They set up right next to the guys, who tried to engage them in conversation. After a few polite exchanges, the ladies settled in for sunbathing, ignoring the key holders like some women do. They never failed to crash a pool, but Karen remembers that as the closest they ever came.

Doreen thinks back to a Halloween evening several years ago. Eon came for a visit. Eon loved Halloween. "Legalized candy extortion," she called it. "When else can you dress up like a fool, knock on a stranger's door, demand candy or else, and be greeted with smiles, open arms, and boxes of sugary treats that are terrible for you but taste so, so good?"

Way too early for trick-or-treaters, Doreen thought as the knock on the front door startled her. She tilted her head in puzzlement and pulled open the door to find Dr. Elaine Olivia Neal, Esq., standing there in a flesh-colored sweatshirt, hood up, hiding behind a pig-snout mask.

She snorted, "Treat or treat," holding out a pink king-size pillowcase. She had an identical setup for Doreen, and after dark, they canvased the neighborhood for Hershey bars, Snickers, Three Musketeers, Twix, M&M's, and Nestlé's Crunch. They disdained Skittles, gumdrops, and Starbursts. The snout theme soon became more than a Halloween tradition.

Lena recalls how lonely and frustrated she was before her friend tripped over a backpack in the coffee shop, and how their friendship originated with their mutual love for mathematics and matured into sharing concerts and movies. They graduated to murder mystery parties, where, if they were on the same team, no one else ever had a chance. She thought back to her doctoral defense. Eon put together a comprehensive attack on her thesis and came at her every which way. She grilled Lena over and over in the days before the defense, so much so that the actual defense felt more like a preyoga warm-up than an Insanity workout. Afterward, they celebrated with triple espresso and cappuccino at Area Four. That time Lena left the tackling backpack at home for safety reasons.

Cav's memories are many and varied, but he calls up two isolated frozen moments in time, Polaroids in his mind. After their alienated junior year in high school, they reconciled as friends for senior year and were like fraternal twins. They managed to manipulate their seats at commencement so that they were side by side. Cav doesn't remember how she pulled it off, but it took some doing because they were to march in and out in alphabetical order. Eon actually arranged for her diploma to be stacked adjacent to his. This reshuffling of the diplomas was the key because each graduate's name would be read from the face of the diploma. At the instant the ceremony concluded, Eon grabbed him into a hug and said with charged emotion, "You will always be my best and most trusted friend." He felt honored. Seven years later, at their law school graduation, they again sat next to one another. But this departure would be different. He was heading back to Lincoln to begin his new life with Joy and the law firm; she was feeling unsettled about traveling north to Boston to a law practice she wasn't sure she wanted to pursue. She again embraced him in an enormous hug, repeating, "That Cavendish boy! What a man! What a lawyer! Go to it, friend."

In a second van, Padraig drives with Sonia, Evangeline, the woman Nad hadn't met yet, and the two girls. Each of them reflects on special times with Elaine. Padraig remembers how Eon befriended him on the plane and then, in the years that followed, helped him edit some of his philosophical treatises and shepherded them through to publication. But, even more than that, he reflects on her kindness and sincerity.

Sonia recalls how excited Padraig had been when he returned from his Bay Area trip, effusively telling the story about this wonderful professor he met. Her first reaction had been to wonder why Padraig was going on and on to her about another woman. But then she met Eon and immediately understood. She remembers how warmly Eon greeted her; she appreciated how much Eon helped her husband. Sonia cherished the closeness that grew between her and her husband's good friend and is grateful for the good times they shared, especially the talks and the duets.

Evangeline can't help but think of her biological mother, Anne, and her surrogate mother, Professor Neal, in the same thought. They were the two women who mostly dramatically influenced her life, molded her into the person she had become. In her mind, the two strong, dynamic women would be forever linked.

Although Nad doesn't realize it at the time, the other woman in the van with Padraig, Sonia, and Evangeline is Cav's wife, Joy, and the girls are their children, Martha and Nicole. Joy's thoughts bring her back to their college days when they first met. She traces the various milestones in their relationship. When her new boyfriend told her he had a very close female friend, she was a bit suspicious. But, she soon understood that Cav and Eon were closer than friends, more like brother and sister. As Joy's relationship with Cav evolved, she and Eon treated one another like real family. They talked openly. Joy told Eon about the kind of teacher she hoped to be and how someday she and Cav hoped to have children of their own. Eon agreed that she and Cav would be great parents and that she hoped she could be like an aunt to their children. In that same conversation, Eon told Joy about how hard it was for her to have a sustained romantic relationship with a man.

"Things just seem to run out of steam after a few months," she confided to Joy. "It's probably a good thing," she went on. "I think I'd be a terrible parent. I saw what my parents did to our family. I'd be afraid that I'd totally mess up my kids."

Joy remembers how Eon helped them persevere through the years of frustration when they were trying to start a family, and how happy they were when the twins changed everything for them. Finally, Joy thinks that Eon was wrong about herself—she was a great aunt and would have been a great mother.

During this whole time, the twins have sat quietly, trying to understand how they are supposed to feel. They would never see Aunt E again. How could that be? She was so much fun to be with. She showed them everything, took them everyplace, taught them games and music and piano. When their parents told them that Aunt E was sick, they thought she would just get better and that everything would be the same. Somebody as full of life as Aunt E wasn't supposed to get sick and die; she was supposed to get better and have more fun.

PARTING

Karen gave Nad a hug and tearfully left the hospice room. Nad settled in to spend a few more hours. He kept the music going in the background. His thoughts churned, harkening back to a dinner in Boston when she wanted to talk about the medieval romances, especially *Tristan and Isolde*. He figured out that she would reveal her romantic emotions through the literature she discussed and the music she would play. That realization helped him reach out to her more openly. He wanted to go back in time to when their paths diverged. He wanted to complete that trip to see her when she didn't return his calls. He wanted to change the past, create a different present.

After a bit, Eon revived and mustered another dose of energy. She reminded him that she had seen Tom Waits in person and that he hadn't. She asked him if he had music with him and could he play his "Take It with Me" for her. He ran out to the car to get his iPod and earphones. She said that whenever she heard that song, she thought of him and hoped that he might feel that way about her. He assured her he did. They sat in silence as Tom Waits crooned.

Phone's off the hook
No one knows where we are
It's a long time since I
Drank champagne
The ocean is blue
As blue as your eyes
I'm gonna take it with me
When I go

He looked right into her eyes—as blue as the ocean—and saw a spark of joy.

Old long since gone
Now way back when
We lived in Coney Island
Ain't no good thing
Ever dies
I'm gonna take it with me
When I go

She was thinking something. He saw a look that he recognized. Maybe the Coney Island reference reminded her of their carousel ride on the Flying Horses. They tried, but neither of them caught the brass ring.

Far, far away a train
Whistle blows
Wherever you're goin'
Wherever you've been
Waving good-bye at the end
Of the day
You're up and you're over
And you're far away

He was grateful that they were here together now.

Always for you, and
Forever yours
It felt just like the old days
We fell asleep on Beaula's porch
I'm gonna take it with me
When I go

All broken down by
The side of the road
I was never more alive or
Alone
I've worn the faces off
All the cards
I'm gonna take it with me
When I go

Children are playing
At the end of the day
Strangers are singing
On our lawn
It's got to be more
Than flesh and bone
All that you're ioved
Is all you own

In a land there's a town
And in that town there's
A house
And in that house
There's a woman

And in that woman
There's a heart I love
I'm gonna take it
With me when I go
I'm gonna take it
With me when I go

At the end, she turned to him and said, "You know, I'm gonna take you with me when I go," just before she drifted off.

He just sat there looking at her. It seemed that he could look right through her skin. It had that opaque look of waxed paper. The flesh above her collarbones sunk deeply, leaving hollows that alarmed him. Her hair looked stringy and grayish sticking out from a hospital cap. Only a few red tones hung on. But even with all that, he could still see the beauty that first caught his eye years ago.

When she awoke, she surprised him by asking to get out of bed so they could take a walk around the building. He went out to talk to her nurse, who said it was okay but that he should be very careful with her. Together they got her out of bed, and she leaned heavily on him, managing to walk, with his support, a few hundred yards before she said it was time to go back to the room. She was exhausted but wanted him to stay and talk with her. He talked about the movies they'd seen together—old classics like *Breakfast at Tiffany's*, *Gone with the Wind*, *To Kill a Mockingbird*, and *Rebel Without a Cause*. She tried to listen but kept nodding off. Whenever she would awaken, she would faintly smile. At one point he reminded her of the some of the details of the Vineyard week—coffee from Alley's General Store, Chilmark, and Edgartown Pizza, dancing in his living room to the Stones, sipping wine with Simon and Garfunkel singing "Bookends" in the background, walks on the Gay Head beach. She then reminded him of the few random dinners they shared in Boston when business trips took him there. She had almost total recall of their walk through the used bookstore on Spring Lane in Boston, reeling off the titles she pulled out of stacks to show him. She then switched back to music, asking if he remembered the time they discussed—debated—a Jane Siberry song, "Calling All Angels." She recited the words they discussed exactly:

Oh, and every day you gaze upon the sunset
With such love and intensity.
Why, it's ah, it's almost as if you could only crack the code,
You'd finally understand what this all means.

Oh, but if you could, do you think you would
Trade it all, all the pain and suffering?
Oh, but then you would've missed the beauty of
The light upon this earth and the sweetness of the leaving.

Calling all angels, calling all angels,
Walk me through this one, don't leave me alone.
Calling all angels, calling all angels,
We're trying, we're hoping, but we're not sure why.

Toward the end, she lost energy again and slept, this time for much longer. He was about to leave when she woke up with a jolt and wanted to talk some more. She kept changing the subject but managed to tell him she was in great pain and that she needed him to look after himself.

"Nick," she said. "Look after Nick and…"

He assumed that this was the morphine speaking; she had always called him "Nad."

"And what?" he asked. She seemed less than coherent.

"Martha," she replied.

"Yes, Martha's Vineyard. Yes, that's where we met." She was clearly struggling. He tried to help her along.

"Yes, Martha. Yes, Nick."

The words came out in fits and starts. She gasped after every one.

"I will," he assured her.

He tried to squeeze her hand, but only a soft twitch replied. As she started to drift off to sleep, she mustered enough strength to pull herself up to a sitting position so that she could look him in the eyes.

"Nad, I want you to leave now. Good night. Good-bye."

"Good night. Good-bye."

He thought the words "I love you" and barely summoned up the strength to say them out loud. She smiled and seemed to mouth an "I love you, too" before she lowered herself and totally drifted off.

Her breathing was shallow but steady. He went to the nurse to ask what to expect. She told him it could be days or even weeks, that her heart was strong but that she no longer had the ability to absorb nutrition. She regretted to tell him that over the next week or two, she would succumb. He could hold back the tears only until he reached his car. This was their final farewell.

FINAL THOUGHTS

She felt his presence leave the room. The pain increased, and breathing became next to impossible; it was shallow and slow. She forced herself to remember as much as she could. She blocked out most of her childhood, but somehow a single scene popped into her head. She and Cav were sitting in his sandbox with a watering can next to them. They used it to wet the sand so that they could make a sand ball to have a catch. It didn't work. Before long they were just throwing sand at one another and up in the air, giggling the day away.

A vision of her and Cav packing up to head for college in Omaha pushed the sandbox away. Her thoughts raced past law school to Cav and Joy's wedding, where she broke the gender barrier by being Cav's "best man." She thought about how happy they were together and how thrilled she was that Nickie and Marti made their lives complete.

It was getting harder and harder for her to keep thinking, but she wasn't done yet. She wanted her final thoughts to be of Nad. She pushed away the feelings of regret; those were not happy thoughts. All of a sudden, they were back in Martha's Vineyard, in Nad's house. The music was blasting. The Boss. "Dancing in the Dark." They couldn't help but spill beer on one another as they twirled and twirled. She couldn't catch her breath. Everything went dark.

THE MEMORIAL SERVICE

The caravan snakes its way through a dirt-and-sand trail littered with boulder-sized rocks that force them off track from time to time. They inch ahead slowly but still bottom out several times. Nad is happy he hasn't taken his little sports car on this part of the drive; he probably would have cracked something or marooned the car. The lurching has a palliative effect on their feelings; smiling and laughing starts to percolate from each vehicle. Finally, they reach a small cutout near a narrow walking path through the scrub brush. This is the trail that descends to the flats. It is long—just short of a mile.

The Brewster Flats swell into being when the tides recede on the western shore off Cape Cod. Tiny pieces of the sky sparkle with solar nuggets in delicate pools of cleansing water as the ocean allows the flat expanse of salted sand to have its day in the sun or its night in the moon. But, let there be no doubt; the ocean is in control. It decides when and how long the flats can come out to play in the daylight, and it decides when the flats must withdraw to repose in the twilight. Negotiation would be futile.

The enclave, united by their devotion to a beloved friend, gathers at the side of the van and starts its procession toward shimmering rays burning from gold to red as the sun resolutely dips toward the edge of the ocean. Cavendish and Doreen hand out paper lanterns and pens.

"The walk down to the flats will take a while," Doreen says. "I'm handing these out now so that you each can carry them. You might want to begin thinking about what you would like to say as a private farewell message. I'll explain what to do with these when we get down onto the flats. Cav will lead the way."

Joy walks next to the twins, who hold one another tightly. Cav takes Nad in tow. Doreen and Carl hold hands, as do Padraig and Sonia, and Karen and Justin. Lena and Evangeline walk in solemn single file at the back of the quiet queue. Soon the dirt trail turns into a sandy path through bushy shrubs. One or another of the troop occasionally stumbles over roots that bubble up through the sand. The group makes its way from the trail to the beginning of the flats. Now, on the fringe of the flats, they continue their resolute march closer to the water. A sheen covers parts of the beach as if some compulsive painter brushed a clear satin shellac to keep it safe from intruders. Puddles of varying shapes and dimensions lay strewn here and there. All the members of the group take the effort to keep their lanterns dry but carelessly splash themselves. Grains of fine, glowing sand cling to their toes and ankles, deposited there by the ocean breeze; the salt water binds it to them. The larger puddles are warm; the smaller ones are hot. They trek slowly. Only the roar of the surf approaching from off in the distance offers a white-noise background sound to their private thoughts.

Nad feels an overwhelming sense of loss. If only that hiatus had never occurred or had ended sooner, maybe they would have had a life together. He regrets that he walked away without making more of a fight, more of an effort. At the time, it seemed the right thing to do.

Back then, his common sense, or maybe it was his ego, told him not to pursue, that if she wanted to see him, she knew how to respond. He didn't foresee today. How could he have?

Now, with the flats fully behind them, they face the ocean; its ebb and flow occasionally cleanses their feet. Doreen takes control.

"Let's just get our feet wet and then go back to the middle of the flats. This will be your chance to write a farewell message to Elaine. Write as much or as little as you want. But, don't hold back. Say whatever you want to say directly to her on the paper lantern. We'll light the candles in the base of each lantern so that they will loft. Cav rigged things up so that at some point, the lanterns should catch fire while they're up in the sky. If the lanterns come back to the flats, we'll burn them ourselves, and then, the ashes of our thoughts will eventually mingle with her ashes forever."

They disperse to think and write.

Nad walks off to the north watching and thinking. He wants to tell her how much he loves her, how much he misses her already, how he thought they'd have time to together, how angry he is that she's been taken from him. He wants to cry and throw rocks at the sun to knock the light out. He thinks of many things but composes himself and decides to write only, "You live on through those of us you have touched." His lantern is ready for ascension.

Cav stands alone writing slowly on his lantern. He, too, keeps his message simple—"To my sister, my friend, my compass, thank you for being such a part of my life." When he finishes, he swivels to survey the group. Lena and Evangeline are still writing. Nad is finished. Carl is finished, but Doreen is still hovering over her lantern. The two young girls are crying. The woman Nad hasn't met has her arms around them. Evangeline looks broken. Lena is stoic, as if hypnotized. Karen glances over at Justin, who returns her look and nods. Padraig and Sonia have finished and look content, but their normally bright smiles have dimmed.

"Another few minutes," Cav coaxes, "and then we'll get started."

He waits as the sun drops a few more degrees toward the horizon, and then he turns toward the tide. The final walk to where the flats give way to the ocean is somberly ceremonious. Finally, Cavendish puts up his hand, and they all stop.

"It's time to light the lanterns."

The lanterns catch the attention of a few very young children who are leaving the beach with their parents. The youngsters make a bee-line to the group, but the parents, sensing that this is not some idle kite flying, bring them back by their sides so they can watch from afar. Cav hands out matches, and everyone fumbles to ignite the candlewicks that will heat the air to send the lanterns skyward and eventually consume the lanterns themselves. The rainbow of orbs ascend heavenward, and everyone bows their heads for just a moment, then looks upward to see several of the lanterns burst into flames. They break into a restrained applause, then quiet down once again. A child who is spectating from off over by the water's edge runs over and asks what they are doing. Evangeline patiently explains what's going on, and the child hurries back to his mother.

After another moment of silence, Cavendish breaks the meditation.

"As many of you know, Nick DiDominico—Nad—met our Elaine at a writers' workshop years ago. Nad wrote a poem about that week as his last assignment in the workshop. He sent that poem to Doreen with the group picture from the writers' workshop. Doreen showed the picture and the poem to me, and the two of us discussed that we should ask Nick to read it as Joy and the girls release Elaine's ashes. But, before he does, if anyone would like to say anything for the whole group to hear, now's the time."

Evangeline speaks first.

"You were my second mother. I couldn't have made it without you. Thank you for reaching out to me that first day and guiding my life. Good-bye."

Padraig is next.

"My bonnie Eon, you lit up our lives and helped me git further dan I ever dreamt. We'll never ferget ya."

Karen's words are also straight from the heart.

"My mentor, my soul mate, I thank you."

When Karen finishes, Cav waits a moment to make sure everyone has had a chance to speak. When no one else speaks, he cues Nad.

"You're up, friend."

Nad had prepared an introduction.

"Elaine and I met in a workshop called 'Heartfelt Writing.' That's what we did that week; we wrote from our hearts. The good Dr. Neal needed some coaxing at first. Early on in the week, her writing, though beautiful, was detached and protected. She eventually opened up some. The way the workshop was set up, we would be given an overnight writing assignment, but we were also given in-class assignments, usually about fifteen or twenty minutes to write something. Then, we would read what we wrote and sometimes have brief discussion, sometimes not. One of our in-class assignments was on the subject 'Regrets.' I think we had only ten minutes. Most of us scribbled out something that we did or said or didn't do or say to a friend or family member or even someone we didn't like—sort of personal essays. Several of our classmates were eager to read what they wrote, but not Elaine. She was the last to go and had to be called on to read. She had written only seven words, which she read staring a hole in her notebook: 'I regret that I have sad eyes.' Her delivery was understated and sad. We talked about that afterward, and she told me something about her life growing up in Lincoln and some of the demons she dealt with. I then understood why she would be so guarded. Cav, she said you were the only constant bright spot from that time period of her life.

"On the next-to-the-last day, our overnight assignment was to write on the topic of 'Eavesdropping.' Everyone would read their work on that last day, and then we would have coffee and cake and disperse. After that class that next-to-last day, we drove to the Aquinnah beach, also known as Gay Head Beach. The parking for that beach is remote, like here. So we carried our stuff through the trail onto the beach, which has great stretches that are covered with stones. At times it's hard to find a place to put a blanket. We walked over to an empty spot under the part of the cliffs that are mostly reddish—like a flowerpot or a brick. We spread out our blankets, set up our chairs, and chilled, quietly thinking about what we were going to write. I was kind of stuck. Elaine just stared off into the ocean. About ten minutes later, two men, one in a blue Speedo, the other in red, clearly a couple, invaded our space. They set up their chartreuse blanket about three feet from ours, pulled out a bottle of red wine and two crystal glasses, and then cut up some cheese on a small wooden board. They chatted away in stage whispers for the next two hours. It distracted me, but Elaine used it as inspiration. She listened intently and from time to time scribbled in her notebook. Every once in a while, she would audibly laugh. The entire time she had this mischievous look on her face. I tried to get her to tell me what she was thinking and what she was writing, but every time I asked, she told me to just wait until tomorrow and to concentrate on my own writing. Well, she wrote this absolutely hilarious piece that had the entire class out of control the next day.

"On the beach that day, I couldn't think of anything to say. I didn't write a single word. The ride home was unusually quiet. I think she was refining her thoughts, and I was having that kind of mental paralysis that comes when you're trying to force yourself to think of something. It never works. I was getting frantic when Elaine reached over and turned the volume up on the radio. Jackson Browne was singing 'My Opening Farewell.' I stopped trying to think and just listened. When we got home, this is what came out."

Nad pauses to pull some papers from his pocket.

'They say that love is touching souls.
Well surely you've touched mine.
For part of you pours out of me
In these lines from time to time.'
Joni Mitchell, 1974.

'Reach out. Be open,' demanded my heart in a half whisper.
To whom, at first, I did not know.
Don't grunt or be one with the tasks of life.
The words will know when to come, and when they do, it will
be at their pace,
Not his or hers.
And certainly not yours.

Be one with the blue.
Not the midnight blue.
Not the king's blue. Not the mourning blue.
But with the iris blue.
Dancing and gleaming onto your face from one that sees and
knows and lives.
Dancing eyes, not dotted *I*'s.
Warehouse eyes, not piercing eyes,
Sad-Eyed Lady from the Heartland to whom all things come.
My heart whispers more, "You need to know what is here for
you, from you, in you. This life."

Sharpen your soul to sever the knot; then sever the edge on
open cupped palms.
Why not?
Why not take this day to share at least one grain of sand or
perhaps two or perhaps all?
Be one with the sun's last beam, the eve's final dropping of
sweet butterscotch on red cliffs.

A flickering candle flame for Dancing in the Dark. The spark to start the fire.
Take the waves in stony salt water, sweet with brown sugar, cooling, tossing, rocking and rolling, together and apart.
A hole and a part.
Struggle to stand but fall to float.
Dancing and gleaming.
Whispering and screaming.
I wish I had an ocean to sail away on.

Be slow.
Don't Rush.
Take long Waits on back roads with no Urge for Going.
And sit and look on Rockport Sundays for the Changes of Ochs and for ways to learn to order nourishment together and then share it.
There but for fortune go you and go I.

Trip the light fandango with wild white horses in the spray of the tide,
Dipping and spinning in the law of large numbers,
Probabilities and possibilities tumbling in a landsliding torrent of starlight,
The distant constellations in a universe ablaze with Changes.

Today, new souls touching mine, one and all,
We part with this Opening Farewell,
So long, Godspeed, adieu.

That heart, a whisper no more, "Love is touching souls."
All romantics do not reach the same fate.
I won't be cynical and drunk and boring someone in some dark café.

No more dark café days.

Not Joni Mitchell

Nad silently peers up through eyes that can't focus to moist faces on bowed heads. The attractive woman and the two young girls produce a simple white urn. They begin dispersing ashes as everyone watches. "'Cast Your Fate to the Wind,'" Nad thinks. He drifts off to random lines from the song.

> You set your sail when the time comes in
> And you cast your fate to the winds.
>
> You shift your course along the breeze
> Won't sail up wind on memories
> The empty sky is your best friend
> And you just cast your fate to the wind
>
> You wonder how it might have been
> Had you not cast your fate to the wind.

When Nad's focus on the present returns, he becomes aware that ocean sounds, often serene and calming, now seem raucous and intrusive. The crash and tumble of the waves rock them every few seconds in measured crescendo. What began as a seeming whisper builds to the din of city traffic to the clatter of a freight train to the stampede of wild buffalo to deafening thunderclaps to who knows would have come next had Cavendish not spoken up, rescuing him.

"We can't have an Irish wake without Jameson's."

Cav reaches into a backpack that nobody noticed he was carrying. Out comes a bottle and a sleeve of plastic tumblers.

"Straight from Cork. Smuggled in by Padraig, who made a special trip to the Midleton Distillery in honor of Elaine, the best of John Jameson—Jameson Rarest Vintage Reserve." He nods to Padraig.

The Irishman waves Pope-like in return with a slight head bow. Doreen hands a glass to everyone, even the two young girls; Cav does the pouring. When everyone is served, Cav, facing the Atlantic, where the outgoing tide carries Elaine's ashes out to sea, hoists his glass.

"To our Elaine, Eon, with all our love. We miss you, girl, and we always will."

Everyone in the entire congregation, in perfect synchrony, downs the elixir.

This bottle of Jameson's is the best finished blend to be found anywhere. Nad feels it slither over his palate and smoothly wend its way, like a raindrop on a windowpane. At first, he glows. But Nad is not accustomed to hard liquor, and after the easy descent, an aftershock splits him in two like a sword from above. He wobbles for just an instant but remains standing. He shudders. A warm rush comes percolating back up; he gets that fuzzy, sort of out-of-body feeling. He clearly is not calloused to Jameson's. The inescapable thought that she would have given him grief for being unable to drink like an Irishman provokes a smile. He looks around to gauge the reactions of the other mourners. Now, everyone is smiling.

"Back to the house for dinner," Cav bellows. "Time for dinner and to celebrate her life with tales of remembrances."

Cav pantomimes a circle-the-wagons gesture.

"Let's roll."

They all turn toward the trail. As they splash back toward the vehicles, the woman Nad hadn't met yet makes her way into Nad's cluster.

"We'll ride with you, Cav," she says.

Nad realizes that he will be riding with her and the two children. They leave shotgun open for him. He's the last to enter the van.

"Nad, that was beautiful. I'm Joy Cavendish."

She touches him on the shoulder from the seat directly behind him with the twins to her left.

"Thank you. Pleased to meet you, Joy, although not under these circumstances. Eon inspired that poem."

NICOLE AND MARTHA: THE TWINS

Cav enters the conversation while starting the bus.

"Oh, I'm sorry. I thought I introduced you earlier. I guess in my rush to get you around the tent, I neglected my own family. My bad. Have you met the girls—Nicole and Martha?"

"Dad, it's bad enough you call us that," the redhead fires right out. "You don't have to have other people call us that, too."

Nad turns around to the girl right behind Cav.

"I'm Nickie, not Nicole and my sister here, she's not Martha. She goes by Marti, Mr..."

"Nad. Please call me Nad. I don't use the mister."

Nad looks at Cav and then turns to Joy as if to ask if it's okay with them that the girls call him by his informal name. He takes the fact that they are both beaming as a sign that it's fine with them. He notices that Marti has also looked to them for approval, and they nod assent. But Nickie's still at the helm.

"Okay, I'll do that, Nad. Dad likes to use our full names, but he doesn't even use his own, so I don't see why we have to. Everybody calls him Caaaaav."

Nickie blurts without restraint. If she has a filter, it's clogged.

"Mr...Nad, that's a different kind of name. Rhymes with 'tad' and 'fad' and 'dad' and 'mad' and 'bad' and 'had' and 'sad' and 'glad.' That's a pretty good name to rhyme with all those words."

Everyone is laughing now.

"Very clever, Nickie. I've never had my name rhymed out that way. The name is really my initials, Nicholas Amadeo DiDominico." He pauses, contorts himself to look directly at each of the girls, then continues. "I'm pleased to meet you both. I'm very sorry for your loss."

He's not sure whether he's supposed to shake hands with pre-teenage girls. He pauses so that he can turn more fully toward then, watching to see how they react. He has a young son, and his niece is only four, so he hasn't had much exposure to girls this age. Nickie answers his silent question by sticking out her hands and grabbing his with both of hers. She gives it an enthusiastic double shake. When she finishes, Marti extends her right hand more demurely. Her handshake is delicate.

"Thank you, Nad," Marti replies.

Nad senses from her tone that she's feeling a bit awkward that she's calling an adult male stranger by his nickname.

"The Amadeo middle name sounds like Mozart's middle name. Aunt E taught us about Mozart. Are you named after him?" Marti presents with strength and confidence but also with a calm, relaxed affect.

"I don't think so, unless my uncle was named after him. My father had an older brother named Amadeo. There was a very famous Italian scientist and mathematician named Amedeo Avogadro, too. Slightly different spelling. I'm A-m-a-d-e-o. He's A-m-e-d-e-o."

Nickie interrupts him. "Oh, he's that chemistry guy, right? He's the guy the mole number is named after."

Nad is shocked. He didn't learn about chemistry until he was well into high school. This girl is not a teen yet!

"Yes, very good, Nickie. Well the name itself means 'lover of God,' but that didn't really fit my uncle. My uncle was very good at math. I don't know about chemistry, but I can tell you he was no Mozart. He was totally tone deaf. I think that Amadeo was just a popular Italian name. So, your Aunt E taught you about music."

Nad is surprised at the maturity level of the conversation from such young girls.

"Yes. Aunt E is not tone deaf. She has a very pretty voice and can play the piano. We sing together all the time."

Marti's face fills with color when she realizes that she's talking about Aunt E like she's still with them. They all recognize what just happened and are sensitive to her, especially her sister, who gives her a hug. Everyone waits supportively for her to take a moment to regain her composure. It doesn't take long.

"She was a lot more than an aunt. Well, she wasn't even our aunt, but we called her that. Sometimes, she was like a friend, sometimes like an older sister, and sometimes like another parent. We love her." Marti chooses her words carefully. Her tone is quiet, thoughtful, and reflective.

Nickie, however, can't contain herself. "She taught us a lot of things," she quickly adds.

"I know how important teaching was to her. And she was a natural. She had a way of breaking things down into small, simple, easy-to-understand parts. So, tell me, how old are you ladies?" Nad is beginning to feel more comfortable talking with them.

"Ladies? Did you hear that, Marti? Ladies, that's us, right?" Nickie puffs out her chest and would have strutted a few steps if she weren't nestled into the microbus. "We're the laaaadies! We were ten in May.

I'm the older big sister. Marti is my little baby sister." Nickie holds out her right hand and shows a space of two inches between her thumb and index finger. "I'm a day older."

Marti rolls her eyes and scrunches up her mouth into a contrived frown. Nickie pats her on the head, but Marti deftly tilts away.

"I'm the exact same size you are, and we may have different birthdays, but you're only a couple of minutes older! Mom wanted to start the next day right by having me a few minutes after midnight," Marti says.

She turns to Cav and Joy, extends her left hand palm up, seeking confirmation. Cav and Joy smile and shake their heads affirmatively.

Despite the occasion, Nickie's charisma and effervescence spill out unfiltered, and it's clear that Marti can hold her own; her personality might be less in-your-face, but she's clearly indomitable. They both seem to be quite well-grounded, intelligent, engaging children. Nad finds himself totally charmed by both.

"Aunt E played with us, read to us, taught us how to read and write. She taught us piano, too. She helped us figure out what clothes to wear and the difference between nice jewelry and ugly things. She said that the right things help people see us better. If people pay too much attention to the 'things' we're wearing, it takes away from seeing us."

Marti seems quite proud that she has remembered this lesson. Under her shoulder-length, wavy brunette hair, Marti's deep-brown eyes fix squarely on Nad. She may have appeared to be a bit shy at first, but she displays a definite confidence in talking to an adult. Nickie and Marti are clearly fraternal, not identical twins. Although, as Marti pointed out, they are exactly the same size, Marti seems smaller for some reason Nad can't quite figure. She's nicely tanned and looks athletic, as does Nickie. Nickie's lighter skin looks like it might burn badly if she doesn't pay attention; her eyes are a bright azure blue, and her reddish hair looks shorter than her sister's, maybe because it is in tight ringlets rather than in flowing waves. Marti wears a blue calico sundress, and her stilt-like legs extend downward into bright-green flip-flops. When they got to the beach, Nad noticed that she had put on a light pink "Vineyard" sweatshirt. It caught his eye because he was pretty sure he had given Eon that shirt that first week on the Vineyard, although it has faded some since then. He had heavily "monogrammed" the small letters "Eon" on both sleeves with a navy-blue marker when he gave it to her. He could still see the letters faintly on the right sleeve.

Nickie is wearing blue jean shorts with frayed bottoms. Nad wonders whether they are actual cutoffs or whether they came that way. She has that same coltish look as her sister, but she is shod in light-pink sneakers with bright-pink shoelaces. Nickie is also wearing an article of her aunt's clothes—a gray Black Dog hoodie. Nad was with Eon when she picked it up that week so many years ago. He remembers the light stain on the bottom front of the shirt, left of center. On the drive to the writers' workshop one morning, he hit a bump, and she spilled some coffee. He apologized, but then when the stain set, he said, "Well look at that. The spill is in the exact shape of Martha's Vineyard. There's Chappaquiddick, and there we are driving right in the stain." Today, he doesn't remark on the girls' attire, but he's glad to see them wearing her clothes.

"So that would put you in fifth grade for this coming school year. Do I have that right?" Nad has an eleven-year-old nephew back home who had just completed the fifth grade in June.

"Nope, we finished up fifth grade already. No more lower school. We're up to sixth grade now. We start middle school this year, and I'm ready for it. I'm going to rock that, too." Nickie has no lack of confidence.

"How about you, Marti?" Nad wants to keep both of them in the conversation.

"I'm definitely ready, too. It's really good to have a live-in homework partner." She shoulder bumps Nickie.

"Well, my nephew just finished fifth grade, too. He learned math problems that have division, multiplication, subtraction, and addition in them. Is that what you studied?"

"Oh, you mean 'Please Excuse My Dear Aunt Sally?' Parentheses, exponents, multiplication, division, addition, subtraction. We did learn that but went on to other stuff. We learned how to use ratios, proportions, and percents. We even started with equations. We had linear equations and quadratic equations, and we worked with polynomials." Marti is controlling this part of the conversation for the moment.

"Wow, that sounds like algebra to me." Nad thinks back to try to remember when he started to learn algebra. He decided it was ninth grade.

"Oh, sure," Nickie intervenes. "We had some algebra and plane geometry, graphing, and data and statistics. We even got started with plane geometry and probability. It was pretty much fun."

"What did you study in English?" Nad figures this will be more in line with what his nephew studied.

"We had normal stuff, but they called it 'Language Arts'—grammar and writing and reading. But, the thing I liked best was what our teacher called 'think out louds.' We would talk about what we had read and had to summarize it out loud and then kind of tell the future, trying to guess what was going to happen next. And we would have to close our eyes and try to see what was described in what we read, try to picture it. And we'd ask one another questions about it. It was a very fun way to learn."

Nickie's description of what they studied and their comprehension of it seem well beyond what he thought was covered in fifth grade. A quizzical look creeps onto his face. Joy notices it.

"Nad, the girls are in a special school for the gifted. They're basically a couple of years ahead of what is studied at their age. But, all of the kids in their class are gifted, so they're in an age-appropriate social environment."

Nad's look relaxes; this explanation clarifies everything. Over the next few minutes, he hears about how they were exposed to informational articles so they could learn how to identify the main idea and supporting details, to interpret graphs, and to write descriptive paragraphs summarizing what they had read. They studied short stories and learned to use various techniques to develop quality short stories. They wrote poetry and persuasive speeches. In the scientific realm, they had an earth-space science course that covered the earth's structure, basic geology, the oceans and the water cycle, the sun, the moon, and the tides. Nad is blown away. These girls, as fifth graders, studied things that he didn't get to until eighth grade and in some cases high school.

"I'm very impressed. You ladies are real scholars."

"Did you hear him, Marti? Not only are we the laaaadies, we're the laaaady scholars, too."

"So with all this learning, what do you do for fun?"

"The learning part's fun. We try to make our studying together like playing games. And there's the music. We both play the piano, and we've started on the guitar, too. It's a lot easier to carry a guitar around than a piano," Marti counters.

Nad begins to notice that although their personalities are very different, they play off of one another in perfect balance.

"Which do you like better?" Nad asks.

"Marti is better at the piano. I'm okay, but she's really good. I like the guitar better, and I'm a little better strumming and picking."

Marti shakes her head in agreement.

"Sounds great. If you have a guitar or piano or both, maybe you could play something for me later on."

"We have both—well, a keyboard and a guitar. We'll play later, okay, Nickie?"

Marti isn't shy about performing. Neither is Nickie, who gives her sister a thumbs-up.

"Aunt E taught us a song called 'Imagine' that we sing together with Nickie playing guitar and me playing piano," Marti says. "It's a pretty song by a guy named John Lennon who is dead. He was in a band called the Beatles. Did you ever hear of them?"

The grown-ups laugh lightly.

"Yes, Marti, I have. They're pretty famous, and I know that song. John Lennon wrote that song after the band broke up. Your Aunt E lived her life a lot like that song. But tell me, with all these activities, I guess you two don't have much time for sports, right? Do you even like sports?" Nad can't imagine that they could cram anything else into their schedules.

"Oh, yes we do," Nickie contradicts. "We love sports."

"Which ones?" Nad is amazed.

"We started out playing soccer when we were real little, but now in the fall we do AAU cross-country," Marti answers.

"Very good. I love cross-country. I do some running, too." Nad is very pleased to hear that they like his sport. "Is the winter the time for chillin'?" he asks.

"In winter we play basketball and swim—I'm more the basketball player, Marti's the really good swimmer, but we both do both."

Nad is now becoming more amazed at how Cav and Joy can keep up with all these activities. Nad swivels to a forward position to give his back a break and to find out how Cav and Joy can keep up with all this activity.

"We just make it a point to carve out time," Cav responds. "Joy's tireless."

"Not so," Joy throws in, laughing. "I get tired, but it's worth it."

Nad turns back to the girls. "How about spring? I hope you take at least one season off." From their abounding energy, he can guess that they probably do something in the spring as well.

"We used to play lacrosse with a club, not for the school, but now we do AAU track. We can do that in the spring, and it goes into part of the summer. We like that better than lacrosse, don't we, Nickie?"

"You got that right, Sis. And tell him about the bow and arrow."

"Oh, and we both shoot the bow and arrow. We started out with regular bows like the kind you see on old cowboy shows. But now, we're strong enough now to pull back a compound bow. They're really fancy. We each have a bow called 'Lil Banshee.' It shoots far and fast, and you can aim with it better, too."

"Do you go hunting?" Nad doesn't know much about the culture in Lincoln, Nebraska.

"No," they both say forcefully in harmony.

"We go on these outdoor 3-D shoots," Marti adds.

"I don't know what they are. Can you explain them?" Nad knows as much about archery as he does about horseback riding.

"There are these targets set up in the woods," Nickie explains. "They're made out of plastic or something like that. They have all kinds of fake animal targets—deer and bear and coyotes, squirrels and rabbits and things like that. You go in with your bow and arrow and shoot at the targets. It takes a long time to go through a whole setup. You keep score and practice your shooting, but you don't hurt any live animals. Sometimes you climb up into tree houses to shoot at the targets. Sometimes you get behind trees. You have to get across streams and over rocks. It's like taking a hike in the woods, an adventure, an expedition. It's better than playing video games, because you're outside and using a real bow and arrow, and nothing gets hurt. We don't want to shoot at real animals. Sometimes when we hit a target, we have a hard time getting the arrow out. Sometimes we miss the whole target and spend a long time looking for the arrow and still don't find it, huh, Dad?"

"Right you are, Nickie. We do lose some arrows."

"You ladies do keep busy," Nad says.

"We have fun, but it's not too much," Marti says. "We have a lot of time where we don't have anything that we have to go to. We don't play any summer sports, like softball or things where we have to be at a practice or at a game. We don't do that stuff because every year we come up here early and spend time with Aunt E."

She catches herself. "Used to come up here early and spend time with Aunt E. She was teaching us horseback riding, too."

"It's very nice to get to know you and hear about your very exciting lives. I'm sure your mother and father are very proud of you. You're really terrific. I'm sorry I never knew about you before today. Your Aunt E was quiet about many parts of her life. I knew about your dad mostly from their school days. She mentioned that you were married, Cav, but Joy, she never went into any detail about you. And she said nothing about the girls."

Nick turns his attention to Joy and wants to keep the conversation going.

"Well, Nad," Joy says, "she talked about you. You probably heard that from some of the other people you met here, too. I'm sure she talked more to Cav about you than to me, but she mentioned you often. She told us how you met and about how she stepped out of your life for a while and about how she came back in again when you were getting married and starting a family of your own. For what it's worth, she said she thought she made a mistake and then waited too long to try to fix it. When she started to get really sick and she knew that she wasn't going to be able to beat this thing, she asked us to give Nickie and Marti the sweatshirts that they have on now, because you gave them to her, and you were so important to her, and the girls were very important to her, too."

"Nad," Nickie says, "Aunt E always talked about Martha's Vineyard, and she told us about the writing up there and about how you played the guitar for her. She said she always wanted to play a duet with you, but she said there was never a guitar and a piano at the same place at the same time."

"She actually talked to us about a lot of her friends, including you," Marti adds. "We knew all about Doreen and Karen, and the airplane story with Padraig always made me laugh."

They finally arrive back at the house ready for the next chapter of the evening—dinner and storytelling.

WAYNE MARLOW

When you are born and grow up in an identifiable, insular area, rarely venture beyond it, and then only for cameo visits to some remote location, it is uncommon for your perspective to broaden as much as it might were your experiences more varied and diverse.

Chas Marlow's wife, Sybil, gave birth to Wayne, their first child and only son, at the Cape Cod Hospital in Hyannis, Cape Cod, Massachusetts, fewer than twenty miles from the family home in East Harwich. Charlene, their second and final child, arrived three years later. Chas and Sybil Marlow owned and operated a local landscaping business in Harwich proper. It started out with Chas mowing lawns and trimming trees and Sybil selling box plants from a roadside stand. Chas had a good business head, and Sybil could picture a garden scene in her mind and then sketch it on paper for Chas to lay out; she was a landscape architect without the title, the credentials, or the formal training. It came naturally to her. Through their consistent hard work, grit, frugality, and creativity, they built their venture into a full-service landscape business, one of the best on the Cape.

Year-rounders and seasonal residents alike tapped into their expertise. Business boomed. When Chas got the idea to provide caretaker services to Cape owners who rented out their properties, the business shot up to another level. They did very well and totally integrated the children into the business.

Wayne and Charlene grew up watering plants, pruning trees, and transplanting bushes. In Chas's mind that was just the way it was supposed to be. The Marlow family structure displayed many of the attributes of "conventional" American families at the time. In business and financial matters and activities that required sheer physical strength, the family was patriarchal. For domestic and educational activities and in matters that involved nurturing, Sybil had more say. The slight twist to this fifties synergy was that Chas and Sybil worked the business together, although that dynamic was more owner-employee than co-owners. Chas called the shots, including the roles Wayne and Charlene would fulfill in the business. He conscripted them as soon as they were old enough to do work, which in Chas's mind was when they hit double digits. From the start it became clear that one day Wayne would take over. Charlene was expected to get married, have babies, and do whatever her husband needed her to do. If that didn't happen, there would always be a place for her in the business, even if just as a hired hand.

Both children picked up considerable knowledge of horticulture along the way. They learned the differences between trees and shrubs and vines and plants, between annuals and perennials, between fruits and vegetables. Their high school experiences expanded their horizons only slightly. They could never learn as much in school as they did working in the business. They both were solid students with social lives typical of teenagers on the Cape. They went to dances and parties and occasionally hit the beaches in the summer when they weren't working at "Marlow's Family Cape Landscaping—Planners, Providers, and Protectors of Beautiful Lawns and Gardens all over the Cape."

At Harwich High School, Wayne played football for the gold-and-blue Rough Riders in the fall. As a two-way player with good athleticism, he became accomplished enough to attract some attention from a few small NCAA Division I programs, which projected him as a linebacker or maybe a tight end. In the spring, he was a power-hitting first baseman with some deftness around the bag. His baseball development became stunted by the time restrictions the family business placed on him; he just couldn't take time off from work to play summer ball, where he could sharpen his skills in competition against the really good players who annually populated the Cape Cod baseball leagues, sometimes on their way to the big dance.

Charlene, attractive, slim, and coquettish with gymnastic ability, quickly took to cheerleading. She could sing and had a flair for the theatrical. The glee club moderator and her peers recognized her as a valued member of the choral group. She played the lead girl in the school plays her junior and senior year and was homecoming queen, just as Wayne had been homecoming king three years earlier.

Despite their good academic and extracurricular records, college wasn't to be in their futures; they weren't that interested—Charlene's boyfriend didn't want to go to college, and although Wayne's girlfriend, Helen, wanted to, her family couldn't afford to send her and didn't want to take out student loans. Besides, Chas clearly envisioned that they would work in the family business full-time after graduation. Sybil deferred to her husband. So, rather than filling out college applications and preparing for the standardized tests, they continued their on-the-job botany lessons. They learned about bryophytes, pteridophytes, gymnosperms, and angiosperms by their everyday names: mosses; ferns; pines, spruces, and firs; and flowering plants. Charlene was more adroit at understanding what kinds of soil, what levels and amount of light, and what kind of watering was required for various specifies. She inherited her mother's creative vision as well. Despite all this, Chas strongly and frequently declared that her role was to use her acumen to support Wayne in his running of the business. It was a role she accepted without question. When she married, her husband joined the business as Wayne's assistant.

Straight out of high school, Wayne married Helen, who hoped that maybe one day Wayne would agree to let her continue her education, after she served her mandatory term at Marlow's. When their daughter, named after her grandmother, arrived a few years later, she bit her tongue and became mother and housewife for the next five years, until she got tired of it and left for the University of Alaska Anchorage to meet up with another former high school classmate, whom she went out with before she dated Wayne. He had gone to Anchorage to study aviation and stayed on to work. He would support her while she earned her degree in social work.

Helen's flight left Wayne dazed and confused. He'd always been in control, always had the upper hand, always called the shots. He had difficulty playing the role of father and mother, and so he decided to go out and recruit Helen's replacement. He expected to have an easy time of it. He knew that many women thought him good-looking, and he knew how to turn on the charm when he thought it would be beneficial. His strong, sometimes brash personality added more than a dash of excitement. He was a good-time guy; he could dance and drink and wasn't reluctant to make a fool of himself singing karaoke. He reeked of charisma.

He kept his eyes open for attractive candidates, particularly at work. Although more than half of his customers were women, only a few were unattached. He checked out each attractive woman who came in head to toe. If he liked what he saw, he immediately focused on the ring finger of the left hand. He would personally serve those without a wedding band. When Elaine Neal came in to get some advice on laying out a garden for her historically certified home in Brewster, he was impressed by her good looks, her spiritedness, and her ringless left hand. He gave her his full attention and a hopeful discount, explaining to her that he was willing to cut his price for her because she was a year-rounder, not just some fair-weather Cape Codder.

"It'll look good for me and the business to be the guy who designed and built a garden at an historically certified Cape home."

She willingly accepted the price reduction.

He made it a point to spend a few long sessions getting her input about precisely what she wanted to accomplish with her garden. Although he wasn't as good at the design part as his mother and sister, he had acquired some proficiency at it, so he started out working on this design himself. As he was sketching out possible designs with her, he inched up real close to her over the worktable, not quite invading her personal space, to see if she would withdraw. She did not. When she left, he brought the sketch over to Charlene, who transformed it from something pleasant and acceptable to a work of art. When he next met with Elaine, he simply told her he had continued to think about the project and made a few adjustments to the plan, understating the changes. Again, he sidled up close to her to review the revision, lightly brushing her hand or arm a few times in the process. Again, no retreat. She loved what he came up with, and she signed off on the project. He moved her job to the top of the list and spent every day at her house until it was over. The next week, he asked her out to dinner.

Elaine welcomed the diversion. Wayne represented a stark departure from many of the other men she came in contact with. Most of them were more cerebral, sophisticated, polite, and often boring—doctors, lawyers, professors for the most part. In contrast, Wayne was earthy and real, a physical man, straightforward without those layers of complexity that often frustrated her. She had more than enough baggage of her own to deal with. She didn't want to be toting around someone else's, too.

After a few casual dates, capped off by polite good-night kisses, she felt he was trustworthy enough to allow the relationship to escalate. It had been almost a few years since her aborted San Diego experiment with a relationship. She was still fighting some demons and made the choice to exercise her willpower to overcome a vestigial aversion to physical contact with men. She wanted to try again. She initiated more frequent and more intimate contact without being too aggressive. She knew he was interested and matched each step he took with one, or a portion of one, of her own. After they spent two consecutive overnights together at her place, he asked if she would like to go away with him for a weekend. She agreed and suggested Marblehead, not too close, not too far. Easy to abort the trip and get back quickly if it turned into a disaster. It didn't.

They both had a good time. She particularly liked the belly clams at Maddie's; he went for the burger. She was pleased that Terry's and Coffey's were two very good ice cream shops. She stayed on the chocolate side; he switched it up with mint or Bing cherry. She felt that the chemistry between them was adequate and that this could be a bit of a thing even if just for a while. She was accustomed to being in social situations where there was less-than-ideal intellectual compatibility, but Wayne was smart enough to discuss certain things with, and his sense of humor, while not sharp and exhilarating, was pleasant and endearing.

Physically, the match was acceptable. She didn't feel relaxed but forced herself to make progress. Irrespective of the physical issues, she knew that the missing elements in this "relationship" pretty much guaranteed that he wasn't "The One," if there was a "The One" out there for her. This recognition relieved her of pressure. She thought she'd be comfortable spending some time with him and that she could do that without having to make a serious commitment.

Wayne's mind-set couldn't have been more different from hers. He had an objective in mind and was biding his time. He knew he had to start out light and easy. Their physical relationship ended a long drought for him. Things were working out just the way he wanted; he would continue to bring her closer and closer. She would be an excellent wife and an involved mother for little Sybil.

When they returned to the Cape, they spent more and more time together. She met young Sybil, and they hit it off pretty well. She discovered she liked reading with a child, and only from time to time did the horrors of her own family situation come rushing back at her. She considered telling Wayne about her family experiences and the resulting commitment aversion, but she decided that might unduly confuse things. She decided to ride the wave for as long as it remained light, pleasant, and drama-free. For the moment, she felt comfortable with the relationship.

Wayne stomped on the gas pedal; his feelings accelerated like a dragster on nitrous oxide. *This is it,* he thought. He mentally started planning the wedding. He saw the flag as green.

Elaine continued to travel quite a bit, often to speak at seminars, sometimes to explore different parts of the country or the world, from time to time to spend weekends with various friends in Boston. Wayne didn't mind her traveling at first, because for the first several months after the Marblehead weekend, they spent every weekend that Elaine wasn't traveling together at his place. She wanted to control when to arrive and when to leave. Elaine would breeze in after work on Friday night and head back to Brewster midday Sunday. They continued to go out to dinner or to listen to music or stay home and watch a movie with Sybil. Wayne was savvy and patient enough to know that he had to let things develop. After all, he worked with plants—hours, weeks, and months of preparation—no dearth of deferred gratification. Impatience led to failure.

After about a year, he decided it was time to dial things up several notches. He started by asking Elaine if she had any interest in helping out with the family business. She liked plants and trees and flowers. The request surprised her some.

"Is there a problem with the business, Wayne?" was her first reaction.

"No, everything's fine," he responded.

"Are you having a hard time finding help?" was her second question.

"No, not at all. It's just that we seem to be getting closer, and I'd like to have you around more. I just thought you might be interested in getting involved in that aspect of my life. You know, another thing to share."

"I'm flattered. Thank you, but with my teaching and writing and traveling, I'm not looking for another thing to do. I love plants and flowers, but I'm not interested in making that commitment. I appreciate your asking me. It's very sweet, but I think it'd be better if I didn't."

She intentionally threw in the commitment part.

Wayne recognized that the yellow flag had been pulled out, but he focused on the time issue. He throttled back for a few weeks. His next attempt to move things along was to ask whether he could come along on one of her seminar trips. Again, she declined.

"When I travel on a trip like that, I'm focused on my presentation, and afterward I socialize with my colleagues. It's very collegial. If you were there, I'd feel obligated to make sure you were having a good time. I wouldn't want you to come and then abandon you. I'm not in a position to be diverted from the purpose of the trip. These are business trips."

Wayne felt put off, pushed away. He tried a smaller request—that she stay over on a Sunday night now and again or at least not go home until late Sunday night. She rejected each proposal. With each rejection, Wayne became more frustrated and wracked his brain to find an acceptable plan to bridge the gap between them. His frustration bested him. He abandoned his patient approach and began questioning the necessity of her travels, especially the discretionary trips, like the ones to Boston to visit a friend or the ones when she went out exploring. They were still spending each weekend together when she was home, and the frequency and intensity of their physical relationship had leveled off for the most part. It was not until she told him about her upcoming trip to Martha's Vineyard did that nitrous oxide back up on him. On a Sunday morning two weeks before she was to depart for the Vineyard, after a very pleasant evening that ended with very satisfying lovemaking, she told him that she would be going away to the Vineyard for a week.

"Great idea," he said. "I need a week off. It'll be great to spend some time on the island. I haven't been for many years. When were you thinking?"

"I signed up for a creative writing workshop. It's in two weeks. It's not a vacation. I want to attend this weeklong workshop…alone." She sensed trouble fomenting.

"Why?" Wayne was totally confused.

"I'd like to think about and write about some things that have been swirling around inside me. I want to address them. I think a writing workshop will help."

"Elaine, what about us? What about our relationship? The way things were going, I thought we were getting closer and closer. Shouldn't we be going away together? Don't you travel enough on your own already?"

Wayne failed in his attempt to keep his voice at a conversational tone. She had anticipated his reaction and was prepared for it.

"We have what we have. It feels okay to me so long as there is no pressure. I like spending time with you, but I want to keep it light and casual. I don't want this to turn into a big deal." Elaine was calm but concerned.

"Casual! Light! No big deal! What the hell is going on here, Elaine? We've been seeing one another for almost two years. Why would you want to go away without me? Don't you want to spend time with me? What's this all about? Don't we have something good going on here? We're a couple, aren't we? Is there something wrong with me? Is there something wrong with this relationship?" Only a modicum of restraint remained.

"It's been fine until now, but I can't plan my life around you and your family and your business. Maybe we should just call this off."

She was ready for this moment. Similar occurrences had happened with others in the past.

Wayne took the comment like a slap in the face. Stunned, he froze in silence. He felt his two-year investment plummet like the crash of Wall Street. He fought hard to pull back his rage and settle down from his feeling of panic. Rather than continuing to react, he turned back to his side of the bed, closed his eyes, tried to take slow, deep breaths like he did when recovering from a difficult play back in high school football. He closed his eyes and thought.

Elaine shuffled out of bed and turned to leave. "Wayne, I'm gathering my stuff. I'm leaving for good." She had known this day would come.

Wayne had quickly sifted through his emotions and decided to make an attempt to salvage things.

"Elaine, I think you're misunderstanding me. I understand that you need your own space. It's just that I miss you when we're not together, and I want to be an important part of your life. You are already an important part of my life, and Sybil's, too. I said those things out of frustration. You go and enjoy yourself. I'll see you when you get back, okay?"

"I'm not sure. I don't think so. I think we might be at different places in this relationship. I'm not sure we want the same things. Maybe it's better if we just call it right here and now."

She knew it would be better to make a clean break right now. She thought first of the Cat Stevens song "The First Cut Is the Deepest," then switched to Paul Siebel's "Any Day Woman." When Bonnie Raitt's voice rattled through her brain, Elaine mentally substituted "him" for "her," and it came out:

If you don't love him, you'd better let him go.

You'll never fool him, you're bound to let it show.

Love's so hard to take when you have to fake.
Everything in return, you just preserve him
When you serve him a little tenderness.

"I know you're mad at me," he said. "How about if we leave it this way? You go to your workshop and have a great time. Write what you're thinking and feeling. Take a few days. Then, give me a call sometime in the week—before you finish up. We can work this out. Okay?"

"I don't think so, Wayne. I think it's best that we stop now." All she wanted to do was leave.

"Come on, Elaine. It's been almost two years. Let's not have it end this way. Just a phone call. I'm not asking for a guarantee. Just think things over, and let's have a phone call. If we can work things out, we can meet in Falmouth for dinner when you get back. Have some fun. Listen to Liam play some songs. Just one phone call. Okay?"

Against her better judgment, she acquiesced. "Okay. One phone call, but I don't think anything will change."

"Great, thanks. Think about the good times we've had and the ones we could still have, and then we'll talk." He was relieved he could get her to agree.

"Okay, but no promises."

She took all of her things from his house as she left.

DINNER

When the sun lowers on the Cape, the air cools quickly, like the coils in a toaster after the bread pops out. You may retain some of the warmth on skin that has taken on a deeper shade than when you started, but the glow of what supplied the heat fades to nothing. Still you feel the tingle. With their arrival back at the house, they watch the moon chase the sun to the west and out of sight. It will rule the sky until dawn, when the sun once again forces its will on the day. The ocean breeze that led to the donning of long-sleeve tees and summer sweatshirts on the flats is now drifting inland toward the house. Everyone stretches out of their vehicles. They find delight in a temperature that is dipping out of the red zone. The day has succumbed.

Nad inhales, heaving his chest and shoulders upward, pulling in the crispness around him, then switching to one deep belly breath to ensnare every milliliter of evening air he can capture. He feels refreshed, sad, and renewed all at once. Everyone begins to make their way back to the tent to eat. What was a snail-paced procession on the way out escalates to a more upbeat saunter back in, not quite a normal walk but more than a shuffle. The mood begins to lighten.

Nad replays parts of his interaction with Nickie and Marti—adorable girls, he thinks. He tries to call to mind as many descriptors for them as he can. He stays away from the commonplace adjectives—smart, pretty, nice, and polite—although all of them fit perfectly. "Effervescent" pops into his thoughts, so he gravitates toward a handful of other *e* words: evanescent, effusive, enchanting, ebullient, and exuberant. He decides to stop there. His awareness that they tease one another good-naturedly with sharp but harmless witty barbs brings a smile to his face. They seem to like and trust one another the way sisters should. He likes that and credits Joy and Cav but speculates that their time with their Aunt E helped nurture their development as well. Nad hopes that he can extend his relationship with the entire Cavendish family beyond this occasion. Maybe he could visit them up here in Brewster from time to time in summers to come. Maybe he could even bring his son up here to meet them, too. All in good time. There's still quite a bit of the evening left for them to gather together and tell stories that celebrate Eon's life. Plus, there's a great dinner ready to be shared.

Joy takes charge. She directs everyone toward the food tables set up beyond a row of bamboo garden torches lit against the nearly midnight-blue sky. The grassy smell of citronella blends nicely with the salt air. A charcoal grill sizzles out on the lawn just behind the buffet now set for a celebratory feast, adding another ingredient to the ocean air. Up close you can hear the grill giving off a slight hiss like a snare drum. From farther back, the sound of cicadas overwhelms it. Despite the charcoal grill, this is no weekend backyard barbeque. There are no paper plates, plastic knives or forks, or paper towels. Copeland Spode Trade Winds dinnerware is stacked up next to the Wallace Grande Baroque sterling silver flatware and Mallorca linen napkins. The main table features lobster, grilled swordfish, grilled asparagus, potatoes au gratin, green beans, corn on the cob—grilled not boiled—and sweet potato fries. Guests can step twice to the right to get to the table devoted to breads: boule, brioche, and baguette. Two more steps in that directions brings them to a whole tabletop where clear ClingWrap protects trays teeming with fresh fruit—watermelon, pineapple, cantaloupe, honey melon, strawberries, raspberries, blueberries, and blackberries. Where you would normally look for the dessert, a sign beckons: Design Your Own Ice Cream Sundae After Dinner.

The spread is catered but self-serve. They line up to help themselves.

"Wow! This is some setup. Spectacular! Who put together the menu?" Nad asks.

"Eon. These were her favorite things," Cav responds proudly.

"Of course she did. What was I thinking? I should've figured that out on my own. Now that I look at everything, I have to say that over the years, I shared meals with her that have everything you have here. I know she loved seafood, especially grilled swordfish, and corn on the cob and fresh fruit and *ice cream*. No meal was ever complete for her without ice cream. Her favorite, I think, was triple chocolate from Ben and Bill's in Oak Bluffs."

It is all flooding back to Nad.

"You're right on target, good sir. There's a Ben and Bill's in Falmouth, too. All the ice cream came from there, including a hefty supply of triple chocolate," Joy says.

"I love triple chocolate best, too," Nickie adds. "It's even Marti's favorite."

Cav, Joy, the twins, and Nad assemble at a round table for six; one chair remains ceremonially unoccupied. A tablecloth that looks and feels more like white linen than the heavy paper it really is adds another element of elegance. Joy rises slowly and turns toward the photo display. She walks almost solemnly to the writers' workshop picture, carefully removes it from its spot, and cradles it carefully as she walks back to the table. Deftly, she positions it upright on the empty chair. The place settings were Eon's—the flatware, too. Other than her piano, a baby grand Steinway, these were her only "fancy" possessions. She gave Cav specific instructions that he was to hold the china, silver, and piano for Nickie and Marti and to figure out a fair way to apportion them. Cav knew he'd have ample time to solve this little puzzle. The five of them settle in for a leisurely meal.

The glow of large, fragrant candles on each table complements the light flickering from the strategically positioned torches outside the tent. The sky continues its darkening. The girls doff their sweatshirts and place them on the sixth chair, taking care not to block the view of the photograph. They are ready to eat.

Cav clinks his water glass.

"Everyone, listen up, please. We already did the toast, so now let's have just a quick moment of silence. Picture our dear girl, and think of all the joy and beauty she brought to us and our world."

Without direction to do so, everyone stands. Heads lower. Eyes close. Cav pauses for exactly the appropriate length of time and then speaks up.

"Thank you. Let's get at it."

Small bursts of chatter break out here and there at various tables.

Nad is still feeling the effects of the Jameson's; he hadn't eaten since early that morning. He's a total lightweight when it comes to hard liquor. He has a slightly fuzzy out-of-body feeling. At the predinner gathering, he was too busy meeting folks to grab any of the hors d'oeuvres; fortunately, the only alcohol he consumed was the Jameson's. But, he really needs some food to balance him out. He starts on a piece of brioche while he watches the twins. Nickie's plate hosts lobster, corn on the cob, and sweet potato fries. Marti went for swordfish to go with her corn and brioche. Nad begins in earnest on a crisp ear of corn. He particularly likes that the black crunchy kernels singed by the grill offset the sweetness of the pleasantly warmed yellow kernels bathed in butter. His eating comes to a halt midbite when he hears the throaty crescendo of a powerful engine. He looks up to the sky, but he can't find any airplane taillights against the netting of stars. Others at their tables also look up. It's not a plane. The sound soon evolves into a roar; it certainly sounds bigger than a car, Nad thinks. And, it appears to be closing in on them. Now everyone has stopped eating, even the twins. In a flash, a bucking pickup truck with mud splattered all over the windshield, hood, and front fenders thunders toward the lawn, bouncing heavily on oversized tires. Even before it stops, Nad sees Cav flash Joy a look of concern. Joy accurately reads his look like a stage cue.

"Girls, I'm feeling really uncomfortable out here. It's getting buggy. I'm getting eaten alive."

She doesn't wait for a reaction.

"How's about we grab our plates and finish off inside? Can you keep me company?"

Nickie starts to protest, but Joy quickly preempts her.

"Nickie, I need you to go along with me, please. Let's go inside. I don't need a discussion here."

Nickie complies. Joy stands over the girls, gathering their plates with hers. She starts to hustle them toward the house. Things are happening so quickly that Nad is a little confused. He jumps up to help Joy and knocks over a chair. He reaches for the plates, but Joy stops him.

"It's okay, Nad. I've got them. You stay and hold down the fort with Cav and Carl out here. We'll be back for dessert."

Nad finally catches on.

"Got it, Joy. We'll finish off out here and then clear things out for dessert."

In the meantime, Cav has motioned to Carl to come over and stand beside him, then turns to Nad.

"Stay ready, friend. I might need some help here in a minute or two. You're part of my backup."

All of this preparation surprises Nad, but he instantly snaps into street mode, calling on all of the instincts he honed back in the old neighborhood growing up.

"I'm right with you. No problem. I got whatever you need."

Although it had been quite some time since he'd been involved in a real altercation, maybe since back in those early days on the city streets, he feels pretty sure that it'll be like riding a bike—everything will come storming back. He expects to be able to react without having to think much, although he acknowledges again that it has been a long, long time. Without even realizing it, he grabs a chair, folds it up, turns it over so that it'll be easier to swing, and places it within quick reach. He checks to make sure he can utilize his belt as either a weapon or a restraint, if necessary. He balls a quarter in each fist in case he has to throw punches. He's pretty sure he won't have to do any slashing with his car key, so he doesn't grab for it. He positions his right foot forward to change his center of gravity; this way he can throw his body weight into a punch with his power hand if he needs to. He's a lefty. The line of engagement, that is, the line of defense, forms with Carl and Nad flanking Cav.

"We'll have to look as relaxed as possible so we don't provoke him," Nad tells Cav and Carl.

Cav agrees and continues with some guidelines of his own. "I think I should do the talking. He knows me, and he'll probably have a quick trigger. If either of you speak, it might set him off. I think he'll be more likely to go after somebody he doesn't know. If he's amped up or liquored up, he'll be more unpredictable. You guys pay attention more to him. I'll get my message across to you clearly and quickly if it comes to that."

Cav inhales deeply and relaxes all the muscles in his face before rearranging them into as bright a smile as he can conjure up, given what he anticipates. He focuses on steadying his heart rate.

Nad has enough experience to control the flow of adrenaline trying to flood his system. He knows that if the adrenaline pours through him too quickly, it won't be there when he needs it.

Carl takes Cav's direction to heart and focuses outside himself. He's pretty inexperienced when it comes to physical confrontation; however, he is naturally even tempered. This attribute helps keep him composed. His ability to focus readies him for a committed response.

The truck slams to a halt well onto the lawn, not far from the tent. It ruts out some grass along the way. The spinning wheels and flying grass and dirt attract everyone's attention. The scene becomes a snapshot for more than an instant. Everyone sees pretty much the same thing. The truck is a heavy-duty crew-cab Silverado, four doors with passenger seating. It's black and accustomed to rugged use, although the body is remarkably free of damage. It's dirty right now but well maintained. The windshield is too muddy for anyone to see inside. After three or four seconds, there's no need to. The driver-side door flies open, and a guy Cav's size unfolds himself and plunges from the cab. His cream-colored polyester shirt with a palm tree running down the front on the left side looks out of place and does nothing to hide strongly muscled biceps, triceps, and forearms. He has a barroom bouncer's neck and shoulders. He's wearing fatigue-green Fire Hose work shorts that come down to his knees, and brown ankle-high steel-toed work boots over heavy gray wool socks that have been pushed down to the top of the boots. He would have to shave if he were going out to dinner, but his growth is okay for work, and, maybe by intention, a bit menacing for a memorial service. He does a quick scan of the crowd and begins a forceful stalk toward the line of defense. He plods on tree-trunk thighs and powerful-looking running-back calves. With each step, he makes quite an impression on the lawn. His hair is dark, almost black, but well-groomed and stylish. Puffy darting eyes undercut what is otherwise a handsome, well-proportioned face with a strong forehead, a right-sized straight nose, and a sturdy-looking but not too prominent jaw. He's tanned and fit. Even from his remote vantage point, Nad notices that the guy is wearing a heavy leather strap watch on his right wrist, signaling to Nad that if trouble starts, the guy would set up left-handed. As one himself, Nad knows where the weaknesses are. He will be ready.

Cav continues to wear that big smile and waves both arms over his head, motioning to Marlow.

"Over here, Wayne."

Cav takes a few steps forward, leaving Carl and Nad just slightly behind him. They now form a *V*. He whispers to them.

"Walk at my pace so that we can separate from the tables. We'll try to meet him halfway. Lag a little behind so that it doesn't look like we're coming for him. Stay ready."

Wayne and Cav are now face-to-face. Carl and Nad stand expressionless a few steps back off of his shoulders. Cav continues his preemptive greeting but doesn't extend his hand for a handshake. He doesn't want to be left hanging. Instead, he lets his arms hang loosely by his sides, hands open.

"Wayne Marlow, hello, hello. It's nice to see you. It's been a while. Sorry you missed the memorial. We went down to the flats at sunset to release Elaine's ashes into the ocean. It was very emotional. You're just in time for dinner. There's all sorts of great food. Salmon. Lobster. Great bread and fruit. Grab a plate, and come over and sit with me."

He keeps his affect slightly up, not overly animated but not deadpan. He's trying to be as neutral as he can be.

"I'm not here for dinner. I'm here for my kids." The words come bellowing out with spit and belligerence.

Cav turns his head quizzically. "What are you talking about? What kids?"

Cav is calm and speaks softly, doing his best to defuse the situation. He waits, but Wayne doesn't answer. He just glares at Cav, then surveys the room. Cav senses that the steam is building.

"Wayne? I don't understand what you're asking. What're you saying?"

"My kids. I want my kids." Wayne's voice naturally projects like a stage actor's. Now there's even more volume.

"Your kids aren't here. Just some folks trying to give Elaine a good send-off. Come on, Wayne. This is a memorial service. Come on, have some food." Cav's voice is still totally neutral, matter-of-fact, as if he's summarizing facts for a jury in an opening statement.

"I want to see my kids, and I want to see them now." Wayne turns his volume all the way up. Veins on his neck and at his temple are prominently visible. The anger spews from him.

Nad has an innate sense of timing about confrontations like this. He can feel the tension rising. He knows he has to be patient so that he doesn't ignite things, but he can't delay when the time is right, or he'll lose control of the situation. *Be patient,* he thinks. *Alert but patient. Patient but ready. No hesitation when it's time to go. But until then, patience. I have to line up an angle so that I can use his size against him. Patient but ready.*

Cav stands his ground. "Your kids aren't here."

He's outwardly calm but inwardly ready. Carl and Nad keep Wayne in sight, but they can also see Cav well enough to detect a signal if one is given. Wayne is still at an appropriate distance from Cav, but it's getting close. Cav raises his left hand as a stop sign.

"Come on, Wayne. We don't want any trouble. Let's have dinner. I don't know who your kids are. But, I can assure you, they're not here."

"Yes, they are. I've seen them around over the past week or so. One of them has red hair, and she looks just like Elaine. The other one has darker brown hair, her twin sister. She looks like me." Wayne is losing all control.

That Cav can remain so unflustered is inspiring. Only Cav is aware that his heart rate is spiking. To Nad and Carl, it looks like Cav could lapse into a nap at any moment. Nad has learned to control his emotions in situations like these, but Carl can feel his heart pounding hard in his chest and in his ears.

"Those girls are not yours. Joy and I are their parents. They're not yours, Wayne."

Even from this distance, Cav smells the liquor on Wayne's breath.

"Yes, they are. I used to see them with Elaine all the time. It took me a while to figure out what was going on. Elaine and I were together about ten years ago. They're the right age for that. They're my kids."

"How about we sit down and have some dinner?" Cav repeats. "We don't want any trouble here."

"Not yours. Mine. I saw her pregnant right after we split. I know those kids are mine—ours, Elaine's and mine, hers and mine. And we'd've all been together if that creep lawyer hadn't come in and busted us up. Is he here? Where's he hiding? I'll show him what happens when you bust up a family. Where's that creep? He's in for some trouble."

Wayne refrains from looking at Nad or Carl directly, but he checks them out in his peripheral vision. They remain expressionless. Carl understands that he can't do or say anything. He tries to look relaxed, like an innocent bystander.

Nad wants to step forward, but knows that if he does, that would surely set off an explosion. He maintains his stolidity. "Patience, patience" becomes Nad's internal mantra.

"There's no creep lawyer here, Wayne. Just me and some friends."

Cav knows that he has to filibuster. In the week leading up to the memorial service, he alerted the police that Wayne might make an appearance at the services or at the house and that he might be hostile. Cav is confident that Joy called them as soon as she saw how Wayne exploded onto the scene and bolted out of the truck. The police promised to cruise the area and be ready. They, too, knew how Wayne's temper had grown over the years.

"We're just having some dinner. We were expecting you for the memorial service. Sorry you missed it. We gave our girl an old-fashioned Irish send-off, Jameson's and all."

Cav knows he is repeating himself, but so far, it seems to be working. He hopes that he can buy enough time for the police to arrive.

"Cav, I've got no quarrel with you, but I know my kids're here and that creep, too. I just want my daughters. I'll leave him alone if I can just see them. I just want to talk to them, tell them who I am. If you let me talk to them, then there won't be any trouble." For the moment, Wayne seems to be settling down.

"Wayne, I don't know where you got this idea. I don't know who your kids are. I know everybody who's here. It's just us. Let's not make this a crazy situa—"

Cav's sentence hangs unfinished because, at that instant, Wayne loses it. He screams.

"Who you calling crazy?"

Wayne lurches at Cav with his left hand in a fist and his arm cocked and ready to fire. Nad felt the escalation coming. He's been poised and ready to catapult himself into action. His timing's perfect. He drops the quarters from his hands and swoops in over Cav's right shoulder, springing to Wayne's left side to pin his left arm down. Neither of them hears the police sirens that were first audible as a faint wail off in the distance and are now ramping up, screaming louder and louder, nor do they see the flashing lights carom through the darkness. Carl storms in from the opposite side and tries to pin Wayne's right arm but slips on the way in, losing balance. Wayne's right arm is strong enough to toss Carl aside. Nad maneuvers around Wayne's back, pressing down the inside of his left upper arm to keep Wayne's left arm helplessly immobile. He reaches all the way around Wayne with his left hand and plants his closed fist on Wayne's sternum. In sequence, he replicates those moves on the right side and locks his right hand around his left wrist. Wayne's body is now a fulcrum. Nad clamps his elbows down to Wayne's side. Both of Wayne's arms are useless for the moment. Nad leans his chin on the top of Wayne's neck and pushes forward so that Wayne has to bow his head. Now Wayne's upper body is totally immobilized, too, but his legs are so strong that Nad can't budge him.

Instinctively, Nad recognizes that Wayne has set his stance for lateral stabilization. He intuits that this makes Wayne vulnerable to forward or backward motion. Nad throws himself back onto the grass, taking Wayne with him. When they hit the turf, Nad spins so that he's now on top of Wayne. They're both facedown. By turning over this way, Nad pins his own arms between Wayne and the lawn. Wayne forces his head sideways so that he's not breathing dirt. He thrashes about but can't toss Nad off. Wayne's attempts to spin and buck dislodge Nad's arms from being pinned to the ground. Just as Wayne is about to free his own arms, Cav and Carl jump in. With Cav on the right and Carl on the left, Wayne is once again completely restrained.

Padraig, who was standing farther back by the food line, makes his way over, but by the time he gets there, Nad, Cav, and Carl have Wayne totally under control.

"We have this, Padraig," Nad shouts. "We can hold him. Get the police over here."

Padraig rushes to escort the police in. They have arrived with backup; there is one police car, one police wagon, and four uniformed officers. They control Wayne facedown and cuff his hands from behind. Suddenly, Wayne relaxes. Totally subdued, he goes limp and gives up the fight. The police get him up, guide him to the wagon, and load him into the secure prisoner-transport unit that over the years has been used almost exclusively to carry underage drinkers whooping it up at some seaside party.

Two of the officers stand guard while the other two take brief statements and gather witness names and contact information. When all that is finished, they make a final check to make sure everybody is okay and start to leave. One of the officers drives Wayne's Silverado from the area, and the three vehicles form a procession to the municipal building where Wayne will be processed.

Finally, after the debriefing and the departure, pulse rates start to settle. Cav and Carl encourage everyone to head back to their tables to resume dinner.

"Let's not let him ruin this, okay? This is about Elaine, not that jerk," Cav says.

He doesn't realize that the words have come out stridently. He's feeling the effect of the adrenaline rush. It will take a few more minutes for his heart rate to settle back down.

After a few minutes, the cicadas are once again audible. Cav, Nad, Carl, and Padraig decide they need a beer before sitting back down to eat. They each grab a Sam Adams Summer Ale and clink bottles. Before the four of them take swigs, Cav acknowledges Carl, Nad, and Padraig.

"Thanks, guys." He hoists his bottle and toasts. "Brotherhood, teamwork—a job well done. We dodged that bullet."

After one deep pull, Nad speaks up. "What to hell was that all about?"

Cav tells the story. "Years ago, Eon warned me about Wayne. She told me she was seeing this guy and the Cape and that she was pretty sure he thought they were going to get married. I met him in passing a few times when I was up with her. Eon didn't want to marry him, or anyone, but not him in particular. She said she liked spending time with him when it was just a casual thing, but that as he got more serious, more needy, she was pretty clear that it wasn't going to work out. She said she would have been willing to keep things on a weekend-dinner-type basis. Typically, she wanted to keep him at a distance. When she felt she was being pressured too much, she ended things. It happened just before she left for that Vineyard trip. He took it hard, but he didn't give her any trouble at first, she said. But not too long after that, maybe a year or two, he pretty much started stalking her. She'd see him parked outside her house for hours. He'd just sit and stare. He followed her to the supermarket. One time, he boarded the bus that she took to Boston for classes and sat three rows behind her. He didn't say hello. He didn't acknowledge her at all. She said she felt like he was staring at her the whole way. One day when she was taking the bus back from Boston to the Cape, he got on the bus and did the same thing coming home.

"For a while he didn't say anything to her, but then one night outside the Brewster Library, he confronted her. She said he was delusional. He told her he knew that she got pregnant with his kid just before they broke up. He said he saw her pregnant, but then he couldn't find her anymore. He asked her if she had an abortion. She tried to walk away, but he insisted that she tell him the truth. She told him she didn't know what he was talking about, that she never had an abortion, and that he was out of his mind. He insisted, and he wanted to know where his kid was.

"For the most part, she was able to keep him at bay. But, sometimes in the summers, the twins would spend some time with her— a week or two now and again. They loved coming up to the Cape. We'd bring them up to spend time with Eon, Aunt E, before our trip. She'd take them to the beach, teach them piano, write with them, take them to Chatham. She was always out and about with them. He would catch glimpses of them, and for some reason, he just decided that they were his kids. He sent her notes and e-mails accusing her of stealing his children from him. She was about to get a restraining order but first asked the police to try to reason with him. He never believed her denials, but after the police talked to him, he seemed to back away. It helped that he saw the girls with Joy and me a few times.

"But, I knew he never totally let go. One time, I ran into him in the supermarket when I was alone, and he made a remark to me about knowing that the two girls he saw with Elaine were his kids. He asked, 'How are Elaine's kids? How are my kids?' I assured him that he was mistaken, that Elaine was watching the twins for Joy and me. He was always agitated about it, but he never gave me a really hard time."

Carl and Padraig have been following along with interest. Nad is beyond mesmerized; he's stunned.

"What a wacko!" Nad says. "Eon and I talked so much that week. If she were pregnant, I think she would have said something. Well, anyway, I'm glad that's over and he's gone."

By this time, Doreen has come over to make sure everyone is okay. She enters the conversation.

"I'm so sorry. I didn't know about any of this, or I would never have sent him an invitation. I feel terrible. It's just that they went out for a few years, and back then he seemed normal. I never saw him after they split up, and Eon never told me about him threatening her or being delusional. I'm very sorry."

"It's not your fault," Cav says. "We all know how Eon compartmentalized her life. She kept lots of things from all of us. Wayne was normal back then, but after Eon split from him, he went off the deep end. The threat of a restraining order seemed to back him off. Until now." Cav is sure to make it clear that neither he nor anyone else is blaming Doreen. "This has been building up in him for years. It was just a matter of time until he exploded." He gives Doreen a light hug. "Not your fault."

"Thanks, Cav. It looks like you and Joy were prepared for this. I'm glad that Carl and Nad and Padraig were here to back you up. Do you think Nickie and Marti are okay?" Doreen is beginning to feel better.

"I'll go check," Cav says and goes inside.

All this while, Joy has been holding the girls securely upstairs in a bedroom as far from the fray as possible. From time to time, she would dart to the window to keep tabs on what was going on. The sirens and the flashing lights frightened the girls. Joy kept explaining that a nasty man from town was trying to cause some trouble. He's upset about Aunt E's death. He had too much to drink. He got angry and confused. She kept assuring the girls that their dad had everything under control and that he had plenty of help from other guests. The police were here to make sure everything stayed okay and that nobody got hurt. The police were taking take care of everything. She told the girls that their dad and everyone else was okay.

When Joy sees that the police have taken Wayne away, she changes her affect from one that is calming and reassuring to one that is upbeat and ebullient.

"We can go outside now and finish our dinner and then *get some dessert. Ice cream!*"

They start to head back outside, when Cav greets them at the door to escort them.

AFTER DINNER

I t takes more than a few minutes for calm to set back in. The Cavendish family comes out together, not laughing but not sullen. Nad addresses them.

"How are you ladies doing?"

The twins' faces light up at the "ladies" reference. As usual, Nickie speaks first.

"We're fine. Mom explained everything to us. We're good. Mom said that you're all okay, right?"

"Yes, thank you. We're all good. Let's finish up this dinner so we can get to important things like ice cream." Nad shouts the "ice cream" part.

As they complete the main course, they begin to fantasize about dessert. Marti opens the subject.

"Dad said that if we want, we could have two small sundaes spaced out instead of one big one. I'm going with triple chocolate for the first one. Lots of chocolate syrup and chocolate chunks and M&M's and nuts and whipped cream with a raspberry on the top. And then, for my second sundae, I think I'll switch to chocolate Oreo with blueberries on top and more chocolate syrup."

They make their way back inside where the ice cream has been removed from the freezer. Nickie mixes mint chocolate chip ice cream with strawberries and whipped cream. Joy and Doreen write down the creative sundae concoctions that the adults conjure up, and Cav, Nad, Carl, and Padraig volunteer to put everything together so that everyone else can head to the back of the house, where a beautiful stone fire pit is ready to be set up. Evangeline, Karen, Lena, and Sonia are charged with the task of starting the fire with the wood Cav had earlier piled up nearby. The women get the fire blazing just as the men bring out the sundaes and a surprise array of pastries, marshmallows, and skewers.

Everything mellows down. Dessert is a serious business, so there's very little chatter; everyone attacks their unique blend. More than a few streaks of brown, white, green, or pink miraculously appear on random chins. Midway through her sundae, Doreen stands up without comment. She ceremoniously reaches into her pocket and theatrically removes a plastic pig nose. Everyone stops to watch her. With exaggerated precision, she slowly pulls the elastic band back behind her head, cautiously places the snout over her own nose, and lets loose a loud, prolonged snort. The laughter encourages her to follow with three more snorts in quick succession. Doreen's ploy is a mood changer. Anyone feeling subdued or melancholy experiences an instantaneous attitude adjustment. The smiles range from subtle ones with lightly sparkling eyes to full-out Duchenne ear-to-ear grins. Without removing her snout, Doreen launches into an explanation of how she and Eon started this silly pig thing.

"Here is my first Eon story of the night," Doreen begins. "Years ago Eon and I went for dinner and wound up walking by a neighborhood bar that was having some sort of a fund raiser. We didn't know what it was for, but the sign out front was very welcoming, something about all the pulled pork you could eat for some ridiculously small amount. Eon says we have to go in, so we do. As soon as we get inside, we see this big sign with an enormous picture of a barbequed pig on a spit. The sign read, 'The top five pork eaters will be crowned Pig Outers of the Night—special prizes awarded.' Eon took this as a challenge. Me, too, but more her, so she reads the 'rules' next to the sign. First prize was a free roasted-pig catered barbeque. Second and third place were pounds and pounds of assorted pig pieces like chops and roast pork. Fourth place was a honey baked ham, and fifth place was five pounds of bacon. As a top 'pig outer' of the night, each of the top five finishers would get to keep a plastic pig snout. Eon says, 'Let's get to it.' For the next couple of hours, we pushed one another to consume obscene amounts of pulled pork washed down with the various beers they had on tap. When the contest was over and the poundage was tallied, we got to come home with a honey baked ham and five pounds of bacon. But, the longer-lasting prizes were these pig snouts. From that time on, without prearrangement, either Eon or I would show up to dinner wearing a coveted pig nose. There were times when I would answer my doorbell, and Eon would be standing there, snout in place. She wouldn't say hello; she would just snort her way in."

Doreen then surprises Nad by reaching into her pocket, pulling out Eon's pig nose, and handing it to him. He carefully puts it on, and they commence a snorting duel to everyone's delight.

The floodgates open, and the stories pour out. For the next hours, they talk and drink and share their own Eon stories, stories that now, through their love for her, bind them together in friendship. The twins hang in for as long as they can, sipping on lemonade and asking questions whenever anything is unclear to them. Eventually, drowsiness attacks. They are old enough to put themselves to bed, but given the occasion and the chaos resulting from Wayne's appearance, Joy decides to make sure they get settled in. They give a hug to each adult at their table to accompany their "Good night."

Nad, as expected, says, "Good night, ladies," to which they in harmony respond, "And good night to you, too, sir."

Joy returns after a short time, confirms that everything is all right and that the girls fell asleep almost instantly. The adults continue late, well past midnight. Evangeline tells how Professor Neal had traveled to East Saint Louis to meet her family and took the time to make a presentation on medical ethics to the staff at her hospital, how she made Evangeline feel like a rock star in the community, how "The Professor's" total belief in her inspired her to overcome any obstacle. Without hesitation she talks about how she used the "WWED" method whenever she had a dilemma and was trying to figure out what to do—"What Would Elaine Do?" From time to time, she couldn't figure it out on her own, so she would give the Professor a call, and without fail, she had worked out a viable solution by the time the conversation ended.

"Dr. Neal kept all these miniature plastic or ceramic pigs in her office," Evangeline tells them. "Doreen, your pig-snout story has certainly added another dimension to those clay pigs. But even better than the miniature pigs was the large photo of a sculpture of the three little pigs she kept on the back wall of her office door. The picture was poster size. She also kept cutout clothes for the pigs in her desk drawer. I could use pins to attach the clothes to the pigs on the poster. When I was particularly stressed out, she would yank open her desk drawer and have me dress up the pigs. Between our conversation and our wardrobing game, I always left her office smiling."

"That picture is of my *Three Little Pigs* sculpture," Karen says. "I didn't know she did that. That's hilarious. I used to see all these miniature pigs Eon had all around her house. When I asked her about that, she just told me that she and a friend of hers both liked pigs, thought they were cute and unfairly maligned. It was those pigs that gave me the idea to sculpt a statue of the three little pigs. I had a piece of beautiful black marble that I was struggling with. The three little pigs just jumped out of it for me."

Karen doesn't mention that *The Three Little Pigs* won her the International Sculpture Center Award, but she does explain how Eon inspired *The Mentor*, which won the Praemium Imperiale Award, and *The Professor*, which won the Spitalfields Sculpture Award. More importantly, Karen talks about the ways Eon helped her aside from inspiring numerous sculptures.

"She was the best friend one could ever hope for," Karen says. "She was always present for you whenever you needed her. She was reliable and candid. She never spouted the conventional line or took a path because it was politically correct. An independent thinker who pulled in many different sides to an issue before she would form her conclusions. Her wise advice shaped my life."

"I feel exactly the same" Lena picks up the thread. "When I began teaching, communicating with my students in speech was very, very hard for me. Writing, no problem. But, talking, oh so very hard. At the beginning, she would listen to the presentations I wanted to make. She would tell me what they would understand and what they wouldn't understand from what I was saying. Without her help, I would never have been able to talk to my students. I would have had to draw on the board to teach them. That would never have worked. Writing the formula out is important, but the formula must be explained, too, in words. She helped me with the words, or I would have totally failed."

Padraig's saga is similar. Although he was regularly published in journals on physical therapy, such as *Perspective* and *PT in Motion*, and was often asked to lecture or give demonstrations at seminars on physical therapy or at schools of physical therapy, like the Institute of Physical Therapy in Dublin, he longed to have at least one of his papers on philosophy published in a philosophy journal. He submitted articles to *Mind* and *Analysis* and others. His lack of academic credentials kept his work from even being looked at. Editors didn't want to take the time to read a philosophical treatise written by a physical therapist.

"Over the years, Eon and I had numerous discussions on epistemology," Padraig says. "She often encouraged me ta write on dis subject. Finally, I did. One art'cle in particular seemed ta intrigue her. I wrote a t'esis on the essential conditions of propositional knowledge, focusing on de conditions precedent for one to have knowledge dat something is so. I tried to present my t'esis by going into de disagreements various philosophers had on trut and belief conditions. She told me it was well-done and dat I should circulate it."

In actuality, Eon thought that the paper was brilliant and eminently publishable. After numerous conversations with Padraig, she persuaded him to submit it for publication. She wrote a letter of recommendation to go with his article, in which she advised the publisher on the efficacy of the submission.

"She talked me into sending it to de *Oxford Handbook of Epistemology*, and guess what—dey accepted it. It was de first philosophy paper I ever had published, and it was all because of her, her belief in me, and her letter." Padraig is glowing. "And it all started with dat flight to San Francisco."

"Nad, what about you?" Cav asks. "Could you retell the Vineyard story for everybody to hear?"

Nad quickly recites a short synopsis of that week but then segues into talking about some of the ethical dilemmas he faced in his career and how she helped guide him through them. He recounts one situation in particular.

"I was representing a national chain of facilities. They owned nursing homes, assisted-living communities, things like that. They were one of the five largest in the country. Well, in one of their facilities out in the Midwest, the state attorney general brought multiple criminal charges for manslaughter, reckless endangerment, assault, Medicare fraud, and so on against the corporate facility, individually against the corporate administrators, and individually against several of the administrators, including the executive director of the facility, the administrator, and the director of nursing. These charges came about as a result of the deaths of a couple of residents in a short period of time. The families of the residents also filed civil malpractice suits. I, of course, was handling those actions, and colleagues of mine in our firm were handling the criminal matters. As the responsible attorney for the client, I had to oversee the defense of everything, including the criminal suits. Our annual revenue in legal fees from this company was high into the seven figures. They were important.

"Early in the matter, the CEO made it clear that he wanted to deflect the blame in the criminal suits away from the company and the corporate executives and toward the facility administrators—the executive director, the administrator, and the director of nursing. He wanted me to set up the corporate defense based on the argument that these individuals had gone rogue and acted without authority on several procedures that resulted in the deaths. Our team carefully sifted through all the facts, in detail, for many, many hours. We could find no evidentiary support for this theory. The CEO didn't seem to care. He was insistent. I was faced with the dilemma of alienating an important client or coming up with evidence against two individuals who appeared to have done nothing wrong. I knew what the right thing was, but I was under quite a bit of pressure not to do it. Eon talked me through the whole ethical issue. It was extremely helpful that she was both an attorney and an expert in medical ethics. It was only through her support and insight that I was able to steer a course. In the end, it cost the firm the client, but we did the right thing, and individuals who had done nothing wrong were not made the scape-goats. Eon was unwavering. She was clear that we couldn't do what the client was demanding. But, she didn't just come out and say that. We talked it out, and she drew out of me what we both knew was the right thing. She helped me face it, bring it to the surface, articulate it."

"What happened after you lost the client?" Cav asks.

"Well, we had to obtain permission to withdraw from the representation without explaining why. After everything was concluded, somehow word got out that we had taken the moral high ground, and after a short time, the largest national chain in the industry contacted us to represent it. It was an arduous process, but in the end, it worked out for the benefit of the firm, but more importantly, we did the right thing."

"That's Eon," Karen says. "She knew right from wrong and would always stick by her convictions."

More stories tumble out over the next couple of hours. Some of them are stories of inspiration and mentoring; others are stories of escapades and activities—concerts, dinners, trips and visits here and there. All of them are tender remembrances of times spent with their departed friend.

EON'S PARTING GIFT

Eventually everyone begins to tire. Dawn is not quite threatening to make its appearance, but it is way past the halfway point between dusk and dawn. The crowd thins out little by little. There are multiple warm hugs and tearful good-byes. Nad is about to do the same when Cav suggests a couple of things. First, he asks Nad if it would be okay to distribute a copy of the poem he read on the flats. Nad readily assents and hands Cav a copy. Next, Cav tosses out the idea of setting up a scholarship fund in Eon's name either at Creighton, for undergraduates or law students, or perhaps at Tufts University Medical School. Everyone eagerly agrees to participate in whatever Cav comes up with. He also asks whether there is any interest in having periodical reunions to try to forge a bond among Eon's close friends, a bond that would help preserve her memory and perhaps even add to her legacy. Again, the group rallies around this idea, and Cav agrees to distribute the contact information from everyone that he and Doreen acquired when scheduling this memorial service—except, of course, to Wayne Marlow.

Finally, only five of them remain: Cavendish and Joy, Doreen and Carl, and Nad. Nad begins to say his farewells.

"Carl, it was a pleasure to meet you. If I'm ever in a barroom brawl, I hope you're there with me."

Rather than the handshake that began their acquaintance, they embrace in a farewell hug. Joy is next up. When she hugs him, she whispers to him.

"Our girl really loved you. And, I know you loved her, too. I hope you'll be able to be a part of our lives going forward. You'll always be welcome here when we're up on the Cape, and I hope that you'll come and visit us in Lincoln before too long."

His eyes begin to well up when Doreen swoops in. She adds a light kiss to her good-bye hug. As they separate, she turns to Cavendish.

"Cav, please remember to give it to Nad. You haven't done that yet, have you?"

"Oh, yes. No, I haven't, but I know right where it is. I'll go get it. I'll be back in a few minutes. Nad, can you chill for a few?"

Nad shakes his head as Cav rushes off. The four remain standing there. He tries to be casual about what Cav is bringing.

"Does anybody know what this is about? I really don't need a parting gift. My memories won't ever fade."

Everybody shrugs. No one answers him.

After a long few minutes, Cavendish comes out of the house carrying a cardboard box that looks to be about two feet long, a foot wide, and a foot deep. The contents can't be very heavy because Cav is hustling along at a brisk trot. He places the box at Nad's feet and draws out a sealed official-looking business envelope with a printed return address:

Dr. Elaine O. Neal
Professor, Tufts University School of Medicine
Boston, MA 02111

It's addressed to "Nicholas Amadeo DiDominico" in cursive that is unmistakably hers. Cav hands it to Nad.

"When she went into hospice, she gave this to me and asked me to give this to you."

The others watch him intently.

"I feel a little awkward about this," Nad says, "like I might be the only one here who doesn't know what's going on. Do I open this now, or do I wait until I'm alone, or don't you know one way or the other?" he asks.

"Your choice," Cav replies.

Nick slowly peels open the envelope and silently reads.

Dear Nad,

I had hoped that I'd be sharing the rest of my life with you, but that was not to be. I can still share my life up to this point with you. I started keeping a diary when I was a preteen. As I matured, it evolved into a journal. While some of the entries are drivel, many of them will provide you with the details of my life that may help you understand the themes in my experiences that brought me to you on the Vineyard and then motivated me to disappear from your life for some time. If I could do it over again with my current knowledge, I wouldn't close the door on you. I warn you that some of the entries about my family dynamic may be difficult for you to read. They were difficult to write, but writing them helped sustain me through that destructive time.

I also want you to know that through you, through my relationship with you, through our relationship, I experienced an epiphany, that I finally mustered the courage to cross the threshold from isolation to intimacy. I'm sorry that we never got the chance to act on that transformation. If I hurt you along the way, I'm sorry.

There's one final thing, and it is more important than anything I've said so far to you or to anyone. I wanted to tell you about this earlier, but at first my own confusion and then life intervened. I hope you will get to know Nickie and Marti. Nickie has my looks and your personality. With Marti, it's just the opposite. Together, they are us. I told Cavendish and Doreen about their true lineage only at the very end. I trust that you and they will work out the best course of action.

Love for eons to come,

Eon

Nick struggles to stand.

ACKNOWLEDGMENTS

This novel began as a very short story in an overly ambitious attempt to sardine all the characters and events into a tiny manuscript. My coffee shop friend and neighbor, Cassandra Krivy Hirsch (*Under the Linden Tree*), read that short story and immediately set me straight.

"This is no short story," she said. "This is a novel. Let the characters breathe."

Thank you, Casey. Without your encouragement, *Brewster Flats* would be a vignette with suffocating characters.

I also want to offer a special thank-you to my brother, Ray, who read an early draft and pointed out more than a few things that needed to be straighted out, and to my son, Pat, who painstakingly read the next-to-last draft and made several incisive observations and suggested a key organizational change that made the story more compelling.

AUTHOR BIOGRAPHY

Tony DeSabato began writing by creating a short-story series, *The Adventures of Merry Moose*, so that he could read original works to his then-young son. From there he began writing short stories about growing up in South Philadelphia. He describes himself as a recovering attorney, having practiced law for more than thirty years prior to his retirement. His full-time residence is in Narberth, Pennsylvania, but he does most of his writing in Martha's Vineyard, either in his home in Edgartown or on the beach at Aquinnah. He is planning to publish an anthology of his short stories.

Made in the USA
Middletown, DE
10 April 2017